D1247893

THANKSGIVING BLESSING

Center Point
Large Print

Also by Marta Perry and available from
Center Point Large Print:

A Christmas Home
A Harvest of Love
How Secrets Die
The Promise of Easter
The Second Christmas
A Springtime Heart
When Secrets Strike

**This Large Print Book carries the
Seal of Approval of N.A.V.H.**

THANKSGIVING BLESSING

AN AMISH HOLIDAY NOVEL

Marta Perry

CENTER POINT LARGE PRINT
THORNDIKE, MAINE

ISBN: 978-1-63808-962-9

*This story is dedicated to my husband,
Brian, with much love.*

CHAPTER ONE

Becca King pulled a wagon loaded with apples and late pears along the lane that led from her orchard to the main road. The farmstand her husband had built had done a good business all summer, but Thomas hadn't been here to enjoy it. The familiar pain grasped her heart.

Hard as it was to believe, she'd been a widow for over a year now. Sometimes it seemed an eternity, while other times she was sure it had been only yesterday that he was here with her, bending over their babies and looking at her with eyes filled with wonder and joy.

With an effort, Becca pushed the memories to the back of her thoughts. With their eighteen-month-old twins to chase and the orchard to look after, she was so busy sometimes she didn't think of him as often as she should, and she felt guilty.

But then some ordinary thing reminded her, and grief stabbed her again, still fresh after all these months.

Get on with the job, she ordered herself. There wouldn't be many more weeks before the harvest season was over and their farmstand closed for another year. The angle of the sunlight and the glow of color showed it.

Becca rounded a clump of overgrown lilac bushes, tugging the wagon loaded with peck baskets of apples and late pears when it resisted turning. There weren't as many pears as she'd hoped, unfortunately, but the pear trees were getting old. She'd have to make a decision soon about planting more of them.

Would her grandfather be pleased with how she'd tended the orchard he'd left her? Sometimes she felt that the trees had borne more fruit for him than they did for her, but that was ferhoodled. Anyway, she hoped it was. Grandfather had always said the trees responded to the owner, and he'd certain sure loved every tree.

She set up the *Open* sign so anyone coming down the road would see it and began putting out the baskets she'd brought. Everything else had been loaded in the pony cart, and her sister Deborah would be along with it once she'd corralled the twins. James and Joanna loved to ride in the cart, but they could be a handful. Still, her fifteen-year-old sister managed them almost as well as Becca herself did.

She glanced back down the lane to see if she could spot them coming but only saw the colors of autumn that seemed to brighten every day. The bronze plumes of the sumac came first, even as the meadow beyond began to turn golden. Beyond that, the trees took over, their yellow, orange, and red leaves calling out to the tourists who had begun to drive along to enjoy the color and hopefully stop to buy.

"Mrs. King?"

The voice behind her startled her so much that the basket of McIntosh apples nearly escaped her grasp, sending apples scattering around the feet of the man who stood there.

She stooped to get the apples, nearly colliding with the man who bent at the same time. "Sorry," he muttered. "I didn't mean . . ."

"No matter," she said quickly, hoping she wasn't flushing. She knew who he was, of course. He'd moved into the old Mueller place next door last week, inheriting it from his uncle, the rumors said. She could only hope, as did the rest of the Amish community, that he'd be a better neighbor than his uncle had been.

"There, that's all of them." He put the last handful into the basket. "You are Mrs. King, yah? I'm Nathan Mueller."

"Next door, I know." She tried for a welcoming tone. "We heard you were moving in. I hope the house is in good shape."

Few people had been inside it for the last several years, given Joseph Mueller's attitude toward visitors. Like as not to turn the dogs on them, so folks claimed. But she shouldn't let that affect her manner toward this nephew of his.

At first glance, she saw little resemblance in the tall, sturdy man who stood before her to the shambling figure old Joseph had become. Except maybe for the frown he wore.

He seemed to be ignoring her comment, and instead was studying the farmstand. His preoccupation gave her another moment to assess what she saw. Brown hair and beard, firmly pressed lips, and thick brows that drew down as if in disapproval over cool blue eyes. She wasn't sure what she'd expected, but this wasn't it.

And what of the beard? She'd heard no mention of a wife and children . . . just a younger brother who lived with him. If he wore a beard, he'd have been married. Perhaps she was waiting for him to get the house ready before joining him.

He'd turned back to her while she was watching him, making her self-conscious. Had he noticed she was staring? She smoothed her apron down over the dark blue dress she wore.

"Are you interested in some apples? Or pears? I'd be happy to give you a basket to welcome you."

"No."

His response was so abrupt that her hands froze on the basket she'd thought to arrange for him.

"I mean, denke," he added quickly, as if he realized how brusque it sounded. Well, maybe he wasn't one for chattering. "But not right now. I hoped we could talk business for a moment."

"Business?" She looked at him blankly.

He nodded toward the farmstand. "I can see

you don't have much produce, and I heard . . . well, someone mentioned you might be willing to sell the farmstand to me. It looks to be well-made, and it could be moved over onto my property easy enough."

Becca's breath caught as she tried to understand what he was saying. For sure the stand was well-made. Thomas had been particular about his work.

But why would she sell the stand Thomas had made? And who was saying things like that?

Just then the pony cart came creaking into view. Deborah drove the shaggy pony and the twins bounced next to her, restrained by their harnesses. Deborah always claimed they needed harnessing more than the mare did.

Grateful for a breathing space before she'd have to answer the man, Becca hurried to help her sister. At least all the baskets on the cart should convince Nathan Mueller that she did indeed have plenty to sell.

Deborah hopped down quickly, reaching out to grab Joanna before she could attempt to get out of her harness by herself. Joanna was the more daring of the twins, and she was likely as not to try jumping down, just as she had from her crib a few days earlier, terrifying her mother.

So while James waited patiently for his aunt's help, Joanna already came toward her mammi at the run that tripped her up more often than not.

"Slow down, little girl," Becca reminded her.

Joanna stopped abruptly, overbalancing at the sight of a stranger, and plopped down on her bottom. James, safe in his aunt's arms, chortled and pointed.

"Ach, don't laugh at your sissy," Deborah scolded, giving a quick glance of her own at the stranger.

Before Becca could reach her, Joanna was up again, and now she headed for Nathan Mueller at top speed.

"Joanna, don't—"

But it was too late. Joanna did her usual trick of throwing her arms around any pair of nearby legs. She looked up at Mueller, probably expecting he'd sweep her up and toss her in the air the way her grossdaadi did.

Becca took a step toward them. "Sorry. That's our little Joanna—"

She stopped abruptly, because she'd caught the expression on Mueller's face. He was staring down at her child, looking as appalled as if he'd stepped into a bear trap.

Nathan realized his mistake in an instant. He knew what he'd done. He'd looked into the rosy, laughing face of the woman's child and seen the tiny, blue face of his own daughter, who hadn't lived to draw breath.

Mrs. King had seen his expression. He could tell by the way she'd swooped down and snatched up her child, her golden-brown eyes turning dark with anger. Well, he was angry, too. No one should ever be able to look so deeply into the heart of his pain.

Forcing a smile, he looked from the little girl to the small boy who'd just gained his feet. They both had cornsilk fine hair as light as flax, round blue eyes, and a dimple in the chin.

"Twins?" he asked.

"Yah." Mrs. King looked as if it took an effort to answer him pleasantly. "My children, James and Joanna. And this is my sister, Deborah Stoltz."

Deborah looked about fourteen or fifteen, and her round, rosy face was the older version of little Joanna's. Her smile was unfettered by the woman's quick resentment.

"Confusing, ain't so?" she said. "I'm a twin, too. And I have twin bruders, also. Twins run in our family," she added unnecessarily.

"I see." He felt as if he walked a tightrope between the girl's cheerful friendliness and the woman's antagonism. "Can I give you a hand?"

"We can manage." Mrs. King was already lifting a bushel of apples from the cart, while the pony dropped its head and nibbled at the grass.

Deborah handed a quart basket of pears to each of the children.

"Careful, now," she said, and steadied them on their way.

James took a few steps, the basket wobbled, and a pear rolled off, but his aunt was there to catch it and reassure him. Clearly the children were being brought up in traditional Amish fashion to work alongside the family. Nathan blocked the vision of himself doing the same.

Seeing Mrs. King occupied with arranging baskets on the stand, he picked up the next bushel and took it over. He'd gotten off on the wrong foot with the woman, and the last thing he wanted was trouble with a neighbor. They'd had enough of that.

The shopkeeper had been wrong, it seemed. He'd said Mrs. King was a widow, struggling to run an orchard on her own. He'd thought she might be eager to sell the stand, and it would save him building one of his own for the truck farm he hoped to run with his brother.

When he carried over a second basket, she unbent enough to nod her thanks. Encouraged, he risked speaking.

"McIntosh, aren't they?"

She nodded. "Yah, they're past their picking, but they're good keepers, and we sell a lot this time of year."

"Good for applesauce and pies, too," he said, remembering. "My mother always wants McIntosh for canning applesauce."

She actually smiled at that. He found himself thinking she should do it more often. Mrs. King wasn't beautiful, but her hair was like glossy horse chestnuts against the background of autumn yellow and orange leaves. Her anger had faded, and he could see the gold tint in her brown eyes.

Deborah must think her sister should try harder, because she joined the conversation. "Be sure and tell your mother that we have plenty of apples when she's ready to can."

"Our mother's not with us. It's just me and my bruder, Peter."

He hoped that hadn't sounded too sharp. He spared a momentary thought for his mother's remarriage, which had taken her off to another settlement. No matter how she tried to explain it, she clearly hadn't wanted to add a troublesome teenager to her new marriage, and that left him responsible for young Peter.

Not surprising, he guessed. Daad had always been the glue that held the family together, the strong leader who took care of everyone, including their mother. He'd told himself that explained why she'd been so helpless after he passed. And also why she'd been so quick to marry again. Somehow it didn't make much difference in the way he felt, or Peter, either, he guessed.

"Peter's probably close to your age," he said, managing a smile for Deborah. "He's fifteen."

"Yah?" Her face lit. "Della and I are fifteen. And David and Daniel are twelve. Tell your bruder to come see us."

"Denke. He'll be glad to know there are other teenagers next door."

"Not next door." She shook her head. "Becca

and the babies live here with Grossmammi, and the rest of us are across the road. The Stoltz farm." She pointed to a prosperous-looking dairy operation he'd already noticed.

"Deborah, do you want to mind the stand for an hour or so? I'll get the twins down for their nap." Mrs. King . . . Becca, her sister had called her . . . was holding out her hands to the kinder.

"Yah, yah. I've got the cash box and the price signs, so I'm ready. As long as you want."

Nathan glanced down the two-lane blacktop. "Not many customers coming by, it looks like," he commented.

"It'll pick up soon," Mrs. King said quickly, as if to counter his remark. "Afternoons are always busier, so that's why we're just opening now."

She had the young ones by the hand and was obviously impatient to leave. He didn't want to hold her up, but he was reluctant to part with her until he was sure he'd made up for his poor introduction to his neighbor.

He fell into step with her as she headed back down the lane, ignoring her surprised glance. Around the shrubbery, the house came into view, sitting at the bottom of the slope leading up to the orchard.

"Back home, we'd usually leave the stand open with a can out for folks to pay." He hoped that didn't sound as if he criticized, but he was curious about his new environment.

16

Shrugging, she nodded. "We did, too, but we have to stop doing that when Halloween is coming up. Seems like the Englisch youngsters have become more destructive with their pranks lately. At least, I hope it's the Englisch, and not our own teens."

Her golden-brown eyes darkened, and he pulled his attention from them and decided he'd have to keep an eye on any friends Peter made. He wouldn't want the boy getting in with the wrong group, especially since Peter wasn't the easiest of kids.

"So it's just you and your brother? You have sisters?" She seemed to make an effort to show interest.

"Three of them, all married with families of their own." And none of them eager to take on a troublesome teenage boy.

"I hope you and your bruder won't find it lonely here without any close relatives."

The woman's concern seemed honest enough, but he wasn't looking for sympathy, even if she seemed ready to give it.

He and Peter were on their own. It certainly wasn't the family he'd once dreamed of, but his duty was to make it work. And he still hadn't straightened up his initial misunderstanding with Becca King.

"About what I said . . . the farmstand, I mean," he began, but she didn't let him finish.

17

"It's not for sale." The words were quick and sure. "I don't know who told you otherwise, but I have no intention to sell anything. The orchard business is mine and my children's. I'll make it work."

It sounded as if she were making a vow, and a glance told him that her expression was intent. So maybe it was a promise. If this had been her dream with her husband . . . well, he knew plenty about having your dreams for the future shattered.

"Yah, for sure," he said. "I'm just sorry I got the wrong idea." They were nearing the house, so he stopped. "I'll walk across the field to my place."

She nodded, her thoughts clearly reaching ahead to her home. "Any help you need settling in, just let us know. I imagine my daad will be stopping by to tell you the same."

"Denke." He began to step away and found his pant leg snared by a small hand. This time he managed to control his feelings as he glanced down.

Little Joanna looked up at him with a tilt of the head and an appealing smile. A flirt already . . . it seemed her mother would have her hands full.

"Ach, Joanna, you must stop grabbing folks." Becca's cheeks flushed. "It started when she was first standing up, but she doesn't need to do it now."

"It's all right." Nate managed to return the child's smile and detach himself gently.

But it would be best if he didn't see much of Becca King and her kinder in the coming days. They were too sharp a reminder of what he'd lost, and he didn't need help realizing why he couldn't trust himself to care for anyone.

The afternoon slipped away, and as usual at this time of year, Becca and her grandmother had brought the children over to her parents' house for supper. Becca sat in the same place she had during all her growing up years, but now with a twin on each side of her. Joanna and James perched atop booster seats made by her father for each of them.

James, especially, loved his little seat, and even now he was bending over trying to trace the letters that spelled out his name.

"Whoa, James." Daniel, on his other side, put out a protective hand. "You'll end up down on the floor that way."

"Down," James said promptly. He didn't talk much, but what he did say was always loud and to the point. "Down, down, down!"

With a look at Becca for permission, Daniel unbuckled him and set him on the floor, handing him his fork and spoon. "Put in the sink, yah?"

James waved them dangerously close to Daniel's face, so that he drew back quickly. "Down. Yah." Then he trotted off toward the sink.

David, Daniel's twin, poked him. "Got to be ready to dodge a fork with him."

"I am." Daniel poked him back. "I learned how dodging you for the last twelve years."

Laughing, Mammi rose. "Enough. Get your plates in the sink. It'll be time for the babies to head back home too soon. It's getting dark earlier every day." She sent a look of dismay toward the window.

"Grossmammi and I will soon have to have supper with the twins at our house," Becca said.

She knew what her mother wanted. She'd love to have Becca and the twins back under her roof for good. Tempting as that might be, she was determined not to do it. She needed to keep the twins in the home that had belonged to her and their father.

The back door opened just then, cutting short anything that Mamm would have said and revealing Becca's brother Matthew, two years younger than she was.

"Ach, Matt, come in." Mamm was already reaching for the pie that was left from their dessert. "Sit down and have some pie before chores."

Matt caught Becca's eyes, and she sent him a sympathetic grin. He had to resist Mamm's efforts to get him and Miriam into the farmhouse, too. They'd only been married a year, and she suspected Miriam was just as determined to keep herself and her spouse in their own place, the story-and-a-half cottage about two hundred yards away from the farmhouse. Miriam probably wished it was farther.

"No, denke, Mamm. I'm stuffed already." Matt patted his flat stomach. "Daad, do you want me to get started?"

"We're coming, too." Daad rose, gesturing to the twelve-year-old twin boys. Daniel and David were so alike with their thick thatch of dark brown hair and brown eyes that people often mistook them for one another, although they weren't identical twins. They scrambled to the door, trying to get out before the babies could follow them.

James let out a wail and smacked the door, but Joanna scurried to her aunt Deborah and grabbed her skirt, probably to keep her from leaving, too.

"Ach, well, if he won't stay, I can still send pie home with him," Mammi said, cutting a couple of large pieces out of the apple pie.

"I thought we'd have that for breakfast," Della declared. "Matt has a wife to make pie for him."

That wasn't the most tactful thing to say, but Della couldn't help being outspoken, it seemed. And maybe it was for the best, because Mammi put down the knife and turned back to the sink.

"Deborah sold several bushels of apples, ain't so?"

Grossmammi, knowing how hard it was for her

daughter-in-law to let go of her kinder, changed the subject, and Becca hurried to help.

"She did. And helped with the picking, too. We have a good crop this year. Ach, I forgot to say we talked to our new neighbor today. Nathan Mueller."

That led to a spurt of chatter about having new neighbors living in the Mueller house, and Becca was bombarded with questions about them.

"Stop, stop," she said finally, laughing and holding up her hands. "We just talked for a few minutes. Go and see him yourself, why don't you? He said he and his brother were eager to meet everyone."

"How old is the bruder?" Della asked, interest lighting her eyes.

Becca smiled. "About fifteen, I think, isn't that right, Deborah?"

Deborah nodded reluctantly. She was probably used to the fact that her sister was the more outgoing one . . . the one who'd be eager to capture a new friend like Peter.

Still, Deborah had talked very naturally to Nathan, even though he was a stranger. Working at the farmstand seemed to be making her more comfortable with meeting people.

A glance at the clock told her they'd best head for home. "We must go. It'll be bedtime for the little ones soon."

Mammi opened her mouth, probably to argue

22

the point, and closed it again. Becca wondered if she was struggling to control herself. Like Della, she tended to be outspoken where her family was concerned.

"Let me have a goodnight kiss, James and Joanna." Mammi knelt, holding out her arms to Becca's twins. Joanna trotted to her. James started out on his feet, but quickly reverted to crawling.

Several hugs and kisses later, Becca and her grandmother had ushered the young ones outside and buckled them in the pony cart. As they started out down the lane, Becca spied her daad coming out of the barn.

"Wave to Grossdaadi," she said, and they all waved to him.

They'd reached the road by the time Grossmammi spoke. "You can't blame your mammi for wanting to keep all her chicks close, ain't so?"

"I know." She glanced at James, who was yawning and drooping already. "Maybe you should remind Matt and Miriam of that, too."

"Ach, it's harder when it comes to a grandson and his wife. I don't think Miriam would like advice from me."

The words struck her, because she'd just been thinking the same thing when Matt had been juggling Mamm's determination about the pie.

"Yah." Her tone was regretful. "I had hoped Miriam and I would be close, like Matt and I are. But she doesn't seem like she wants that."

"Take it slowly, and . . ." Her grandmother looked around as they reached their own lane. "Ach, how could I be so foolish? I've left my knitting bag at the other house. Well, I'll do without it tonight."

"You don't have to do that." Becca hopped down and handed her grandmother the reins. "I'll run over and get it. It won't take long. I'll be back in a couple of minutes."

Grossmammi started to shake her head. "You don't need . . ."

But Becca was already running back across the road. It was a little thing to do for her grandmother in return for everything her grandparents had given her.

Besides, it was refreshing to be out in the evening air by herself. The sun had slid behind the ridge, but the western sky still glowed with colors from pink to purple. With the babies and the rest of her family always around, Becca seldom had a moment to herself to do something so simple as stand and admire God's handiwork.

She inhaled, looking up at the sky. The moon was a pale disc opposite the setting sun. It was very quiet, with only a few soft sounds in the bushes where some small creatures went about their business.

Despite appreciating a few minutes by herself, she wouldn't want to be as alone as Nathan

24

Mueller and his brother seemed to be. That would be sad.

The farmhouse was quiet as she slipped into the kitchen. Everyone must have scattered. But there was Grossmammi's bag, right by her chair. She bent to pick it up and was startled by voices that seemed to be in the room with her.

Straightening, Becca realized it was Mammi and Daadi, talking in the living room. Mammi spoke, and at the words, Becca froze.

". . . just wish your father had made a different decision about the orchard. Now if Matthew and Miriam had it . . ."

"It was his decision, and he always said Becca had the gift for it." Daad's voice was a low rumble. "And with Thomas . . ."

"But she doesn't have Thomas now, and it's just too much for her. If only she'd be sensible and let Matthew take over the orchard, we could have her home."

Daad murmured something indistinguishable, and Mammi went on. "Or maybe the new neighbor who took over the Mueller place will want to add the orchard to his property. You know old Joseph Mueller always wanted to do that."

"My daad would never have wanted that."

Daad's voice was louder, and Becca realized he was coming toward the kitchen. Grabbing the knitting bag that she'd let slip from her hand, she fled silently to the door. The last thing she wanted was to be caught eavesdropping.

She raced outside, closing the door silently and letting the night hide her. Maybe the cool air would help to chase away the shock that rocked her.

She'd been taking things for granted, it seemed . . . assuming that her family was behind her in her desire to fulfill the dreams she'd shared with Thomas. Now it seemed that Mamm, at least, wasn't as approving as she'd thought. She felt as if the beam that held her in place had suddenly snapped beneath her feet.

CHAPTER TWO

"Hush, now." Becca made an effort to frown at her son over the breakfast table, but it was no use, not while she was suppressing laughter and Joanna was chortling at her twin's antics.

She started again. "In your mouth, not on the table." She guided James's hand, clutching a spoon, toward his mouth. "Your oatmeal will make you strong."

He swallowed once before sputtering oatmeal on his bib and allover his fat little face.

"Ach, stop." She mopped it up with the wet cloth she kept handy whenever the twins were eating. "Or at least be a little quieter. Grossmammi isn't up as early as you."

"Gr . . . grommy!" Joanna declared in her own version of Grossmammi. She pointed with her spoon toward the hall.

"Yah, I'm here." Becca's grandmother emerged into the kitchen and bent over one, then the other twin, distributing kisses.

"Careful," Becca warned, smiling. "They'll get oatmeal all over you."

"Won't be the first time," her grandmother replied, pouring her morning cup of tea from the pot. "And don't worry about keeping them quiet when they get up. Folks my age don't need so much sleep."

Her grandmother had probably slept more than she had, Becca realized. It felt as if she'd been up half the night, replaying her parents' conversation in her head. It sounded a little worse each time she did it. Sitting here in the familiar kitchen, with sunlight streaming across the worn floorboards and touching the geraniums she'd brought inside at a light frost, she could barely convince herself it had happened.

How could she have assumed, as she did, that her parents were happy with her decision to continue running the orchard after Thomas died? She hadn't had any doubts. In spite of the grief, pain, and confusion of that time, she'd never doubted that this was what Thomas would have wanted.

It had been their dream—one that they shared. She'd loved the orchard behind her grandparents' house from the first time she'd been allowed to go there on her own. There was something so beautiful in the rows of trees, each one producing leaves and buds, blossoms and fruit, in their season.

Unlike the garden that had to be planted every year, the trees in the orchard went on and on, giving her a place to work with her grandfather or to sit and dream on her own. Some of the trees were like Grossdaadi . . . older, a bit crooked or bent with the winds and storms, but still producing. Even now, Becca seemed to feel his presence there.

"Fruit!" Joanna declared, pulling her out of her thoughts. Having gotten her mother's attention, she handed her bowl over with a sweet smile, tilting her head to the side. "Apples?" she questioned.

"Yah, apples, funny-face." She touched the tip of her daughter's nose and then reached for the bowls of apple slices she had ready for them.

"It's a gut thing to like what you grow," Grossmammi said. "Should I start some more applesauce today? We'll want to have plenty for the pantry. And there's the Fall Festival in town coming up next week, too."

Grossmammi was like an apple herself. A little wizened, but with rounded pink cheeks. Her hair was all white now, but still thick where it was smoothed back under her kapp. Her eyes were innocent, yet somehow wise. She and Grossdaadi had run the orchard for years and years, and she knew everything there was to know. So the suggestion about the applesauce was a reminder, just in case it was needed.

Becca smiled, remembering how Thomas used to describe her grandmother. "A little tart, a little sweet . . . sort of like rhubarb sauce."

She brought herself back to the present. "Yah, we'll be busy. We ought to figure out how many baskets we want to take to the festival. What do you think about taking more of the small baskets? They seem to sell more quickly each year."

Grossmammi nodded. "Yah, there's not as many folks canning as there used to be. I guess that's why." She was silent for another moment, her gaze on Becca's face. "Now how about telling me what happened last night and why you look so tired this morning?"

Becca blinked in surprise. She hadn't thought she was giving anything away, but Grossmammi seemed to see right through her.

"I just didn't sleep so well last night," she murmured, looking for some reason to evade the question.

"And why? Was it something to do with what happened when you ran back to the house?" Grossmammi leaned across the table to pat Becca's hand. "A trouble shared is a trouble halved, you know."

Her lips twitched. That was one of her grandmother's favorite sayings, and her mother's, as well. But she certainly couldn't tell her mother what she'd overheard. She pressed her fingers against her eyes for a second, wishing she didn't have a face that gave everything away.

"It wasn't so much, but—" She stopped, then started again. "I overheard something. I shouldn't have listened."

"No, but you did, ain't so?" Grossmammi had the air of someone who knew everything.

Becca grimaced and was instantly sorry because Joanna, watching her mother, made the same face, too. "Ach, don't be such a copycat," she said, tickling Joanna under her chin until she giggled.

"Mamm and Daad were talking. I guess she was just worrying about me, but I never realized she didn't approve of my having the orchard."

"Ach, she surely never said that," Grossmammi exclaimed.

Becca frowned, trying to remember the exact words. "She said it was too much for me. That it was all very well when Thomas was alive, but I couldn't handle it alone. And it would have been better if it went to Matthew."

"Now that's nonsense." Grossmammi's hand gripped Becca's tightly. "Your grandfather and I talked it over many times, and it was up to us, ain't so? You are the one who loves the orchard, so you were the one to have it. I'm sure Matt doesn't feel that way, ain't so?"

She hesitated. "I . . . think you're right, but I guess he wouldn't show it if he did."

"I'm sure," she said firmly. "It's done, anyway. And it's foolish to keep going back to the past and thinking things should have been different. We're just given each day, one at a time, to work with. It brings enough, ain't so?"

She stood up and lifted James from his chair. "Now let's get these kinder ready for the day, and then we'll sort apples."

Becca nodded. Her grandmother was right, she

supposed. And she hadn't dared mention what Mammi had said about maybe someone buying the orchard. That would have set off an explosion.

Her mother didn't have the same feelings for the orchard, that was all. The orchard had been in the Stoltz family for generations. Even though Daad wasn't interested in running the orchard himself, he wouldn't want it to pass out of the family, would he?

Becca tried to push all of that out of her mind. All she could do was deal with today, that was certain sure. No one could do anything else.

"Come on, Peter, send up another few shingles."

Nate leaned against the wooden ladder they'd propped up against the barn. Uncle or not, Joseph Mueller had let the place go—not quite to ruin, but close enough. This barn roof wouldn't have lasted another winter the shape it was in.

"Peter!" More sharply, since the boy didn't move in response to the first call.

"They're coming." Peter finally grasped the rope they'd run through a pulley and pulled the platform loaded with shingles up to where Nate could reach them.

Grabbing a few shingles, he looked down at his younger brother. It was too bad they weren't a little closer in age. The gap between them was nearly nine years . . . too much for them to form any kind of friendship, he supposed.

"Cheer up," he called down. "Once we finish these, we'll take a break."

Peter muttered something that might have been "Who cares?"

Nate pretended not to hear him. Peter had been unhappy with the move here, but what else could he have done? Their mother had made it clear she didn't want to take Peter with her to start her new marriage, and Nate couldn't say he blamed her. Nobody would want to take a sulky, complaining teenager along on their wedding trip.

His sisters would have been a possibility, but they were wrapped up in their young families. And Peter seemed determined to grouse no matter who he was with.

As for himself, after losing his wife and baby, he'd sworn he wouldn't make himself responsible for anyone else ever again. Now, like it or not, he had Peter on his hands to finish raising. When in doubt, he struggled to think what Daad would have done in each situation.

He drove the nails through the last of the shingles with more than necessary effort. "Okay, bring that back down," he called, and started down himself.

He'd taken on the boy because no one else could or would, so he'd make the best of it.

"How about pulling out the smaller wagon, Pete? We can load it up with a few of those pumpkins." He nodded toward the orange pumpkins

33

scattered across the upper field, apparently the one thing their uncle had bothered to plant this year. Or if he had planted anything else, it hadn't survived.

He may have been wrong about running the farm Onkel Joseph had left him, but at the time, a fresh start seemed a good idea for both him and Peter. He could sell out, if he had to, but he felt he owed it to his onkel to give this a try.

"What are you going to do with the pumpkins?" Peter asked. He never said *we* Nathan noticed. He seemed to be deliberately cutting himself off from this new start.

Still, the good Lord knew that they both needed a fresh beginning, and when the word came of Onkel Joseph's bequest, it seemed like the answer.

"There's no point in letting the pumpkins rot in the fields. Someone might want them." An idea hit him that might solve two problems at once. "We'll check with Mrs. King, next door. Ask if she'll sell them in her farmstand for us. I don't believe she has any."

Peter paused with a large pumpkin in his arms. With his sandy hair and bright blue eyes, the straw hat on his head, he looked like a good advertisement for pumpkins.

But he shook his head. "From what you said, she'd probably rather see the back of us. Sounded like you got off on the wrong foot with her."

Nate shrugged, putting an armload of pumpkins

in the wagon. "She's probably forgiven me by now. I hope, anyway. We don't want to be on bad terms with any of our neighbors, do we?"

Peter flared up in an instant, suddenly sure that expression was aimed at him. "I keep telling you it wasn't me who knocked over the Millers' shed. Why don't you believe me?"

"I wasn't thinking of that at all." He rubbed his hand across the back of his neck. Was this ever going to get easier? "It's Onkel Joseph. He didn't have a good reputation around here. Folks might be cautious about us, that's all."

"Onkel Joseph was under the Bann because of his drinking. Why don't you come right out and say it? Everyone knows."

"Well, the sooner the neighbors learn we're not like Onkel Joe, the better. Komm on. A few more pumpkins, and we'll head down to the farmstand."

And once they were there, he could only hope that Peter would make a good impression. The boy needed to have some friends—good friends, not like those rackety Englisch boys he'd tried to hang out with after Daad passed. They'd led him straight into trouble.

He told himself again that they both needed a new start. If Peter met a pretty Amish girl like Deborah at the market, maybe she'd get him in with some decent friends. Maybe. Unless Becca didn't want her sister hanging around with him.

Before he'd prepared something to say, they'd rounded the curve in the lane and were within sight of the farmstand. A car had pulled up, and an Englisch woman was talking miles a minute to Becca while she bought apples and Deborah put them in the car for her.

It would make a pretty picture, except that the twins saw them first and came running. He braced himself, but neither of them ran for him, thank goodness. Instead, the little girl . . . Joanna . . . flung her arms around Peter's legs, startling him so much he nearly fell backward.

But then he was laughing down at her, grinning and answering her jabbering. He'd been around their sisters' babies enough not to be thrown off-balance.

"Hey, Nathan, better grab that one," Peter said.

Nate turned to find little James making a spirited enough climb into the wagon. Just when he thought the little guy was giving up, James threw one leg over the side, lost his balance, and headed for the ground.

Nate's heart nearly jolted out of his chest as he grabbed the child just in time. Heart thudding, he held him up at arm's length. James wiggled. Nate held him closer and then realized James was still trying to get at a pumpkin.

"Yah, all right. I'll give you one, okay?"

A smile spread over the baby's face, and James reached out to pat Nate's cheek. Startled, Nate tried to control his reaction to that chubby little hand touching his skin. He put the boy down quickly, relieved, and got out one of the small pumpkins they'd put in the wagon.

"How about this one? It's just your size." Relieved that he'd managed to sound normal, he smiled at the boy.

James wrapped his arms around the pumpkin and loudly proclaimed, "Mine." He trotted to his sister. "Mine."

Joanna's face clouded, so Nate quickly grabbed another one, giving it to her. Again she tilted her head and smiled up at him, blue eyes sparkling.

"Joanna, you are such a flirt," Becca said, shaking her head. "Really, you don't have to give them your pumpkins."

"That's why Peter and I are here." He gestured toward his brother. "This is Pete. Peter, that's Deborah Stoltz you're talking to, and this is Mrs. King, who owns the farmstand."

"Becca," she corrected quickly. Her lips tilted up as she looked at him.

So, apparently Becca had forgiven him. And judging by the way Deborah was looking, Peter had made a friend already. Maybe this wasn't going to be such a bad place after all.

Becca realized she'd been standing there smiling at Nathan for just a bit too long, and she looked quickly away, hoping the warmth she felt in her cheeks didn't show. At least her mother would be happy that she was on good terms with the new neighbors.

She found she was looking at the wagonload of pumpkins, and the words Nathan had said finally registered.

"Seriously, what are you going to do with all those pumpkins? I noticed that the top field is covered with them."

Nathan nodded, glancing back toward his new property without showing much enthusiasm. If he'd expected to find a working farm, he'd obviously been disappointed. Nothing had been done over there for most of the growing season, and not much for the previous few years. The pumpkins were volunteers, most likely, popping up and sprawling everywhere.

"I was hoping you could answer that question for me." Even the slightest smile chased the grimness away from his strong-featured face. "I saw you didn't have any pumpkins at your stand. Would you be willing to take some?"

"On consignment, you mean?" She couldn't deny that pumpkins would give some needed variety to her stand, but it was best to have terms spelled out in advance.

He shrugged. "Any terms you like. I'm not expecting to make anything, but it would be better than letting them rot in the field."

"I could help, Mrs. King. I mean, if you

38

wanted." Peter spoke quickly, and he turned scarlet when everyone looked at him. "I mean, I mean . . ." He stammered into silence, sending an apprehensive look toward his brother.

Problems with the brother? Becca couldn't tell.

Still, she'd seen enough awkward young boys flushing and stammering and stumbling over their own feet that she was sympathetic, whatever the cause. It was a tough age.

"We'd be glad of any help," she said, smiling at him. "Maybe you and Deborah could set up a display of pumpkins. It would draw the attention of people driving by, anyway."

"Sure." Deborah grabbed the twins by the hand. "Joanna and James can help." She headed for the wagon, tossing Peter a smile over her shoulder that had him flush again to the roots of his hair.

Becca stared at her sister. She'd never seen Deborah, the shy one of the twins, actually flirt before. Maybe she hadn't seen a boy who interested her until she met Peter.

Becca turned back to Nathan. "I won't take advantage of you. If Peter can help with the stand, I won't expect any share of the pumpkin profit."

"That wouldn't be fair, either," he said quickly. "You don't know yet how helpful Peter is likely to be."

Becca glanced at the two teenagers, their pumpkin moving assisted, or more likely hampered, by the twins. Still, Deborah's kind heart was leading her to put young Peter at ease. He needed something, to judge by the strained look that kept sliding onto his face when he wasn't actually talking.

"Is Peter happy about moving here?" she asked impulsively. Nathan stiffened, frowning, and she could see that he thought she was being nosy.

Well, maybe she was, but she hated seeing any young person feeling so . . . what? Unhappy? Out of place? She wasn't sure, but Peter, young and awkward and a little lost, touched her heart.

She waited, wondering if he would answer her.

Nathan's face was tight, and a muscle twitched in his jaw as if he were trying to control himself. "It takes some getting used to," he said finally. "For both of us."

His lips clamped shut. He might as well have held up a sign that said *Closed*.

Before the moment could become too awkward, a buggy came into view on the road and a moment later pulled over to the farmstand. Her brother Matthew nodded to them. His gaze lit on the pumpkins, and his eyes widened.

"Where'd all the pumpkins come from? You haven't been snatching from the neighbor's field, have you?"

Becca made a face at him. "Nathan, this is my brother Matthew. You'll have to excuse him. He thinks he's funny."

Matthew hopped down, nodding to Nathan. "Gut to see you. Daad and I planned to come over later to see if you needed any help."

Nathan's expression relaxed. "Mostly advice, I think. There's a lot to do. And it looks like conditions are different here than in upstate New York."

"Yah, I guess the weather, anyway. You get a hard frost up there pretty early, ain't so?" Matt then plunged into conversation with Nathan, from which words like *winter planting* and *cover crops* emerged now and then.

At least Matt could talk to the man without tripping over awkward comments that caused him to freeze up. Relieved, she moved over to where the others were working on the pumpkin display, watching with a grin as Peter tried to cope with Joanna, who thought he was stacking them up so she could knock them down.

Bending over to help them, she glanced cautiously at Nathan. Peter actually looked very like his older brother, although his hair hadn't darkened yet to his brother's sun-streaked brown, and his blue eyes were shy and hopeful instead of icy and accusing.

Now why did she think accusing? That wasn't the right word, surely. What could he accuse her of? If anything, she'd expect him to be apologetic for his uncle.

Hopefully he planned to be a better neighbor

than his uncle had been. But however he managed the land, Becca had an edgy feeling that he could be just as disturbing to the neighborhood as his uncle had been, with his determined manner and his quick reactions to anything he thought was interest in his business.

Her gaze lingered on the deep lines that marked his face . . . too deep for his years, she thought. Grief? She recognized that, for sure. But there was something else there . . . something hiding behind that steely facade, and she didn't know what that was.

CHAPTER THREE

Becca turned her attention to the children, thinking that they would be less distracting than her new neighbor. Then she had to laugh at herself for being naive, because she could see trouble coming from them, too.

James was carefully stacking one pumpkin on top of another, then putting a tiny one on top. Deborah was talking to Peter, bringing a smile to his face. And Joanna, standing back a little, watched her brother with a mischievous twinkle in her eyes. Becca knew what she was up to as surely as if she'd already seen it.

James took a step back from his creation, looking proud. Before Becca could move, Joanna trotted straight for his pumpkin tower and into it, sending the pumpkins rolling.

James let out a roar and pushed his sister down, and Joanna promptly burst into sobs. Peter looked horrified and helpless, while Deborah shook her head, sighed, and grabbed Joanna just as Becca caught James up, before he could cause any more mayhem.

"Enough, you two." She tickled James until his roars turned to giggles.

"I'm sorry," Peter muttered. "I should have been watching them."

"Forget it." Smiling, Becca shook her head.

"Nobody can watch them every second, and that's what it would take to keep twins from fussing at each other."

Deborah laughed. "That's for sure. As a twin, I can promise that. Come on, let's finish this." She jostled Joanna. "How about if you help this time, you little schnickelfritz?"

Becca planted a kiss on her son's fat cheek. "Go build it with Aunt Deborah."

Nathan was frowning. "Shouldn't he be punished?" It could have sounded like an obnoxious question, but it didn't. It seemed he really wanted to know.

"For what?" Instead of being offended, she found she was wondering how his mind worked.

"He knocked his sister down."

"Yah, but she knocked down his pumpkin tower first."

"But . . ." He looked as if he wished he hadn't said anything. "Sorry. It's not my business."

She could have agreed, but she just smiled at him. "Believe me, trying to be fair and find out who started what is useless when it comes to twins. Or probably any child that age. They'll go back to babyhood trying to say why the other one is to blame."

Overhearing them, Deborah nodded. "For sure. Della and I have arguments going back ten years. Just yesterday, she reminded me that I took her teddy bear when I was five."

44

"I remember that one. But she got over it," Becca said, and wondered if Nathan thought her heartless.

He didn't seem to be used to the kind of squabbling that was second nature to the Stoltz family. From what he'd said, she knew he had sisters besides his brother Pete. She'd think that was a large enough family for him to be used to it, but obviously it wasn't so.

She took her own relaxed parenting style from her mother, and she had to say it worked pretty well. Maybe Nathan's parents had been different. His father had passed away fairly young, she thought.

Nathan was standing back a little from the pumpkin building, his eyes on the children. "Guess I should keep quiet. I don't have your experience."

"I'm sorry," she said softly. She winced at the pain in his voice. "You and your wife . . . you didn't have any children?"

"One. A little girl." He seemed to force out the words, as if he didn't often say them aloud. "She and my wife both died."

"I'm so sorry." Her throat choked on the words, and she was relieved when Matt came over and interrupted them.

"I almost forgot to tell you, Becca. Daad heard that there was some vandalism in town last night."

Peter glanced at them. "Yah, I heard that when

we were in town this morning too, Nate." Nathan looked about to ask him something, but Peter hurried on. "There were some guys hanging around out front of the hardware store talking about it."

"There always are," Becca said. "Along with the lumberyard. Biggest gossip places in town."

Peter smiled at her teasing. "I don't know about that, but they said that someone pushed over a shed and then started a fire in a stack of trash."

"Over at Benninger's place," her brother added. "Other end of town, but that doesn't mean they won't come out this way. Daad says better lock everything up tonight. If you need any help, just give us a shout."

"Yah, I will." Becca tried to close down the nerves that fluttered in her stomach at the thought of someone prowling around her property. The idea of someone outside in the dark, maybe watching them through the windows . . . that was frightening. "I'll be careful." She managed not to show how much that news affected her. She didn't want Matt thinking he had to look out for her as well as his wife.

Then Nathan spoke her name quietly behind her, and she jumped.

"Sorry," he said quickly. "I didn't mean to startle you. I was just going to say that Peter can help put everything away from the stand." He hesitated. "I can, as well."

"Denke." She tried to make light of it. "The idea of vandals prowling around seems like nothing out here in the sunshine, but after dark . . . well, I hate to think of someone coming near my house."

Why had she told him that? She was trying not to show it, but she'd blurted it out to Nathan. She hardly knew him.

And she certain sure didn't want her parents knowing she felt that way. They'd consider that another good reason why she and Grossmammi and the kinder should move back home.

"You have dogs that will make a racket?" Nathan asked, his tone reluctant as if he thought she was asking for his help.

The warmth of embarrassment rose in her cheeks.

"Yah, of course." She took a step away and tried to sound brisk and in control. "They'd raise enough noise to be heard halfway down the valley. We're perfectly all right."

And yet she'd poured out a worry she'd never shared with anyone else. What was the matter with her?

Nate nodded, not quite sure what else he could say. He wanted to be a good neighbor, wanted to be accepted here. It was already a challenge since his uncle, having been under the Bann, hadn't had a good reputation among Amish or Englisch, as far as he could see.

So yes, he wanted to do what any neighbor would. It was just unfortunate that the neighbor in question was Becca King. He barely knew her, but he could already see her heart in her caring manner, her quick kindness to Peter, and her welcome to both of them.

But he had to draw a clear line between them. He couldn't risk getting involved with any woman, especially not one who almost seemed designed to fill the empty, aching place inside him.

Good thing little Joanna distracted him before that train of thought could get going. She picked up one of the small gourds he'd brought along with the pumpkins, turning it around in her hands. She shook it, held it up to her ear, and then ran straight for him. She clutched his leg and held the gourd up with a quizzical expression, as if expecting some explanation from him.

He knew what he should do. He should talk to her, should get her to put the gourd with the pumpkin display, then smile and turn away.

But he couldn't. Not when looking down at that sweet face sent so much pain grasping at his heart. He tried to move his leg, but those small, chubby hands had a grip of iron.

Before he could find something to say, Becca swept in and picked her daughter up. "Komm with Mammi, Joanna. Nathan doesn't want that gourd. We'll put it on display, yah?"

She pointed to the pile of pumpkins, setting her

daughter down. Without looking at him, she took Joanna's hand and led her away.

He had to get out of here. Nathan's heart twisted. He had to.

"Peter!" He was too sharp, and he knew it, but he couldn't help himself. "We'd best get things ready to plant a cover crop in the big field tomorrow. Matt says winter rye does best around here."

"But I thought you wanted me to stay and help?" Peter hefted a pumpkin as if weighing it, but his eyes were on Deborah.

"You can come back and help close up later. Right now I need you." He grabbed the handle of the empty wagon, forcing himself to look at Becca. She was very definitely not looking at him. "Denke," he muttered, and started walking.

Peter tagged along behind him, muttering to himself. Nate tried his best to ignore him. He wasn't proud of himself, but Peter didn't have the right to judge him.

But Peter seemed determined not to give up. He caught up to Nate with a couple of long strides and raised his voice. At least he'd waited until they were out of sight and hearing of the others.

"I don't get it. First you're pushing me to make friends and be accepted here, and then you're being rude to the neighbors."

"I was not rude." He wished he could believe that himself.

Peter made a face. "I don't know what else you'd call it. Deborah probably thinks you're . . . I don't know what. Just when I was making friends with her, too."

"Okay, okay. I said you can go back later. Maybe she'll have forgiven my behavior by then. If she even noticed."

"She noticed, all right. And so did Becca." Peter, apparently feeling he'd made his point, stamped on ahead, and they went the rest of the way without talking.

Nathan knew he should find a better way of dealing with the boy. Peter was enough younger than him that he couldn't say they knew each other well. That hadn't been a problem when Daad was alive.

But afterward . . . Mammi seemed to fall apart, unable to take care of anyone. The only logical thing was for him to take on Peter, and the truth was, he wasn't any good at this parenting business.

Maybe, if he'd had a chance . . . But he hadn't.

The memories came back, tumbling over each other as the pictures formed in his mind. Molly, her delicate face flushed, blue eyes glowing as she'd talked about the baby who was coming.

She'd been eager, so very eager. Sure that she could handle everything about being a farm wife and a mother. So happy, even when she'd felt sick, even when the baby's kicks kept her awake at night. She'd loved every minute of expecting their child.

Nate tried to stop thinking about it. Tried and failed, as he always did. Once started, the pictures didn't stop. It was like a film rolling in his head, relentlessly moving toward the end just as if it were yesterday instead of six years ago.

He stopped outside the barn, planting one hand against the wall and leaning on it, feeling his heart twist.

He'd gone to get the last of the hay in before the storms came. He'd said he'd be back in time to put a coat of paint on the room where the baby would sleep. But things kept going wrong . . . one of his helpers didn't turn up, another had to leave early. Then the fire alarm started to wail from the township fire hall.

He was a volunteer, and it was his duty. He'd run down to the road to catch a ride with the neighbor. He hadn't even thought of stopping at the house to tell Molly. If he had, he could have stopped her, convinced her to wait until he came home.

It hadn't taken long to put out the fire with the help of the rainstorm. When he'd finally headed for the house, rain was pouring down in buckets. He'd shed his wet, muddy shoes, calling out to Molly. But the only answer was a faint sound, almost like a kitten's mewling.

Up the stairs, stumbling in his haste, he'd

rushed into the room and found the picture that had already been forming in his mind. The upset ladder. The bucket of paint spilled and dripping. Molly, lying there.

She'd seen him, there at the last, but her thoughts had been on the baby. By the time paramedics arrived, it was too late for both of them.

Nathan blew out a long breath, feeling again the pain and the emptiness. He hadn't been able to save them. They had been entrusted to his care, and he'd failed them.

He'd never trust himself with such a responsibility again. Never.

Becca didn't say anything for a spell after Nathan and his brother left. Deborah glanced at her, opened her mouth as if to comment, and wisely changed her mind.

Several customers stopped by, and there was a lot of chatter. Everyone seemed to admire the pumpkin display, and Becca could see Deborah begin to glow at their praise.

It would be good for Deborah, she thought. She was so often outshone by her twin. She must get tired of Della's accounts of all the people she waited on and talked to at the grocery store in town. Every night at supper Della had some story to tell, it seemed.

Deborah was happy in her role of helping with the twins. Becca didn't doubt that. But once in a while she might wish to have her own story to tell. She'd be sure to bring it up at supper tonight, if Deborah didn't do it herself.

But when a lull came in customers, that wasn't what came to her mind. It was Nathan.

What was wrong with the man? The first time it had happened she'd managed to ignore it. Well, not entirely, but at least she hadn't said anything to anyone about his reaction to the twins.

But now . . .

"I can't imagine what that man was thinking." The words came spurting out without thought.

Deborah glanced at her, eyes wide and startled. "What man? Where?"

"Nathan Mueller, that's who. Didn't you see how he reacted when Joanna tried to show him a gourd, and he acted as if she'd poked a knife into him."

"I guess I must have missed it," Deborah said carefully. "What did he do?"

"He . . . he tried to yank away from her, but you know Joanna. She has a grip of iron when she gets hold of you. And then he absolutely glared at her."

"Are you sure about that?"

Becca sniffed at her sister's doubt. "I guess I can trust the evidence of my own eyes. He looked like he thought my baby girl was . . . was contagious or something." She frowned at Deborah. "Don't tell me you didn't notice anything."

Deborah bent to remove an apple from James's

53

hand before he could throw it. She straightened slowly. "I saw that he looked uncomfortable. But maybe that's sort of natural."

For an instant Becca felt a flare of annoyance with her sister, and then she thought how foolish that was.

"Okay, I know everyone doesn't think my twins are the cutest babies in the whole wide world. But it just seemed like . . ." She stopped, unsure.

"Peter told me that Nathan's wife died. He said their baby died, too. Don't you think that might make him sort of uncomfortable around other people's babies?" She watched Becca cautiously, as if waiting for an explosion.

But there was no need. Her little sister's careful words convicted her of judging poor Nathan without thought or kindness. And she knew of his loss, too, so there was no excuse.

She studied Deborah's face as she stood watching her apprehensively. Becca shook her head at her own foolishness.

"How did you get so wise, little sister?"

Deborah relaxed, smiling in relief. "By watching my big sister," she said pertly. "Grossmammi and Mammi, too."

"That's certain sure." She laughed, giving her sister a quick hug. "Okay, you're right and I'm wrong. Just don't let it become a habit, will you?"

She was still smiling as another car pulled up beside the stand.

The Englisch woman who got out was familiar to Becca as a customer, but it took a moment to remember her name. Then it popped into her head just as the woman exclaimed over the pumpkin and gourd display.

"It's gut to see you, Mrs. Larkin. What can I help you with?"

"Well, I came for apples, just as I do every year." She pushed her sunglasses up on her head and smiled at them, bending over to exclaim about how big the twins were getting.

"Yah, they're growing faster than the weeds in the garden. They're trying to help," she added, a little apologetically as Joanna held out a gourd to the woman.

Mrs. Larkin accepted the gourd, laughing a little. "Oh, how I wish my grandchildren lived close to me. Our daughter's little Amy is just three, and they remind me so much of her."

Tears shone in the woman's eyes for a moment before she blinked them away, and Becca felt a wave of thankfulness that she and her children were surrounded by family.

"Do you want the Idared apples again this year? I have several baskets of them here, as well as these nice Winesaps. Good keepers, Winesaps," she added.

"No McIntosh?" Mrs. Larkin sounded disappointed, depressing Becca. She always wanted to have what the customer wanted.

"I'm afraid we didn't have a very big crop of them this year, and they're about gone. And of course, they come on earlier. But my grandmother has been using Winesaps for her applesauce, and she thinks they're the best we've ever had."

Mrs. Larkin gave a brisk nod. "I'll have a bushel of the Winesaps and one of the Idared. And now, about those pumpkins . . ." She moved to the pumpkin display.

Becca gestured to her sister to load the apples as she followed Mrs. Larkin.

"These are from the farm next door," she explained. "Not really pie pumpkins, I'm afraid."

"That's all right. It's not for baking, it's for decorating. Somehow or other I got on the committee for decorating the downtown area, and we're going to need a load of pumpkins and gourds. Thing is, I'd want them by Saturday, when we start decorating."

"I see." Becca's thoughts whirled. Did Nathan have enough? And if he did, would he want to be involved in anything like this right when he was eager to plant cover crops?

Mrs. Larkin must have sensed her hesitation. "You won't know until you've talked to the farmer, of course." She pulled out her wallet to pay for her purchases. "You talk to him . . . say we'll need at least a hundred for what we want, and if he has more, that'll be great. We'll pay top market price, of course."

Becca quickly calculated the amount. Surely Nathan would want to take it on, assuming he had enough pumpkins.

"I'll talk to him later this afternoon, and I can call you as soon as he decides," she said quickly.

"Very good." The woman handed over the money for her apples. "And here's a card with my phone number on it."

In a few moments they waved goodbye to Mrs. Larkin, and Becca's thoughts were still in a jumble. She'd have to talk to Nathan as soon as possible. And this time she'd have to control her feelings.

"I guess you'll want to speak to Nathan," Deborah said, as if reading her thoughts.

"Yah." She tried to control her expression. "He did say he'd come back to help us put things away for the night. I'll talk to him then. Right now I'd best put the twins down for their naps."

James, hearing the dreaded word, looked up from the pumpkin he was rolling and let out a roar. It turned into a yawn before it really got going, making Becca laugh as she scooped him up. She held out her hand to Joanna.

By the time she saw Nathan, she could only hope she'd have figured out how to talk to him.

CHAPTER FOUR

When Becca headed back to the farmstand a few hours later, she was driving the pony cart, knowing they'd need it to bring everything back to storage. Maybe all this caution wasn't necessary, she thought hopefully. Maybe the pranksters had had their fill of causing trouble.

On the other hand, maybe they were all keyed up and ready to do something worse than set trash on fire. It was best to play it safe, that was certain sure. They'd put everything in the barn or the storage shed, and she'd close and lock the shutters on the farmstand.

Thomas had made it to be secure because that was the kind of person he was. Always careful. But sometimes an accident occurred that no one could have anticipated, like the one that took his life.

He'd always been so careful with the chain saw, but no one could predict a second's inattention or the stubborn knot in the tree trunk that caused the chain saw to kick back. He'd been alone, and by the time someone found him, it had been too late.

She didn't relive those moments quite as often as she once did. She'd learned that it wasn't good for her or the children if she persisted in dwelling on it.

Chasing the thought away, Becca spotted Peter pulling the wagon he'd brought before. Maybe Nathan had sent him instead of coming himself. But that was a foolish thought, because if so, she'd still have to talk to Nathan about Mrs. Larkin's offer.

The lane rounded the lilac hedge, and she realized that Nathan was a few yards ahead of his brother. They glanced back, and Peter waved his hand at her, making her smile. At least she'd gotten off on the right foot with him, if not with his brother.

In a few minutes all four were gathered around the stand, and usually quiet Deborah, eyes sparkling, was talking excitedly about how many sales she'd had that afternoon.

"And several people bought pumpkins, too." She pulled a slip of paper from the cashbox. "I've made a note of them so we can split the money."

Nathan got the stubborn, frowning look that announced he was going to argue about taking any profit from them. Becca was beginning to find she could read him easily, and she spoke quickly before he could start.

"Gut job, Deborah. And I see all the pears went. Excellent! Suppose you and Peter load up the wagon with the rest of the apples, and I'll help Nathan take the pumpkins to the barn until tomorrow."

As Deborah nodded and grabbed a basket,

Becca turned to Nathan. "I hope you don't mind, but there's something I need to discuss with you."

Nathan gave her a cautious look, probably wondering if this was about pumpkin profit. But when she didn't say anything else, he just nodded and started loading pumpkins. Peter and Deborah were busy with the apples and talking . . . at least, Deborah was talking and Peter was giving her a shy smile and a nod now and then.

The kids were done first, of course, and Nathan shook his head at Peter's offer to help them. "You two go ahead. We'll be right there."

So Peter and Deborah headed up the lane, and Nathan took the last of the pumpkins from Becca's hands once they were out of sight and hearing.

"What is it we need to talk about?" he asked, setting them in the pony cart.

"Actually, it's about pumpkins." Turning back to the stand, she stretched to reach the shutters that closed over the opening. "I'll just lock up, and then we can be going."

Moving behind her, Nathan reached over her head to get the latch she was struggling with. His hand closed over hers, and for a moment it didn't move. Becca, startled, found she was holding her breath.

She let it out slowly, stepping back. With his face averted, Nathan pulled the shutters down into place, bolted them, and then stepped out and waited while she locked the door.

"Now about the pumpkins," he reminded her, with an air of needing a bit more patience.

"Yah, sorry." She swung herself into the pony cart before he could give her a hand, sliding over so that he could join her.

"Not long after you left—" she began, only to have him stop her with a gesture.

"About that." He was silent, frowning for a moment. "Peter tells me I was rude, and he's right. I'm sorry. I don't know what got into me. I—"

"Don't think anything about it. I'm the one who's sorry." She took a breath, knowing she must say more, but afraid of hurting him. "I should have realized what was happening when Joanna kept forcing herself on you. The loss of your own babe . . . I can't imagine the pain."

Her eyes filled with tears, and she dashed them away with her fingers, wishing she had more control.

Nathan's face was as tight and rigid as a stone wall. If she'd said too much, made it worse . . .

"It's not your fault. Or Joanna's." His lips softened for a moment. "She's got a smile that will capture the boys' hearts one day. But I just find . . . well, it's better for me to steer clear of little ones."

A dozen thoughts rushed into her mind at once. Surely it would help him to heal to . . . But it wasn't her concern, and the wound he carried was obviously too deep. She couldn't meddle, no matter how she longed to help him.

Becca paused a moment to be sure she could speak naturally. "There's no need for you to be around the babies, ain't so?"

She hesitated, but he didn't speak. Her mare, tired of waiting, jingled the harness, and Becca clicked to start her moving.

"Now, about the pumpkins," she said again. "One of my regular customers, Mrs. Larkin, stopped by, and she was so pleased to find a place where she could get pumpkins. She wants to buy a good bunch of them . . . one hundred at least . . . and she'll pay market price for the whole lot of them."

"A hundred?" Nathan looked startled. "I certain sure didn't expect that. She must be wanting a lot of pumpkin pie."

His tone was lighter now, as if he was relieved to be safely away from an awkward subject.

"What you have are not really pie pumpkins . . . at least those big orange ones aren't. Anyway, she wants them for some decorating they're doing downtown. Thing is, she needs them by Saturday morning, or even tomorrow night, if you can manage."

He nodded slowly, but she suspected he was thinking about too many things to do and not enough time to do them in. Surely that just meant he could use some extra help.

"My little brothers will come over and help to pick and load them. Now don't argue . . . that's what younger brothers are for."

Nathan's face relaxed. "I guess I'd have to agree with that. But if we're doing this, you have to accept a fair share of the money."

"No, no, that's not necessary," she said quickly. "I didn't do anything, and—"

"You're the one who sold them to begin with," he pointed out. "We'll have to be partners in pumpkins, or there's no deal."

He smiled at her, a real smile, for the first time. Goodness. With a smile like that, he could persuade anyone of anything. As for her, well, the warmth she felt in response startled her, making her want to get much farther away from him than the small seat of the pony cart allowed.

She must be ferhoodled. How had she let herself become so entangled with the man in two short days?

Nathan swung himself out of the cart as Becca came to a halt at the barn door. He hadn't missed the . . . well, call it confusion . . . she'd experienced for a moment. Had he really been so standoffish that she'd been confused by a sign of friendship?

He grasped the barn door and slid it open, standing back as she drove the pony through and considering the point. Well, if he had been, he'd best watch himself around all the new people he and Peter would be meeting. He wanted to be accepted here, for both their sakes.

He and Peter both needed a fresh start in a new community. Maybe here they could heal and live a normal life.

"Do you want everything unloaded?" he asked, following her into the barn.

"No, I think just leave it loaded until tomorrow." She began unbuckling the pony's harness. "We'll have to keep it away from Sweetie here, though. She'll eat anything that's not nailed down."

"Sweetie?" He moved to the other side of the shaggy pony to help with the harness. "Unlikely name for an Amish pony, ain't so?"

She chuckled. "I forget how strange it sounds to someone who hasn't met her before." Becca checked to be sure the mare was free of the harness. "Step up, now, Sweetie."

The pony stepped clear of the cart shafts and promptly tried to turn and reach the pumpkins. Becca grabbed her. "What did I tell you? She eats like a goat instead of a pony."

"And why is she called Sweetie? I can't say she seems all that sweet," he added, suppressing a laugh as the mare tossed her head in disapproval of being led firmly away from the pumpkins.

"I made the mistake of letting my little brothers and sisters name her. Sweetie was actually the best name they found. Speaking of names, you should have heard the names they came up with for my twins. They had Thomas in stitches most of the time."

"I can imagine." In spite of the loss of her husband, Becca didn't seem to have trouble talking about him, even to strangers. Why did he find it so difficult in his own case?

He leaned against a stack of straw bales, watching as she turned the pony in to a stall. He was just relaxing when a scrabbling noise in his ear sent him jerking away from the bales.

"Is that what I think it is?" he said, staring at an improvised chicken-wire cage.

"That depends on whether you think it's a squirrel." Becca scooped some grain from a metal can and dropped it into the cage with the squirrel, which dropped from the wire to begin downing the grain.

"Daniel found this guy lying behind the barn with a broken leg. Poor thing looked pretty far gone. Matt said we should put him out of his misery, but Daniel wouldn't hear of it. He brought him to me."

Nathan studied her face. Gentle, nurturing, but with an extra spark that appeared when you didn't expect it.

"So you're the resident squirrel doctor, are you?" He couldn't say he was surprised to find that her caring extended beyond her children and family.

"Just common sense, for the most part. He was as much stunned as anything, but he's coming along now. Before long, he'll soon be ready to go back to his family. Won't you?" She addressed the creature, reaching through the mesh to pet the animal with one finger. The squirrel seemed to like it, rubbing against her finger like a cat would.

He found himself smiling instead of having his instinctive reaction against making a pet of a wild creature. "Any other wild pets I should watch out for?" He glanced around, making a joke of it, but Becca didn't seem to feel that way.

"You think it's foolish, yah?" She read his expression easily.

He shrugged, finding he really didn't want to disagree with her. "I've always thought wild creatures should take care of themselves."

"Usually they do. But sometimes they can use a little extra care, just like humans." She gave him a look that challenged him to disagree. "After all, God gave Adam the job of caring for all the creatures He created. Not just the useful ones."

He might have argued about that, but he didn't think he had a leg to stand on . . . somewhat like the squirrel. He certain sure couldn't disagree with the amount of love and caring Becca seemed to pour out on anyone and anything that crossed her path. Whether he thought it foolish to waste it on a squirrel . . .

The barn door rattled as Peter poked his head

around it. "Deborah's grossmammi says for us to come in and have some lemonade and cookies. Okay?"

"We'll be right there," Becca said, apparently assuming Nathan agreed.

They walked toward the house together, and he noticed the phone shanty next to the back porch.

"Should we . . . I get in touch with that Mrs. Larkin?" he asked. "She might be waiting to hear back about the pumpkins. I'll need to know the details, too."

"Ach, yah, you're right. She's expecting a call." Becca pulled a slip of paper from her apron and handed it to him. "Use our phone, if you want. Any time. I'm sure your uncle's was disconnected."

She nodded toward the phone shanty and then went on into the house.

When Nathan came out ten or fifteen minutes later, he was rubbing his ear. Mrs. Larkin was a talker, that was certain sure. But generous. She'd send someone over with a truck to pick up the pumpkins late tomorrow afternoon, and the price she'd offered was far higher than he'd expected.

But then, he didn't know anything about prices in this area yet. It was another thing he'd have to catch up on before he could make a success of truck farming.

Nathan walked in the open back door to find

himself in a typical Amish kitchen . . . linoleum floor, wooden cabinets, a rectangular oak table with chairs all around it, and plants blooming in pots on the windowsills.

The twins were in their high chairs, apparently having a snack. Joanna put her hands up in front of her and peeked around them to look at him, but James kept trying to stuff a whole cookie in his mouth.

"Don't mind James," Becca said. "He's a messy eater."

He was just glad they were confined to their high chairs. It would make a getaway that much easier when he decided to leave.

"Wilkom." The woman who was obviously Becca's grandmother smiled, looking like a much older version of Becca for a moment. "You'll have some lemonade, yah?"

"Denke, but I think we should go home and get started. Mrs. Larkin is sending a truck for the pumpkins tomorrow afternoon. We can't miss that opportunity."

"You'll come for supper sometime soon, then," she said. "It's wonderful gut to have the Mueller family back in Promise Glen."

He nodded, hoping her feelings were shared by the rest of the community. "Komm, Peter, we'd best be going."

Peter got up and went out with him after thanking Deborah and her grandmother. Then he glanced toward his brother. "You think everyone else in the community will feel like that?"

There was a touch of bitterness in the boy's voice that Nate didn't like, but he tried not to let it put his back up.

"Probably not, I guess. We'll just have to give it time."

Peter didn't respond, but the sulky look on his face wasn't encouraging. Daad would know what to do. But all Peter had now was Nathan, and he surely didn't.

"Are you sure we have enough sugar?" Grossmammi put scrambled eggs in front of the twins the next morning, but her mind was clearly on making apple butter.

"There's an extra twenty pounds in the pantry." Becca hoped she sounded assuring and not irritable. The family party to make apple butter was Grossmammi's favorite thing, and Grossmammi did fuss about it.

Becca's grandfather could always tease her out of worrying, but Becca didn't seem to have that talent.

"Ach, I know, I know. I've got a bee in my bonnet about it." Grossmammi shook her head, laughing a little. "That's what your grossdaadi would say. I just don't remember so gut as I used to, so I have to keep checking."

"You're doing fine."

Becca gave her a quick hug. Grossmammi had always been the rock of the family, and it saddened Becca to see how she seemed to slip since Grossdaadi died. It wasn't just her memory, but she seemed frailer, too.

"It'll be the best apple butter making ever, ain't so?" Grossmammi said, sounding upbeat.

Responding to the tone of her voice if not the words, Joanna beat her spoon against the high chair tray, laughing.

"And you won't forget to invite Nathan and Peter." Grossmammi shook her head. "Whatever is wrong between those two boys? Seems like they're always at odds."

"I don't know." They'd both heard Peter's tone as they were leaving.

There seemed to be a lot of things she didn't know about Nathan. He and Peter were more of a mystery than most newcomers, mainly because Joseph Mueller had been alienated from the church.

"We'll have to do what we can for them," Grossmammi announced firmly. "It's our duty as neighbors."

Becca didn't speak for a moment. She wasn't surprised her grandmother felt that way, but she'd just been hoping to avoid that particular duty. She had enough to do without involving herself in their struggles.

She knew exactly what her grandmother would

say if she tried to use that for an excuse, so she didn't bother. Besides, just thinking it made her feel ashamed of herself.

"I'll be sure to invite them to join us tomorrow," she said, trying to sound enthusiastic. "And then Sunday they'll meet the rest of the community at worship. Right?"

Grossmammi nodded, but she was eyeing the window of the sink, looking distracted. Becca turned to find her father coming to the back door. She flung it open.

"Just in time for some coffee." She smiled, the twins welcomed their grandfather with crowing and banging on their trays, and Grossmammi reached for the coffeepot.

"Ach, not for me." He shook his head. "I was just checking on the farmstand. You brought everything in, ain't so?"

"Yah, of course." She met his gaze, wincing a little at the worry in his face. "Daadi, was ist letz? Has something happened?"

He nodded, his face tightening. "Fence broken down over at Eli Miller's place, and somebody drove right through his planting of winter wheat. Looked like they were racing each other. Eli ran out, but they shot off toward town before he could get a good look at the cars."

Grossmammi shook her head, moving closer to the babies. "That's bad."

"Kind of thing to upset folks. Next thing you

know, some of the farmers will be running out with shotguns at every noise. Before you know it, somebody could be badly hurt."

Daad looked more worried than Becca had seen him in a while. With his lean, weathered face and his twinkling blue eyes, he was usually relaxed . . . not one to worry needlessly. But not now.

"There's always trouble this time of year," she reminded him. "Halloween is next week, so that should make an end to it." She tried to sound comforting, knowing the main reason for his worried frown was the thought of her and his mother alone here at night with the babies.

"A lot of things can happen before then." Daadi moved toward the door. "I'm going to see what help young Mueller needs today. And I'll let him know about what happened so he'll keep a lookout."

Becca's instinctive reaction caught her off guard. She didn't want Daadi giving Nathan the idea that he should look out for her. But there was no way of saying it so that Daad would understand. Naturally neighbors looked out for each other.

She stepped out onto the back porch, wrapping her arms around herself in the chill morning air. The back of her property marched back side by side with Nathan's, hers stretching gently upward to the orchard while his fields reached on toward the woods.

Daad had crossed over to Nathan's property already. Nate, working with Peter in the pumpkin field, spotted him and started toward him.

They met, two Amish figures alike in their black pants, blue shirts, suspenders, and straw hats. Daad spoke, then Nathan. Then Daad again, and they both turned and looked back toward her. Becca shrank back against the door she was holding, hoping it would shield her from their gaze.

Was she trying to fool herself? It wasn't *their* gazes she was concerned about. It was Nathan's. What was he thinking? Did he suspect her family of pushing him on Becca?

They weren't, but if they did, they'd be disappointed. Nathan didn't seem to be remotely interested in marrying again.

CHAPTER FIVE

Becca was getting ready to head out to the stand that afternoon when the back door opened and her sister-in-law, Miriam, came in, looking around tentatively.

"Miriam, wilkom!" Becca suspected she always sounded too enthused when she saw Miriam, just because she sensed a barrier between them.

Miriam glanced at her with a timid smile, but when she saw Joanna and James in their high chairs, her face simply glowed. She hurried to them, bending to kiss first one and then the other.

Becca's heart clenched, and her gaze met Grossmammi's. An unspoken understanding moved between them. Miriam longed so much to have a baby of her own. Why had her prayers not been answered?

Becca swallowed the lump in her throat. "I'm glad you came over, Miriam. Did you see the pumpkin picking going on up in Mueller's field?"

Miriam managed to tear herself away from the babies to pay attention to the grown-ups. "Yah, I heard about it. I thought you might need some help. I can watch the babies and help Grossmammi get things ready for tomorrow."

"Wonderful gut idea," Grossmammi said briskly. "There's plenty to do, and now Becca can get off to the stand. Friday afternoon is always busy."

Not to mention Saturday, Becca thought, but she'd have to let tomorrow take care of itself. "Yah, denke," she said, grabbing her heavy black sweater from its hook. "I'll be off, then."

She bent to kiss the babies, suspecting she knew what was in her grandmother's mind. Grossmammi was longing for some time alone with Miriam, no doubt hoping Miriam would open her heart. After all, she didn't need to suffer alone when she had women here ready to share and comfort. And probably offer some advice, if she knew her grandmother.

Waving goodbye, she hurried out to the barn. Poor Miriam. And poor Matt, struggling so hard to understand and to say the right thing. If only she could help them. But the fact that she had produced two healthy babies within little over a year of marriage while Miriam still struggled seemed to stand between them—on Miriam's part, at least.

Parenting was never easy—she'd learned that already with the babies. How hard it must be, as a parent, to rejoice with one child's happiness while mourning another child's sorrow. She remembered Mammi saying in frustration that after they'd grown past being babies, she'd never had all of them happy at the same time.

Becca had laughed at the time, but she was a little older and wiser now, and she understood.

She went to the paddock to catch the pony, rattling a little grain in a bucket and remembering Thomas laughing at her for her inability to get Sweetie any other way. He had a sure hand with horses, but he'd soon learned that Sweetie's stubbornness matched his own.

The memory made her smile, but it gave her a pain in the heart, as well. Still, it was worth the pain to have the memories.

"Let me help you." The voice surprised her, and she turned, holding onto Sweetie's bridle, to see Nathan approaching.

Trying to hide her surprise, Becca began leading the pony toward the barn. "I thought you were tied up with gathering pumpkins and getting your upper field ready for planting."

"The young ones are having such a gut time doing it that I decided to trust them for a few minutes." He vanished into the barn and came out pushing the loaded pony cart and carrying the harness.

Becca craned her neck to see the field. Everything looked under control, with her two sisters and brothers helping Peter and a certain amount of laughing and talking going on.

"Was ist letz? Is something wrong?" Nathan began settling the harness on Sweetie.

Becca was surprised into a laugh. "Only that you're showing a lot of confidence in my siblings." More than he seemed to show to Peter, she thought but didn't say. "The girls are okay, and Daniel is usually dependable. But David . . . well, sometimes David gets carried away. He's not as mature as Daniel is."

He handed her a harness strap. "Should I go back and send Peter down to help you?"

Becca shook her head. "I think they'll be okay with both of the girls there, at least for a bit. Kids that age are so unpredictable, ain't so? Don't you find that with Peter?"

Nathan frowned, turning toward the shed where the small wagon was with apples. "I'll get the rest of the things and be right behind you."

Becca studied his tall figure as he strode off. It looked as if she shouldn't have asked the question, but she couldn't help noticing that things were strained between the brothers. As always, she saw and wanted to help.

Nathan must think her a busybody. Maybe he was right, but at least it wasn't because she wanted to gossip, just to help. Peter wasn't her responsibility, but she still felt sorry for the boy with the lost look.

At least Nathan showed some consideration in letting the kids enjoy themselves together. She glanced back. If she saw a pumpkin rolling down the hill, she'd know who the culprit was. But they all seemed to be in their proper place. She could certain sure trust Deborah. It would be nice to think they'd all make a good impression on Nathan, but she feared that was too optimistic when her younger brothers were concerned.

Becca clicked to Sweetie, heading down the lane toward the road and hoping for good sales this afternoon.

It had been a good season, she reminded herself. Surely she'd shown her parents that she was managing very well. Still, Mammi would worry, no matter what. Each time she got impatient with that worrying, she'd think about herself and the twins and understand, at least a little.

A few minutes later, Becca was opening up the stand while Nathan carried a bushel of apples from the cart. He set it down, still frowning, and then moved to the outside of the counter. When he spoke, his tone was abrupt.

"How does it happen that you understand teenagers so well? Your own kinder are just babies." He acted as if they were continuing a conversation they'd just begun, and in spite of his tone, she sensed that he genuinely wanted an answer.

"Having younger siblings helps, and obviously I have plenty." Although Nathan was also the eldest in his family, it hadn't helped him. "Besides, I can easily think back to what I was like at that age." She hesitated, but decided to take a chance and prod him a little toward understanding. "It wasn't so long ago that you were Peter's age, ain't so?"

For a moment Becca thought he wasn't going

to answer. Frowning, he carried another basket over. Then he shrugged, as if trying to shake something off.

"Now that you remind me, it feels like a lifetime ago, maybe because so much has happened. But I guess it wasn't so very long." He sounded surprised. "Our daad was alive then, though. He seemed to hold everyone together."

Her heart was touched by the suddenly bereft look on his face. "I'm sorry," she murmured, reaching out to touch his hand lightly where it lay on the counter. "You've had a lot of losses." She hesitated a moment. "So has Peter."

His gaze met hers. This time the blue eyes weren't icy. They were shadowed with sorrow. His hand turned so that he was clasping hers, palm to palm.

Becca's breath caught. Despite the counter between them, she felt close to him. Too close.

His hand was warm and strong, but she could have pulled away in an instant. The trouble was that she didn't want to.

By the next day, Nathan figured he should have come to terms with himself over that moment with Becca when emotion and need had swept over him. Somehow, he hadn't. He was still thinking about it, no matter how he tried to ignore it.

He paused to sight down the row across the

field to be sure it was straight. With the pumpkins delivered and some extra money in his pocket, they'd made a start on the winter cover crop. With the two of them working, it shouldn't take too long.

Sure that the row was where it should be, he nodded to Peter. Standing at the far end with the planter, Peter waved acknowledgment and started guiding the planter along, the seeds dropping evenly into the row. It was an old-fashioned way of doing it, but the area wasn't all that large, and it would work. By the time they'd had a year of running the place, they'd surely be more organized.

A glance in the other direction told him that the members of the Stoltz family were gathering behind Becca's house, hauling firewood and bringing apple baskets from the shed. Becca seemed to be everywhere at once, organizing, helping, encouraging.

Becca. If he had it to do over again, he'd have invented some reason why he couldn't come to their apple butter making this afternoon. He'd be better off staying away from Becca King altogether. How many times did he have to remind himself?

Anyway, Becca probably felt the same way about him, or at least she would if she'd felt the huge wave of warmth and longing that had hit him when their hands touched.

Maybe she hadn't. Maybe it was just him. Either way, the remedy was the same. Stay away from her. Stay away, so he wouldn't risk caring for anyone again . . . caring and then letting her down.

Or them, in this case. Not just Becca, but the two babies, as well. He'd lost whatever trust he'd had in himself the day his wife and baby died.

Seeding, tamping the rows down gently, the routine went on, until Peter paused and Nathan caught up with him.

"You want to trade places?" Nathan rested his hand on the planter.

"Yah, I guess." Peter sounded discontented. "Daad never planted cover crops this late."

It wasn't really a question, but it needed an answer, he guessed.

"Gets cold earlier up in New York State. Up there, they've probably had a hard frost this week. You heard what Becca's brother said."

"Yah, I guess." Peter didn't sound convinced, and his gaze strayed over to the next farm. Looking for the kids, or maybe especially for Deborah.

"If I'm wrong, all we've lost is some seed and a few hours of work." He smiled, relenting, and tapped Peter's shoulder. "Finish another two rows, and then you can run over to Becca's and see if you can help while I finish up."

Peter grinned, nodded, and took off along the row.

Was that the right thing to do? He didn't know. He never did. He was only Peter's brother, not his father, and for a moment he missed Daad fiercely.

They finished quickly, and he cleaned and put away tools while Peter dashed to the house, emerged ten minutes later in a clean shirt and pants, and then sauntered toward the people gathering in Becca's backyard.

Nathan's lips twitched at the boy's effort to be casual. Thanks to Becca's prodding, he did remember that period, being so anxious to impress someone and fearing failure.

Well, he wanted Peter to make some decent Amish friends here, not like those kids he'd hung around in the past. The Stoltz kids ought to be a good influence, he'd think from what he'd seen of them.

Nathan took his time going across to Becca's property, dallying over clearing up. They'd understand that, but he'd offend the family if he didn't show up at all. He knew only too well that he could never explain to anyone why he didn't want to get too close to this particular neighbor.

Or maybe the truth of it was that he was afraid to get too close. *Afraid?* He rejected the thought as soon as it occurred. He wasn't afraid. But even so, it lingered at the back of his mind.

"Here you are." Becca's brother Matthew,

carrying an armload of cut firewood, greeted him. "Here, take this over to the fire, will you? I need to fetch the apple butter paddle before those boys make a mess looking for it."

"Sure thing." Nathan accepted the wood and carried it over to where a fire was glowing in a stone-enclosed firepit.

"Denke." Becca's father, Abram, wielded a poker to get the logs into the exact position he wanted, and Nathan had a quick memory of his daad doing the same thing.

"You've got a nice even heat," Nathan commented.

Abram glanced at him and smiled. "You've done this before, yah?"

"For sure. My daad loved apple butter. We had a big old tree of McIntosh apples that we used for everything."

Funny, to have that pang of remembrance when he'd been away from the old farm for so long.

"Good apples . . ." Abram began, but broke off when Daniel and Peter between them carried the heavy black apple butter kettle over. Abram moved quickly to help them get the kettle hung from the framework in place to hold it, murmuring encouragement to the boys.

By the time they'd gotten the kettle situated over the fire, Matthew was back with the long-handled paddle, smooth and worn from years of use, Nathan could see.

"Grossmammi gets the first stir," Matthew declared, and there was a murmur of encouragement, a few claps, and a whistle from David. Laughing, their grandmother came forward to wield the first turn of the paddle.

The young ones cheered, then broke into a laughing argument about who should go next.

This led to a complicated discussion about who had done what when, until Della settled it by grabbing the paddle while the boys were still arguing.

Someone put a cup of cider in Nathan's hand, and Abram gestured for him to sit with him on a rough-hewn bench pulled up by the fire. The fire warmed his feet and the comforting hum of family talk flowed around him like a blanket.

Amid some shoving and laughing, Peter took over the paddle. He was flushed and smiling, and Nathan thought that he hadn't looked like that in months. It was good to see. Why hadn't he realized that it had been missing?

"The young ones will be distracted eventually," Abram said. "They'll get tired of standing still and stirring. Then the rest of us have to take over."

"Sounds gut," Nathan said, smiling at his own memories. "I'll be glad to take a turn. My daad used to say that anyone who let the apple butter stick to the kettle would get tossed in the duck pond."

Abram nodded. "Sounds like your father would have gotten along fine here."

Thinking about what his daad would make of this place and these people, Nathan knew he was right. Abram wasn't like his father physically, but Nathan perceived the same sense of fairness and patience that his father had. That was probably what attracted Peter to these people, too.

Deborah and Becca came out of the house just then with the twins, leading them a safe distance from the fire where a playpen was set up.

James, seeing what was coming, started to wail, but before Joanna could echo him, Matthew tossed a ball into the playpen, distracting them. Joanna made a dive to grab it first, but James quickly sat down on it, grinning from ear to ear.

Nathan joined in the laughter as his gaze swept around the circle of people.

Not just people. Family. Not his family, but an ordinary Amish family working together, playing together, laughing and sorrowing together, just as they should.

That was what he missed the most, he realized. That was what Peter missed, as well . . . that solid sense of belonging somewhere special by right of acceptance. Family.

Becca woke early on Sunday morning, as she always did, hearing the twins jabbering back and forth between their cribs in the room across the hall. That was enough to get her feet on the floor.

Then she heard Deborah answering them, and she relaxed a little. She remembered Mamm's insistence that Deborah stay last night to help out after all the work of making apple butter. Deborah had been eager to do it . . . it made a nice change to be away from home, even just at her sister's place.

It was all too easy to accept the help her family offered so freely, but Becca was determined not to get used to it. Especially now that she knew her parents, or at least her mother, didn't entirely approve of her decision to carry on with the orchard.

Becca grabbed the dress hanging from the peg on the wall and scolded herself. She wouldn't keep going over it. She knew where her duty lay. It was to carry out the plans she and Thomas had made for their family, not to go back to being a girl in her parents' house. She'd do just that, and lingering in her bedroom wouldn't get anything done.

There was the usual rush to get everyone fed, dressed, and ready to go to worship, complicated by the need to pack everything the twins might require for several hours. Finally it was gathered together and loaded into the buggy.

Deborah took the lines, obviously pleased to be driving instead of stuffed into the back of the family carriage with her twin and the two boys.

Becca helped her grandmother up, handed her one twin, and carrying the other, she took her place next to her.

Deborah waited until everyone was settled and snug, with a lap robe protecting them from the crisp morning air. Then she clicked to the mare, and they were off.

A moment later she glanced toward the neighboring property. "Look, there's Nathan and Peter leaving, too." Deborah waved and sent a mischievous glance toward Grossmammi. "I could race them to the road," she ventured.

"Behave yourself, Deborah." Grossmammi gave her a reproving look. "Just remember that there's always someone to see if you misbehave."

"I know. I was just teasing. Anyway, Peter said they'd follow us to the Unger farm this morning. I guess they aren't sure which place it is."

Becca stole a glance at the buggy traveling parallel to them on the other lane. Peter and his brother both looked suitably solemn in their black suits for the trip to worship.

Grossmammi smiled and nodded as they rode virtually side by side for a minute or two. "I understand the bishop came to call on them a few days ago," Grossmammi said. "That will make it easier for them, this being their first time at church here."

"That's good." Becca couldn't help wondering why Nathan had confided in Grossmammi, not her, and then scolded herself for the thought.

The buggy went around the bend in the lane, and they could see Daad with the carriage waiting at the gate across the road. He nodded and pulled out, they fell in line behind him, and Nathan and Peter drew up behind them. In a few minutes they'd all joined the line of buggies headed toward worship, getting longer as they passed more farms and homes.

Joanna, sitting on Becca's lap, wiggled instead of sitting placidly the way her brother did. "Stop it, little wiggle-worm." Becca bounced her in time with the buggy wheels. "If you're restless now, worship will be a long three hours."

"Ach, we can always take the babies out and feed them if we need," Grossmammi said, never worried about things like that. "No one will be bothered by a little baby noise."

Joanna tilted her head back to look at Grossmammi when she spoke, then glanced at her mother as if she understood and was plotting that exact thing.

Becca shook her head. She couldn't understand, could she?

The drive to church always felt like part of worship to Becca . . . a time of quiet preparation and getting in tune with the peace of the Sabbath. She loved being part of the long line of friends and relatives all headed for the same place.

It seemed no time at all before they were

pulling up at the Unger farm. One of the Unger boys, obviously on duty as hostler today, hurried up to help them unload. Looking more serious than Becca had usually seen him, he then took the horse and buggy off to a shady spot behind the barn.

As they arrived, people had already started forming lines, men on one side, women on the other, to file into the barn that the Unger family would have ready for worship. After checking that Becca and her grandmother were ready, Deborah hurried off to join her twin and the other teenage girls, and her brothers seemed to have taken Nathan and Peter under their wing. In a moment they had disappeared to join the men's line, which was snaking around the far side of the barn.

Carrying Joanna, Becca moved with Mamm and Grossmammi toward the women's line, with her mother carrying James. Grossmammi had the lighter diaper bag, while Becca juggled the one containing food for the little ones until Miriam grabbed it.

For a moment, Becca thought longingly of the time, a few more years from now, when they could come to worship without bringing much of the nursery with them. Just as quickly she rejected the idea. She couldn't wish away these precious baby years. They'd go fast enough, any-way.

They neared the entrance and came within sight of the men's line again. She could see Peter taking a place in line with her younger brothers. Daadi ushered Nathan into line with him and Matt. Anyone who looked would see that her family was welcoming their new neighbors.

Soon Nathan would be part of the background of her life. Soon, too, she wouldn't bounce between resenting him and feeling that completely inappropriate interest.

Someone touched her arm and Becca turned to be caught in a quick hug by her cousin, Leah Stoltz, now Leah Burkhalter.

Leah was blooming; that was all Becca could think when she looked at her cousin. Marriage to Josiah Burkhalter had brought a new serenity and happiness to her lively face. Becca felt a momentary pang and dismissed it. Leah deserved all the happiness her marriage had brought her.

But Leah's mind was on something else, even as she tickled Joanna's chin and smiled at her. She gestured to where the men's line moved on. "So, what are your new neighbors like? I hear they are kinfolk of Joseph Mueller."

Becca nodded, untangling herself and Joanna from Leah's hug. "His nephews, Nathan and Peter Mueller."

"No Mrs. Mueller?" Leah lifted her eyebrows in the question.

"Nathan is a widower, I understand," Becca

said. "And Peter's around fifteen. Apparently Joseph left the farm to Nathan."

"They'll have a job with the place, I'd think," Leah responded. "Everyone says Joseph had let it go downhill."

Hilda King, who was Becca's aunt-in-law, passed near enough to hear Leah's words. She stopped and then shook her head, her thin lips pressed together in disapproval, as usual.

"Wouldn't want them moving in next to me, I can tell you that. It wouldn't surprise me if they were just like their uncle. There's bad blood in that family, you mark my words."

"That's a dreadful thing to say." Becca spoke without thinking and was instantly aghast. She should never speak that way to a sister in faith, especially a relative of Thomas's. And at worship, to make it worse.

Hilda King stood with her mouth open, her face turning red. Speechless for the moment, she marched off to her place in the line, leaving Becca mortified and angry and Leah suppressing a laugh.

Leah cleared her throat. "If she weren't your aunt, I'd say she's got a tongue like a copper-head."

Becca blew out a long breath, hoping against hope that they'd not been overheard. "She's no aunt of mine," she murmured. "Thank goodness."

She could always count on Leah's loyalty, no

matter what. But what was it about Nathan that roused such extreme and opposite feelings in her? She had to get hold of herself before people began talking.

CHAPTER SIX

"I can't believe I said that," Becca murmured to her cousin as the line for worship moved into the barn. "Do you think anyone else heard?"

Leah glanced around. "No," she whispered. "But Hilda's probably enough, ain't so?"

They exchanged glances, both knowing Hilda's reputation as a blabbermaul. Anything she thought or heard would come out her mouth, that was certain sure. They passed through the doorway into the barn and fell silent.

Filing into the row of benches that would have been brought here from the last worship site, Becca tried to quiet her thoughts and prepare her heart for worship.

Unfortunately, her mind wouldn't cooperate. She grasped hold of her thoughts and silently began murmuring the first verse of a Psalm, focusing on each word.

Her tension started to slip away, but before she'd even reached the tenth verse, Mammi was nudging her. With gestures, she indicated a switching around of who held which of the babies. Becca understood. Her grandmother always wanted to do her share, but they'd both noticed how she sagged toward the end of the long service.

Mammi handed James to her mother-in-law,

since he was the more placid twin, and she took Joanna. Becca and her sister-in-law Miriam would take over later.

Della and Deborah were seated with the other girls their age and enjoying it, of course. She couldn't hear anything from the girls' row, but a certain amount of movement seemed to ripple constantly along the bench, as if they communicated even when heads were bowed and hands clasped.

Her lips twitched. She remembered so well the eagerness to see her friends on church Sundays, the longing to share secrets and talk all day if possible. Even now, she'd love to hear Leah's thoughts about her predicament. Fortunately, she had a bit more control over herself now.

Leah, as if reading her thoughts, nudged her and nodded toward where the men were settled into their benches on the opposite side of the barn. It didn't take much to realize that she was indicating Nathan, and she had a question in her eyes.

Again Becca suppressed a smile. Maybe they weren't so grown up after all. *Later,* she mouthed.

As usual, taking the babies to worship was an adventure. Joanna wiggled and squirmed, but Mammi had a firm grasp on her, and finally she settled down, gnawing on a teething biscuit while she glanced from face to face around her. James, with his easygoing disposition, leaned against Grossmammi smiling, and then drifted off to sleep.

They stayed quiet until just about an hour before the end of the service. Then, first Joanna, then James, began stirring. This time there was no comforting them. Joanna fussed, but James decided he was hungry and let out a wail that seemed to his mother the loudest cry she'd ever heard in worship.

Flushing, Becca grabbed him and the bag containing their food. A silent discussion then took place over who would go out with her, and finally Grossmammi joined her. They hurried outside, afraid of another loud outburst from James.

As soon as the door closed behind them, James's crying shut off. Laughing, Becca tickled him. "You're a faker, James. You're not hungry at all."

James wasn't listening. Instead, he spotted the remains of a teething biscuit in his sister's hand and successfully snatched it.

"Look out," Grossmammi warned, but Becca had already grabbed the sloppy little hand.

"You don't want that," Becca told him. "Yucky." She wiped his hand with the washcloth she'd brought.

"Yucky," he repeated, grinning at the thought of acquiring a new word.

Grossmammi laughed. "We'll hear that now until we're tired of it."

"I should think before I speak. Being the mammi is harder than I thought." She looked ruefully at the messy cloth. "Let's sit down and get them something better to eat."

Picnic tables had been set up under the trees for the after-worship lunch. It looked as if the Unger family was trusting on the continued warm weather, at least for this week. They settled at one, and in a few minutes both babies were provided with dried apples and milk cups.

"Now, that's gut." Grossmammi leaned back against the edge of the table and gave Becca a curious glance. "So what was going on with Hilda King this morning? I saw her say something to you, and you answered. Then she looked as though she'd bitten into an apple and found a worm."

Becca found herself giggling even while she considered how much to tell her. One thing that influenced her . . . Grossmammi was never surprised by anything. Maybe it was a benefit of old age. What could happen that she hadn't already seen at one time or another?

"You know how Hilda is." She tried to make it sound casual even though the memory of Hilda's face made her wince. "Leah was asking about our new neighbors, and Hilda, who's never even spoken to them, said she wouldn't want them living near her." Her anger flared up again. "She said they had bad blood. Imagine talking that way about someone you don't even know."

Grossmammi was eyeing her patiently. "And what did you say?"

Maybe Grossmammi was never surprised, but she was also persistent. It would be no good avoiding the question.

"I said that was a terrible thing to say." Her own cheeks flushed the same way Hilda's had. "I shouldn't have. I'm so ashamed of myself. And there's no end to the number of people she'll repeat it to."

"True." Grossmammi spooned some applesauce into James's mouth when he looked up from investigating the grass beneath the table. "Still, everyone knows how she talks. I don't suppose most folks believe even half of what Hilda says."

"I hope you're right. I've had enough trouble with Thomas's family." She regretted those careless words almost before she said them. "Ach, I don't mean . . ."

"You mean with Thomas's little bruder, ain't so?"

Becca rubbed her temples at the thought of Abel, Thomas's younger brother. "Yah, I guess I do. At least since he's been working out of state with his uncle he hasn't been trying to convince me to marry him. I hope he's gotten over that foolishness."

Grossmammi looked up, frowning. "I hope so, too, especially because he's not still away. He's

99

at worship this morning. Didn't you notice him?"

"Oh, dear. No, I didn't." Becca's heart thumped down to her stomach, it seemed.

It wasn't that she didn't care for Thomas's younger brother. She loved him like a brother. But his determination to take care of her had become a nuisance in the months after Thomas's death.

Her grandmother patted her hand. "Don't worry so much. Surely he's grown out of that by now. And if he hasn't, you'll just have to talk to his parents about it. They're sensible people."

"I can't." She felt a stab of pain at the thought. "His mother would be so grieved, and I just can't hurt her like that on top of everything else. I can't."

"Yah, I know what you mean, but you might have to. That's for his parents to deal with at his age, not you."

Becca nodded, knowing what her grandmother said was true, but cringing from the possibility.

Nathan had thought they might leave soon after customary lunch was over. He'd eaten with the Stoltz men, and he'd met a few other neighbors who'd sat with them. He felt as if he'd already heard too many names to remember, and he was about to round up his brother.

But Becca's father seemed to have his own agenda for the day, and he grasped Nathan's arm.

100

"Come along, and I'll make sure you meet some folks."

Nathan hesitated, but the truth was that Abram Stoltz still reminded him so much of his father that he just naturally followed along.

Not that they looked much alike—his father had been tall and wiry, while Abram was short and stocky, with arms that looked capable of lifting a cow or two effortlessly. Still, their attitudes were similar, and he suspected Becca's father was as honest and upright as Daad had been.

He glanced around for Peter, but he had been scooped up by the twins and led off to a pickup game of kickball in a nearby field. He looked happy enough, and Nathan guessed any boys who were here at worship would be unlikely to lead him into trouble.

Abram guided him easily through the crowd as people shifted away from the tables and got caught up with their neighbors. He was clearly looking for particular people he wanted Nathan to meet, and he wouldn't be deterred by casual chatter.

Nathan caught a glimpse of Becca, deep in conversation with a young woman about her age, and then lost her again when Abram piloted him over to a group of men.

"Here's someone you must get to know. Our new neighbor, Nathan Mueller." Abram's announcement took in the whole group, and then he started introducing one at a time.

Nathan thought he saw a few cautious looks when his name was mentioned, but Abram charged on with his self-imposed duty.

In a few minutes Nathan caught on to what Abram was up to. He was seeing that Nathan met the young married men of the church, and especially those he'd probably do business with—the owner of the grain mill, the fellow who ran the hardware store, then the one with the harness shop, and so on.

He had to smile. Abram had it right—these were all folks he'd do business with at some point, so it was smart to put names to faces as soon as possible.

That was if he could remember them, after the way Abram rattled the names off. Still, after a few awkward minutes of trying, he found himself talking to someone with a name he remembered seeing on a sign. Josiah Burkhalter ran a carpentry business with his father just a few miles down the road from his place.

"Leah's going to be jealous that I met you before she did," Josiah said with an easy grin. "Leah's my wife, and cousin to Becca King. She was a Stoltz before we married."

He chuckled. "I guess there's lots of people named Stoltz around here. Is that her, talking to Becca over by the tables?"

"Yah, that's my Leah." There was a certain amount of pride in the way Josiah spoke, making

Nathan wonder if they were newly married. "She's spotted us. I'd best make you known to her or I won't hear the end of it."

Since Leah was clearly on her way toward them, he guessed Josiah was right about her desire to meet him. For a moment he thought Becca would join her, but then she was intercepted by a young guy, probably not much older than Peter, who grasped her hand fervently and plunged into speech.

"You're Nathan, yah?" Leah was saying when he focused on her. "Becca was just telling me what a helpful neighbor you are."

Nathan smiled but shook his head. "The shoe's on the other foot, I think. Becca . . . all the Stoltz family have been making us wilkom and jumping in to help us get settled."

"Yah, I'm sure they would," Josiah said. "Leah's grossmammi likes nothing more than cooking for a whole big bunch of people. And her pies are almost as good as my Leah's."

Leah flushed at the compliment from her spouse. "Becca feels the same, but she's so busy with the orchard and the babies I don't suppose she can do as much as she'd like to."

Nathan nodded, interested in Leah's view of Becca but at the same time reminding himself he should be drawing back, not getting more involved.

Unfortunately, just thinking her name drew his

gaze back to Becca. His view of her was blocked by the back of the young man he'd seen a few minutes ago.

"Who is that talking to Becca now?" The question popped out before he could censor it.

Josiah craned his neck to see around several people. "That's Abel King. I didn't know he was back in town until I saw him at worship. Becca's brother-in-law."

Nathan stole another look. Now the guy . . . Abel . . . had hold of Becca by both wrists. Nate couldn't see her face, but she seemed to be leaning away from the guy.

"He seems very . . . intent," he said, wondering what would happen if he walked over there and took Abel by his shirt. He'd ruin his own reputation in the community from the start, he guessed.

"Oh, dear." Leah looked distressed. "Poor Abel. He's so persistent. I think I'd best go and interrupt."

"We'll all go," Josiah said after a glance at Nathan. "I'm sure there are other folks ready to catch up with Abel. He doesn't need to monopolize Becca."

They moved toward Becca, and Nathan could see her more clearly now. Her face was set, and she was attempting to pull her hands away without success. Apparently no one else had noticed. He quickened his steps, and they came up to the two.

"Look who's here, Josiah. It's Abel King." Leah's voice was louder than Nathan expected. Loud enough to bring Abel swinging toward them, wearing a thunderous look.

"Abel!" Josiah clasped him firmly by the arm. "Just the person I wanted to see, right, Leah?"

"Yah, for sure." Leah moved beside her husband. "Let's get another cup of coffee, and you can tell us all about your job in Maryland. We've been eager to hear what you thought of living down there for a bit."

"Maybe later . . ." Abel began, but Josiah had a firm grip and was already steering him toward the coffee setup. Leah hurried to link arms with the boy on the other side. He could hardly shake himself loose.

Boy was the right term, Nathan realized as he got a good look at him and confirmed his earlier guess. Probably not twenty yet. What could he have been saying to upset Becca?

He turned to her with a smile, hoping to pretend he hadn't noticed anything, but her brown eyes had darkened and her usually cheerful face was drawn and pale.

"Becca . . ." He stopped, sure anything he blurted out would be the wrong thing. He started again. "Let's take a little walk and look at that fine pair of Percherons in the field."

He was rewarded by a flicker of relief from Becca, and an instant later they were walking side by side toward the draft horses. As for him, he felt about ten feet tall for having rescued her.

To Becca's relief, Nathan didn't ask her what was wrong, so she could pretend for a moment that he hadn't noticed. He had, of course. He was quite observant for a man who usually hid behind such a withdrawn expression.

She had so hoped that Abel would have forgotten his obsession during his time away from Promise Glen. Why couldn't he have met some nice young Amish girl in one of the Maryland communities? There must be plenty of suitable girls his age.

Well, he hadn't, and she'd best focus on what she was doing before Nathan felt driven to ask about her conversation with Abel. She tripped over a clod kicked up by one of the horses and felt Nathan's hand on her arm, steadying her. His hand was withdrawn so abruptly that she felt she could ignore it, but the warmth of even that quick touch lingered.

They stopped at the field gate, and she put her hand on the top bar. "They are beautiful, aren't they? Several people in the valley have draft horses, but I can't think of any that match these."

One of the horses lifted his head to look toward her, and Nathan laughed. "Looks like he appreciated the compliment."

She'd returned to normal, she realized thankfully. Now she just had to be careful what she said to him. Abel's notions were embarrassing enough without other people knowing about them, especially Nathan. Why Nathan in particular, she didn't quite know, but that was what she felt.

She glanced at him where he stood leaning against the gate, his eyes still on the horses. Was he waiting for her to speak? It looked as if she had to say something.

"Denke for stepping in." She spoke quietly. "I was relieved. Abel . . . well, he can get intense sometimes."

Nathan shrugged. "Probably goes with the age. What is he? Eighteen? Nineteen?"

"Not quite twenty." Her voice sharpened, and she said more than she intended. "Old enough to know better."

She stopped short, but it was already too late. Nathan's gaze was intent on her face. "Better than what?"

Becca took a deep breath. "The fact is that, like most younger brothers, he was devoted to Thomas, my late husband. Abel . . . well, he thinks he ought to take care of me."

Nathan seemed to search for some encouraging words. "Looks to me like you're doing a fine job of taking care of yourself."

"I have plenty of assistance from my family," she pointed out, but she couldn't help being pleased by his words. "I don't want to shut Abel out, but he can be so persistent. Anyway, thanks for interrupting him. I really wasn't ready to hear all about his feelings today. He's been away, you see."

"I heard. And no need to thank me. It was all Leah and Josiah, not me." He smiled. "So if he's mad at anyone, it will be them."

"I don't suppose it will bother them." She chuckled, but then sobered. "I don't seem to be doing very well with Thomas's family today."

Nathan raised his eyebrows in a question, but she could hardly tell him about Hilda's unkind comments. That might make him withdraw even more.

But his mind still seemed to be on Abel. "Boys that age take things hard. I suppose he was very close with his brother."

"He adored Thomas." She could remember Abel at their wedding, upset that he wasn't old enough to participate, maybe a little jealous of her. "There were only the two boys in the family. Rather like you and Peter. I guess it's natural."

"Not so natural after all this time. I mean, it's been over a year, ain't so?"

"More than that. The twins are over eighteen months now. It hurts to think Thomas didn't get to see them growing . . ." She saw his expression, knew he was thinking about his own wife and baby, and let that trail off. "Anyway, Abel is just being foolish, thinking he can somehow take Thomas's place."

She had babbled on, trying to chase the grief from his eyes, and she'd stumbled right into something else she shouldn't have said.

"Take his place?" Nathan's eyebrows lifted, and his face showed more understanding than she'd expected. "You mean actually take his place? He wants to marry you? But you're too old for him."

Nathan sounded so incredulous that she was almost insulted. "I'd rather think that he's too young for me," she said tartly.

He blinked, and a smile tugged at his lips. "Yah, for sure."

"Well, you know what I mean. It's just silly." She frowned, staring absently at the Percherons. "When he first brought it up, I was still in so much shock that I barely registered what he was saying. I guess you'd say I brushed him off. Afterwards I thought of a dozen easier ways to let him down, but at the time I had too much on my mind to listen to something so . . . foolish."

"I take it he didn't give up."

"No, unfortunately he didn't. He insisted it was biblical, that it was the duty of a brother, most of all that Thomas would have wanted him to." She felt the familiar combination of frustration and pity at the thought.

Nathan seemed to be considering Abel's

argument, and he looked at her questioningly. "You don't think he was right about Thomas?"

"No, of course not. Thomas loved the boy, but he was realistic. He'd have been the first one to laugh if someone had said something like that to him."

She felt her face soften as she thought of Thomas's laugh, always so joyful it made others want to laugh with him.

"Abel has been working in Maryland for nearly a year," she went on. "I really thought he'd have found himself a nice girl and forgotten all this nonsense. But he's back and just as insistent as ever." She shrugged, trying to shake it off. "Sorry. I shouldn't be unloading this on you, of all people."

"Sure. You hardly know me. For all you know, I might be the biggest blabbermaul in three states."

Becca couldn't help the chuckle that burst out at his expression. "I do know you better than that, thank you." She turned toward the tables, beginning to move in that direction, and he kept pace with her.

"Seems like there ought to be someone Abel will listen to if he won't take no for an answer. Any older relatives who would advise him?"

Her thoughts flickered to his aunt Hilda. Goodness knows what she'd say about this.

"I'll have to think on that. His parents, of course, but I'm afraid of hurting them by bringing it up." She shook her head. "They are so grieved already. But I hope Abel is not going to make a scene about it every time I see him."

They'd nearly reached the spot where Deborah was sitting on a blanket with the babies.

"You'll figure it out. A smart woman like you."

He nodded at Deborah and then strode off toward the kickball game.

She watched him for a moment. Nathan had listened to her foolish outpourings. That was good of him, but he'd rushed off so fast he'd probably had enough.

Becca felt herself blushing at having told a relative stranger so much. He'd probably steer clear of her now.

Oddly enough, that didn't come as a relief, either.

CHAPTER SEVEN

On Monday afternoon Becca waved Deborah off to the farmstand, wondering just what was behind her sister's eagerness to work at the stand instead of watching the twins. Peter, maybe? Becca had to admit that she hadn't been paying a great deal of attention to them. Maybe she'd better start.

Something clanging on a high chair tray had her spinning back to the kitchen. As usual, James was signaling that he'd finished lunch by making as much noise as he could with his utensils. She took the cup from his hand before he could take another swing and turned to check on Joanna.

Her small daughter looked as innocent as could be, which was a bad sign right there. A closer look told her that Joanna had been dipping the remains of her bread into her milk and then dropping the pieces onto the floor.

"Naughty girl." She snatched away the milk, frowning at the sloppy mess on the tray. "We don't waste food like that."

Becca swept a damp paper towel over the tray, gathering up the remains of the meal, which certain sure were wasted. When she lifted Joanna to the floor, she put the soggy paper towel in Joanna's hands.

"Put it in the trash," she said, pointing. "And don't drop it."

It would be useless to say that to James, because he couldn't yet carry things and walk with any chance of getting there without dropping. She tried to suit their chores to their abilities, just as her mother had always done. That was tricky with twins, and she wouldn't want James to think himself less than his sister.

Joanna deposited the soggy mess into the trash, rubbed her hands together, and announced, "Gut Joanna."

Grossmammi, who'd just come in from the grossdaadi haus, chuckled at Becca's expression. "You think it's hard now. Just wait until this one is a teenager."

"I'm wonderful glad to have time to prepare for that." Becca laughed as she lifted James down and glanced at Grossmammi again. "Are you going somewhere?" Her grandmother carried a basket on her arm.

"Yah, I thought I'd help your mamm with some canning. Do you need help with anything before I go?" Grossmammi glanced around as if looking for Deborah.

"No, nothing. I'm just going to put the twins down for their naps. Deborah wanted to work the stand this afternoon."

"Hoping to see Peter, I imagine," Grossmammi said, and Becca realized she'd been paying more attention to the young ones than Becca had. "Nice for her to have some company, yah? I'll see you later, then." Kissing each of the babies, she headed out, easily thwarting an effort by Joanna to get out the door.

Becca scooped up both twins and carted them off to the room they shared, wondering what else she had missed that her grandmother had noticed. As the oldest, she should be doing a better job of looking out for her young sister.

It took a few minutes to get the twins mopped up and settled for their naps. Predictably, they kept popping up again, but a few soft songs finally seemed to do the job.

She'd just tiptoed out of the twins' room when she heard someone coming in the back door. She hurried down to find her cousin Leah heating a kettle on the stove.

"Leah, how nice."

Leah held up an assortment of the herbal teas she made. "Which do you want today?" She took another look at Becca's face. "Chamomile for stress, ain't so?"

Becca smiled, nodding. "I love your chamomile, but I don't think I'm stressed." She set out a plate of apple raisin muffins and got the mugs for tea.

"Tell that to someone who doesn't know you as well as I do," Leah said firmly. "You're stressed, and it's no wonder with Abel King being such a nuisance. Komm, the tea will relax you. It doesn't help him for you to be upset."

"I don't know that I'd say he's a nuisance exactly," she said, loath to say anything negative about Thomas's little brother. She tried to be honest. "I mean, I suppose he thinks he's doing the right thing."

Leah poured boiling water into the teapot, as familiar with this house as she was with her own. They'd grown up going back and forth between the farms, helping Grossmammi and Grossdaadi, and they were as much like sisters as cousins. Closer, in fact, than Becca was with Deborah because of the age difference. The realization made her feel guilty all over again.

"Maybe that's what he thinks," Leah said, pouring the pale, golden tea into mugs from the earthenware teapot. Released, its delicate aroma filled the air. "But maybe he's just dramatizing himself, pretending he's the hero who will save the day. And you."

"Whatever it is, I wish he'd stop it." Becca lifted the cup to her lips, inhaling the scent of it before sipping.

The heat and aroma seemed to flow through her, and she did feel more relaxed, though whether it was real or the power of suggestion, she didn't know. Whatever it was, the tea and the company made her feel better.

"What did Nathan have to say after we tore

Abel away?" Leah's bright eyes were intrigued.

"I wish you'd stop looking at me as if you're waiting for romance. I'm not interested in men— at least, not that way."

She hoped she was convincing Leah, because she couldn't be sure she was convincing herself.

Leah touched her hand gently. "Maybe it's too soon now. But you have too much to give to want to spend the rest of your life alone, ain't so?"

Becca didn't really have an answer for that. She moved impatiently, brushing her kapp strings back over her shoulders and looking down at the black dress she wore today. Widows wore dark colors, of course, but this one made her think of Thomas because Thomas would have hated to see her in black.

"I don't know," she said finally, her thoughts flickering to Mammi's worries over her running the orchard alone. "But I had first love once, and nothing else would be like that."

Leah's eyes were troubled. "People marry for other reasons. For family, for companionship, for help, yah?"

Becca shook her head slowly. "I don't think I could. You understand, don't you?"

Leah nodded, her gaze dropping. "Yah, I guess."

"And if I were going to marry again, it certain sure wouldn't be to Abel. Now all I have to do is convince him of that."

Leah's lips quirked a little. "We're right back where we started. Did Nathan have any suggestions for discouraging Abel?"

"None at all," she declared. "In fact, he acted as if the whole thing was a great big bore."

Actually, he had made one suggestion, and she'd thought about it more than once. She might, she guessed, find someone to talk to about her difficulties with Abel, someone Abel respected and would listen to. But if she did, it certain sure wouldn't be Nathan.

Nathan had been trying to make sense of Peter's behavior since Sunday afternoon, and he still didn't know what had happened.

"Look, you might as well tell me what made you walk away from that kickball game yesterday. I could see by your expression that someone said something that upset you."

They were washing up from lunch on Monday, and that was sometimes a good time for talking. Something about standing side by side at a sink full of dirty dishes seemed to encourage conversation. At least, it usually did. This time it didn't seem to be working.

Peter grabbed a plate and rubbed it hard enough to take off the blue line around the border. "It doesn't matter. I don't care what those hicks think anyway."

Hicks? Where did he get an insult like that, when

they'd always been country people themselves?

"They're no more hicks than we are," Nathan pointed out, holding on to his temper with an effort. "I figured you were making friends. The Stoltz boys weren't calling you names, were they?"

The boy shrugged. "David and Daniel are okay. And they weren't the ones I had trouble with. Just because Onkel Joseph was a drunk, doesn't mean I'm going to be one." He hesitated. "It doesn't, does it?"

Nathan's heart sank. He had realized some people would have feelings about Onkel Joseph's failings. Just because Becca's family treated them well didn't mean everyone would.

"No, it doesn't. You can count on that. I don't know what sent our uncle off the rails, but whatever it was, it's nothing to do with us."

"Some folks don't see it that way," Peter muttered.

"Forget about them." His control slipped a little. "It's not worth getting mad about." He glanced at the clock. "Isn't it time you went to help at the farmstand?" Maybe Becca or Deborah could soothe Peter's ruffled feathers.

"Don't want to." Peter seemed determined to hang on to his bad mood.

"Now listen. I heard you tell Deborah you'd be there to help this afternoon. You can't tell someone that and then let them down."

"Let me alone!" Peter threw the dishcloth at the sink, where it splashed into the soapy water. "Just leave me be!"

Before Nathan had time to respond, his brother ran out the door, slamming it behind him.

He could go after the boy, but what good would that do? *Daad would have known how to handle Peter,* he told himself again. He rubbed his damp hand on the back of his neck. What would Daad have done? Or Becca's daad, for that matter?

Nathan dried his hands and left the dishes in the drainer. Grabbing his jacket, he walked out on the back porch.

Peter was nowhere in sight. Maybe that was for the best. A good long walk over the hills might improve his disposition. But in the meantime, it seemed like it was his job to go down and let Deborah know not to expect him. He could spare the time to help her set up.

But when he came within sight of the farmstand, Deborah seemed to have everything under control. She spotted him, and the welcoming smile faded from her face as she wilted. Clearly he wasn't the one she'd been looking for.

"I came to see if you needed any help. Looks like you've already made a couple of sales." He nodded toward the peck baskets she must have emptied into a customer's bag.

"Yah, that's so." Deborah was doing a good job of pretending she hadn't been looking for his brother. "All of a sudden more people are picking up gourds and pumpkins. I guess because it's Halloween on Friday."

He nodded, lifting a basket of apples to the counter for her. "I'll be glad to see the last of it. Halloween, I mean."

"Did you hear about the trouble in town last night?" Her eyes widened. "The lady who was here last said that a lot of the decorations they'd put up in Market Square were torn down."

Deborah looked frightened at the thought, and her lips trembled a little. "You don't think they'd come here, would they?"

Nathan set himself the job of being comforting. "Ach, we're well out of their way. Sounds like they wanted to make a mess right where everyone would see it."

"I guess you're right." But she didn't sound quite convinced. She glanced back at the curve in the lane that shut off the house from view, a little apprehensive.

The farmstand was more isolated than he'd thought. It couldn't be seen from either Becca's house or his, and the Stoltz place across the road was far enough back that they weren't likely to notice anything unless it made a lot of noise.

"Seems like it would be better for you not to be here alone." Obviously she hadn't expected to be alone. It was clear she'd thought Peter would be with her. His jaw clenched. He'd have something to say to his brother when he showed up. Once again he felt he'd been given a responsibility he couldn't handle.

"Suppose I hang around until Peter comes," he suggested, hoping that would happen. Maybe he'd best steer the conversation away from his brother. "What a shame things were messed up, after all that work folks did to decorate the town, ain't so?"

"Yah. I heard someone called the police, but by the time they got there, everyone had run away." She shivered a little, rubbing her arms. "I don't see why anyone would want to do something like that. The lady that bought all the pumpkins must be upset."

"Yah." Maybe he ought to take another load in to make up for them. "I guess we could donate some more, if it would help."

Deborah brightened at the thought. "That's nice of you. I could get my bruders to help load, if you want. Maybe Peter—"

But whatever she was going to suggest for Peter was interrupted by the shriek of brakes as a pickup truck came around the bend. He had just time to see that some teenagers were riding in the back when a pumpkin arced through the air toward them . . . then another and another.

Grabbing Deborah, he pushed her down behind the counter. The only thing he could think was that he needed to get the license number. The police would be glad to pounce on some of the vandals.

In the meantime, they were making a mess, throwing pumpkins and tomatoes that splattered against the sign. Another hit him on the shoulder, splashing into his face.

Nathan's temper got the better of him for the second time that day. He headed straight toward the truck, intending to yank a few of the culprits right out of it.

They must have seen his purpose in his face, because the truck tore back out on the road, throwing up gravel, just as Peter came running up the lane.

"What happened? Where's Deborah?" he shouted.

Deborah stood up, looking a little shaken. "I'm okay."

"Sure you are." Nathan spoke cheerfully, giving Peter a warning glance not to make things worse. "You'll want to wash up a little, ain't so? Peter, why don't you take Deborah back to the house so she can tell her sister what happened? I'll start cleaning up here."

Peter, seeming to stifle his alarm, nodded quickly. "Sure thing. Come on, Deborah. It's all right. We'll see to things." He clasped her hand reassuringly. "Just listen to Nathan."

Nathan's lips twitched in a smile. That was a far cry from his own attitude not long ago. It sounded as if their quarrel was over.

But this wasn't funny. Those kids had made a mess and left it for others to clean up. That was bad enough.

But what if Becca and the twins had been here, as they sometimes were? The twins certain sure would have been scared and maybe even hurt.

It was no good his thinking they weren't his responsibility. A thing like this was everyone's responsibility. This had to be stopped.

Becca was putting away the containers of herbal teas that Leah had brought. At the sound of voices, she glanced out the window and saw Deborah coming toward the back door, with Peter beside her, holding her arm protectively.

She reached the door and swung it open. "Deborah, what has happened? Are you hurt?" She reached for her sister, but Deborah managed to smile as she shook her head.

"Don't touch me unless you want to get squashed tomato and splattered pumpkin all over you." Deborah held out her arms, displaying the mess of her dress and apron. A glob of pumpkin dropped onto the floor.

"Ach, what a mess." Becca's heart started beating again at her sister's smile. "But how did it happen? Did you fall?"

"Only when Nathan shoved me behind the counter." Deborah fumbled with her apron tie.

"Nathan did what?" Deborah wasn't communicating very well, but at least she was all right, it seemed.

"A bunch of guys in a pickup truck," Peter said, as if that was an explanation. Well, maybe it was. It wouldn't be the first time an Amish person had things thrown at him or her from a passing vehicle.

"I was on my way down the lane when I heard it," Peter went on. "Seems like a pickup truck veered off the road, and they started throwing things. Nathan got Deborah behind the counter, and then he started after them." He looked as if he wished that had been him.

"They were scared by then, I guess. They rushed off down the road." Deborah wiped away a stain on her arm, her voice shaking a little. "I'm so glad I wasn't there by myself."

Becca's breath caught at the thought of it, and she forced herself to be practical. "Just run up to my room and find something to wear." Such a short time ago Deborah had gone off with a happy smile, wearing the deep pink dress that made her eyes sparkle, all fresh and ready for a pleasant afternoon. Now . . . it made Becca's heart hurt to see her this way.

Peter turned to go out. "I'll go down and help Nathan clean up. Maybe a bucket of soapy water . . ."

"For sure." She quickly supplied the bucket, soapy water, and a sponge. "Tell him . . . denke."

She wanted to see him herself, to tell him how thankful she was that he'd been there.

But she couldn't. She was needed here, at least until she was sure Deborah was settled down. She'd have to wait.

Peter went out, and he must have run into Daad, because she heard Daad's deep voice saying something. Then Peter went on, and Daad hurried inside.

"Deborah's all right?"

She nodded. "She's changing. How did you know what was going on?"

"We were out in the field nearest the road. I didn't like the looks of it when that pickup came tearing down the road. We came over, and I left the boys to help Nathan."

"Thank the gut Lord Nathan happened to be at the stand. If Deborah had been there alone, I'd never forgive myself." Becca rubbed her temples, feeling torn.

Daad patted her arm. "Ach, now, don't get all upset. She's all right, you said. We'll just have to be careful until this Halloween nonsense is over."

"Let's hope that's the end of it. The tricks people play get worse every year."

"Yah," Daad said. "It's one thing to put out pumpkins and cornstalks and pretend, but when it comes to destroying people's property, that's something else."

Becca found it hard to concentrate, her thoughts

spinning off to her sister, then down to the stand, then back again. "I'd best check on Deborah . . ." she began, when she heard her sister's step in the hall.

"No need to check on me. I'm fine." Deborah hurried to hug Daadi and then lingered a few minutes with his arms around her, as if needing that comfort.

Daad put his hands on either side of her face, looking into her eyes. Communion seemed to pass between them, and Deborah smiled.

Becca's throat closed. That was what her babies would miss . . . that loving understanding between father and child, as if Daad passed some of his strength along to his child when needed. At moments like this her heart rebelled at the loss her children had suffered when they were still too young to understand.

She had to hurriedly wipe her eyes at the sound of someone on the porch. This time it was Nathan. Becca opened the door. "Is everything all right?"

"Yah, sure, no worries. The boys are going to dump the broken stuff in the compost. Daniel says is it okay to keep the stand open? There are a lot of folks stopping by. I guess they're curious."

Nathan looked as if he didn't approve, but Becca smiled.

"They're buying things, ain't so? I'd say that means they're coming to support us. I'd better go down."

127

A cry from upstairs punctuated her words, but before she could move, Deborah started toward the stairs. "I'll take care of them, Becca. You go ahead."

Nodding, Becca went out, Nathan following. When they reached the lane where their ways parted, Becca turned to him, surveying his tomato-splattered clothes.

"You'll drop that off for me to launder, yah?"

He shook his head. "I'll take care of my own washing." To her surprise, he clasped her hand. "Just you make sure you and Deborah aren't down there alone. They might decide to come back."

Becca looked up at him, very aware of how her pulse was racing and wondering if he could feel it. "Denke. Deborah told us how you helped her. I can't say how thankful we are to you."

"Never mind that." His voice was brusque. "Just be careful." His fingers moved for a moment against the skin of her wrist, and then he turned and started off.

"Nathan," she called when her mind began working again.

He half turned, glancing back at her.

"Drop those clothes off, or I'll have to come after them."

He smiled, lifted a hand in a wave, and went on.

128

CHAPTER EIGHT

Whatever hope Becca had that the incident with the vandals would fade away and be forgotten, she realized she'd been wrong when a township police car pulled up at the back porch the next morning. Not that she wasn't happy to see the police car, but the Amish had often found that reporting incidents just led to more trouble with neighbors. Besides, the Amish aimed to live in peace with all.

It was so early that she and Grossmammi were still at the kitchen table with the twins, who were dawdling over their breakfast. Becca exchanged glances with her grandmother and moved slowly toward the door. This was bound to be about the vandalism. Of course she would cooperate, as anyone would.

She just didn't want to cause any trouble or get folks talking about her.

Opening the door, Becca was relieved to recognize Jack Reynolds heaving his considerable bulk from behind the steering wheel. Everyone in the valley liked Jack, except for the few teenagers who got into trouble with him. And even then, they surely knew that he was always fair.

"Officer Reynolds. Please, come in." She held the door open and tried to feel welcoming.

"Jack," he corrected her. "Since I've known you since you tried to teach me Amish when you were four or five, I think we can call each other by our names."

Stepping inside, he nodded to her grandmother, and almost instantly walked over to the high chairs. "Well, now, if these two aren't the cutest babies I've ever seen. Hi, sweetie."

He bent over Joanna's chair. She lifted a spoonful of applesauce, and for a moment it looked like she'd throw it. Becca darted toward her, but instead Joanna held it up invitingly toward him, tilting her head and smiling.

Grossmammi laughed as Jack pretended to taste the applesauce. "Be careful with that one. She likes to flirt."

"I can see that." He tickled Joanna under her chin, then turned to James. "What about you, young man? Are you going to grow up to be a big strong man like your daddy was?"

Becca winced for a moment, but then she felt warmed. Jack had been one of those who came that terrible day, so calm and understanding. If he was dealing with this situation, she wouldn't have to worry.

"Komm, sit down." She pulled out a chair. "You'll have some coffee, yah? And a piece of shoofly pie?"

"Just the coffee. Black, please. I have to watch it with the shoofly pie." He patted his stomach, smiling. "My wife tells me if I'd quit eating on the job, I'd be in better shape."

When they were settled at the table, he took a gulp of the coffee and turned to her. "Now about this vandalism yesterday—"

"How did you know? I didn't call the police."

Jack smiled, shaking his head. "No, but you can almost count on it, someone will. One of your customers saw what had happened when the boys were still cleaning up." He shook his head. "A nasty mess."

"Yah, it surely was. It took a couple of hours to get everything straightened, even with everyone helping." She smiled. "But when the news got around, it seemed like everyone in the township stopped in to buy something."

She felt a glow of thanks when she thought of how proud David and Daniel had been when they'd handed her the overflowing cashbox.

"They wanted to support you, that's certain sure," her grandmother said. "They're good people around here."

"Most of them," Jack added. "But some of their kids go running off the track this time of year." He hesitated. "Most of the tricks have been what you'd expect. Like yesterday. Not meaning to hurt anyone."

Grossmammi flared up at that. "Whether they meant to or not, it could have happened. Sometimes these babies are down there at the stand.

Can you promise they wouldn't have been hurt with things flying around?"

"Grossmammi . . ." Becca warned, afraid she'd start scolding the wrong person.

The officer backtracked quickly. "No, ma'am, I sure can't. I just meant that they probably didn't intend anything serious. That's the trouble. They don't see the possible consequences."

"Can't understand why their parents don't teach them better," her grandmother continued, sounding querulous for someone who was usually so pleasant and uncomplaining. "What are they thinking of?"

Jack caught at her remark. "That's just what I feel. With both parents out working all day, they don't know what their kids are doing. I can understand that, but parents need to know."

Grossmammi nodded firmly. "That's so."

Encouraged, Jack leaned toward her. "Now, if I go calling on them when the parents are home and tell them about all the damage their sweet kids caused, maybe they'll wake up and make sure it doesn't happen again. And that might keep the kids from getting involved in something more serious."

Becca thought it a good moment to interrupt. "You said most of the tricks were ones you'd expect. Does that mean some were more serious?"

Jack blew out a gusty breath. "We don't want to alarm people, but the fact is that there have been

132

two or three efforts to start a fire. Fortunately only one of them got going, and that was caught quickly." His face darkened, growing serious. "And someone used fireworks to blow up a shed at the township garage just last night."

Becca rubbed her arms to chase away the goose bumps. "That is frightening. I'd think people should know, so they could be extra careful. If a barn caught fire . . ."

"That's a good point." Jack agreed with her. "Thing is, the powers that be don't want to panic folks, especially with tourists around and the Fall Festival coming up. Still, this damage at the township shed is sure to be in the paper."

"Foolish to try and keep it quiet." Grossmammi looked ready to go after someone with the coffee-pot she was holding. "It's more important to keep people safe. And livestock."

"Sure is," he said heartily. He glanced at Becca. "That's why I stopped by. I don't suppose you'd be willing to close down for the rest of the week? Once Halloween's over, things should settle. Unless there's a real fire bug out there."

Becca was already shaking her head. "I can't, not possibly. This is my busiest week. I can't afford to lose it."

She thought of her need to show she could make a success of the orchard. She couldn't do that if she shut down at the slightest problem.

"No, I didn't think you could. Well, you be

sure you always have somebody with you down there, okay? Nobody should be there alone."

She was nodding when he started toward the door, still talking.

"I'll just stop by and see what your neighbor noticed. I understand he was there and saw the kids and the pickup."

"Yah, that's right. We've been selling some pumpkins for him at the stand. I was wonderful glad he was there when it happened."

Jack nodded. "New, isn't he? Related to Joseph Mueller, right?"

"His nephew." She felt like saying he wasn't a bit like his Onkel Joseph, but feared that would do no good.

"Well, maybe he'll be able to give me enough of a description to narrow down our search. He ought to have seen something."

All she could do was nod and tell him goodbye, but she cast an apprehensive look at the police car. She had a feeling Nathan wouldn't like seeing it parked outside his house. And that he might consider she was to blame for their interest.

Nathan wasn't surprised that Peter disappeared after the township officer left. Neither of them had relished having a police car at the door. He didn't know what Peter was thinking, but he couldn't help wondering how folks would react at the sight. He was trying to make a good impression here, especially after his uncle's problems.

His mind worrying at it, he finished the morning chores. Then he stood for a moment, surveying the farm that was now his. It was good land, and the situation was all that could be desired. But would they be able to make the farm pay enough to stay here? And could they find a real home here?

He glanced toward Becca's property and saw the back door open. She came out, carrying a laundry basket that seemed full of washing. Dropping it to the ground under the clothesline, she began pegging sheets on the line.

Would she be opening today? It might be safer to close up until after Halloween. Or even for the season.

With a last glance around for Peter, he strode off toward Becca. Best thing to do might be to talk to her about this business with the police. Let her know what he'd said. At least it would clear the air.

He realized he was watching her as he walked. Becca's movements were smooth and sure as she took a sheet from the basket, shook it out so that the breeze caught it, and then began pinning it to the line. He'd never really noticed the grace of her movements, but now that he thought about it, he realized she did everything that way—smoothly and confidently.

He shook off those thoughts. He didn't have

time to be thinking about that, not with trouble right on the doorstep.

Nathan saw the exact moment when Becca became aware of him. Her cheeks flushed, and her gaze slid away from his as if embarrassed.

"I didn't think you were going to call the police." The words sounded accusing, and he wanted them back. After all, it was her property, and if she wanted to report it, she had the right, even if it meant they came to his door.

Becca tossed a wet towel back in the basket and straightened herself, her gaze meeting his squarely. "I didn't."

"How do you suppose they knew about it? It was a bit of a shock to see the police car at my place."

She seemed to relax, as if she were on surer ground. "One of my customers called. She must have come by after you left to bring Deborah back to the house."

Feeling a bit foolish, he nodded. "I see. Sorry if I sounded . . . upset."

He stopped, thinking it was better not to go in that direction. He stood there awkwardly, not sure what to do next.

Becca began hanging towels on the line. "I hope you don't think I shouldn't have answered his questions. Jack Reynolds is a good man, always respectful of our traditions."

"I didn't mean . . ."

136

Becca swept on as if he hadn't spoken. "Jack wants to know who the vandals are so he can stop them before they do something worse. He says maybe that will wake the parents up. That's a good thing, ain't so?"

"Yah, I guess. As long as they don't pick on the wrong people." The memory came back, the memory that for Peter was like a black cloud following him.

"That couldn't happen!" Becca was horrified at the thought.

Nathan had no intention of telling her. It wasn't any of her business. But the words came out anyway.

"It could. It happened to us. To Peter."

She dropped the wet towel she was holding. It missed the basket and fell on the ground, but she didn't even notice.

"What? How?" Sympathy flooded her face. "Poor Peter."

"Yah." He took a deep breath, not sure of anything, even now. Still, Becca's first thought had been for his brother. "It happened back home. We had Englisch neighbors . . . nice people. Peter grew up playing with those boys. Only when they grew up, they turned out not so nice. They got involved with some older guys who thought it was funny to see how much they could get away with." He rubbed the back of his neck, feeling the tension there, wishing he hadn't started this.

"I'm sorry." Becca's voice was very gentle. "What happened?"

"They were all in a car together when Peter found out what they were doing. He says he didn't want any part of it. He wanted them to let him out of the car, but they wouldn't. When the police stopped the car, they questioned all of them. They called me because Peter was underage." His jaw was so tight that Nathan could hardly speak, remembering the shock he'd felt. The guilt.

"That's . . . that must have been terrible for both of you. Poor Peter. But surely he wasn't blamed. He didn't do anything."

Becca was holding his hand in both of hers, and he didn't even know how it had happened.

"No, of course he didn't." He was appalled to hear the doubt in his tone.

Becca dropped his hand, staring at him. "You didn't believe him." The shock in her voice made him feel worse.

He shrugged, trying to avoid the accusation. "Nothing came of it. I guess the police didn't have any evidence. Anyway, they let all the boys go. But word got around. It always does."

She made a gesture as if to brush away the gossip. "Surely you trust Peter." She wasn't going to let him get away from facing it.

"I didn't say I didn't trust him," he protested, but it didn't sound convincing, even to him. "But how could I be sure? I was responsible for him, and I didn't know what to believe."

Becca stared at him for a long moment, her face pale and her eyes shadowed. "Nathan, he's your own younger brother. Are you saying you can't tell if he's lying? It sounds as if it's yourself you're doubting, not your brother."

He stared at her blankly, speechless. Maybe it did sound that way. If he'd expected sympathy, he hadn't gotten it. Becca's sympathy was all for Peter, not for him. He couldn't even argue about it, because he was afraid she was right. Walking so fast he was almost running, he headed for home.

By the end of the week things had calmed down for Becca. Business had continued to be good, either because people were still decorating for Halloween or because they wanted to make up for the trouble she'd had with the vandals.

As for those vandals . . . well, there had been no news from the police, for which she was just as glad.

She hadn't seen Nathan since Tuesday morning. That wasn't surprising. He wasn't likely to forgive her interference. Why hadn't she thought before she spoke? She'd likely spoiled any friendship they'd had by interfering.

Becca had gone through it time after time, regretting what she'd said. Yet when she thought of apologizing, she feared she'd make it even worse.

He was wrong. She was convinced of that. Oh, not because she was sure Peter was innocent. She couldn't know that.

But Nathan was still wrong. First, because he hadn't known his own brother enough. And wrong because he'd gotten it all turned around to make it his fault. Nathan blamed himself for the loss of his wife and baby . . . that stood out a mile when he even thought of them. He was convinced that he couldn't trust himself, and poor Peter was caught in the middle.

Whether Peter had done the damage or not she couldn't say. She didn't know Peter as well as Nathan did. Or should. But Nathan's vision was clouded because of what had happened to him.

She'd been no help at all. If only . . .

"Was ist letz, Becca? Is something wrong?" Miriam hesitated, holding the ball she'd been about to toss to James, leading to some gibberish from him that was probably a complaint.

"No, nothing." She held up a small outfit from the basket of clothes she was folding. "Just wondering if James will start walking instead of crawling before the knees are worn out."

Miriam laughed, reaching out to tickle Joanna before she could grab the ball. "He can walk. He just goes faster on his hands and knees."

Grossmammi had invited Miriam and Matt for supper, and while she supervised the chicken and dumplings in the kitchen, Miriam sat on the living room rug playing with the little ones. Becca was folding a load of wash and had to confess she'd let her mind wander. She'd best keep focused.

Grossmammi was still convinced that Miriam needed someone to confide in, and she seemed to think that person was Becca. Maybe she should say something to keep conversation going.

"I'm relieved today is Halloween. Maybe this will be the end of any mischief making."

Miriam shivered at the reminder. "Matthew says I shouldn't worry about it. He says they're probably done with such foolishness for this year."

Becca hid a smile. Anyone who was around Miriam had to hear what Matt said on any subject. Since as far as Becca was concerned, Matt was still her pesky little brother, she had trouble not chuckling at Miriam's reverent quotes.

"I hope he's right," she said, wondering if every young bride was like that. She didn't think she had been, as much as she'd loved Thomas. Still did love him, she corrected her thoughts. "I did hear that someone started a fire in one of the chicken coops over at the Miller family's place last night. Thank goodness they spotted it right away. The chickens made so much noise, folks said it was as good as a fire alarm."

Grossmammi had maneuvered the two of them into this private conversation, but she probably didn't expect they'd be talking about chickens.

And she couldn't very well come right out and ask Miriam if she had anything to confide.

Most of the time all Miriam talked about was the twins. Right now she held James on her lap, smoothing his silky hair and looking at him with so much yearning that it hurt Becca's heart.

"Becca . . ." Miriam began, and then came to a stop, absently running a plastic horse across the rug until James grabbed it and Joanna grabbed it from him.

Becca waited, hoping she looked encouraging.

Miriam frowned and then started again. "You know my sister Abby."

Becca nodded encouragingly. Everyone knew Abby—cheerful, laughing, talking, giving orders—Abby knew everything, including just what anyone should do on any occasion. Becca found it hard to believe sometimes that Abby and quiet, gentle Miriam were sisters.

"She always thinks she knows what everyone should do." Miriam echoed Becca's thoughts. "And then she tells you, whether you want to hear or not!" Her voice rose on that, rather surprising in Miriam.

Becca hesitated, thinking Grossmammi had been right. Miriam did need to confide.

"She likes to give advice, ain't so?" Becca smiled encouragingly. Clearly it had been some particular advice that Miriam had resented.

"It would be all right if she really knew

something. Or even if I asked her, but I didn't." Miriam was fuming as much as was possible for someone with her gentle personality.

Becca suspected her sister-in-law would burst if she didn't come out with it, so she tried to help her along. "Do you want to tell me about it?"

Nodding, Miriam looked down at her hands, clenched in her lap. "Abby says . . . she says if I'd only relax, then I'd be able to have a baby." Her cheeks flushed at bringing out the words.

Poor Miriam. Her big sister was certain sure a trial to her. Becca struggled to speak calmly.

"I've heard people say that, but they don't really know. I think sometimes it just takes time to get pregnant. That doesn't mean there's anything wrong."

She prayed that was the right thing to say. Maybe she should suggest a visit to the woman doctor in town. Or even the midwife. They'd have better advice than Miriam's sister.

"But how can I know? If I couldn't give Matthew a son or daughter, I'd never forgive myself." Her voice wavered, and she was very near to tears.

"Maybe it would be best to see what the doctor has to say," she ventured. "Surely it's better to know than to grieve yourself by wondering."

Please let me be saying the right thing, she prayed. This was the first time Miriam had confided in her, and she couldn't fail her.

"I would. But I'm so scared. What if it's bad news?"

The pain in her voice echoed in Becca's heart. If she didn't have the babies, how could she survive without Thomas?

"Listen," she said, reaching out to clasp Miriam's clenching hands in hers. "What if I went with you?" she asked.

Miriam looked up then, her blue eyes filled with tears. "Would you?" It was just a whisper.

"For sure I will." Becca scooted across the rug and put her arms around her sister-in-law.

Joanna apparently thought this was a group hug, because she threw herself at them, followed by James. Arms full, Miriam hugged them all, laughing a little despite the tears on her cheeks.

"Denke, Becca. I hated to ask you, but that makes me very happy. I'll call right away."

They were in a happy scramble on the rug when Grossmammi popped in from the kitchen. She surveyed them, looking satisfied. "I see Matthew coming, and supper's ready to dish up."

"We'll come and help." Miriam stood, taking James with her. "James will help, won't you, James?"

James chuckled as if he understood, and Joanna threw herself at her mother. "Me help," she announced.

"Okay, everyone will help," Becca said, and chased them into the kitchen, laughing.

"What's going on in here?" Matthew came in, wiping his boots on the mat. "Tell me what the joke is, so I can laugh, too."

Grossmammi shook her head, waving a ladle at him. "It's a secret, can't you tell? All women have secrets."

"What about James?" he said, sweeping his nephew into his arms. "James isn't a woman."

"He doesn't know the secret, either," Miriam said, laughing. She went up on her toes to kiss his cheek and then James's. "You go play with your niece and nephew while we get supper on the table."

Such a simple thing to say yes to, Becca thought as they ate chicken and dumplings, to bring so much happiness. Miriam continued to smile more than she had in days, and Matthew's teasing kept them all laughing throughout the meal.

By the time Matt and Miriam had left, Becca had settled the children in bed. She came down the steps, seeing darkness closing in against the windows.

She switched on the battery lantern that they kept in the living room, its gentle glow chasing the shadows away. Settling in her usual rocking chair across from Grossmammi, she reached for the basket of mending.

"You were right," she said, smiling at her grandmother. "Miriam did need to talk—"

She stopped, startled by a sound from the

window behind her. She turned to stare and saw nothing but her own face reflected against the darkness outside.

"What was that?" Grossmammi half rose, looking startled.

As if in answer, a handful of what sounded like gravel hit the first window again, and then the next one. Alarmed, Becca hurried to put her arms around her grandmother. "We should . . ."

But before she could think what they should do, footsteps sounded on the front porch and someone yelled. Something smashed against the steps, maybe one of the planters.

Matthew had been wrong about this. The vandals weren't done for this year—at least not for them. She looked instinctively toward the stairs, but the babies were all right. Please God they'd sleep through it.

Something hit the glass of the closest window, and the pane cracked. Panic froze Becca for an instant, but then anger surged through the fear. What did they think they were doing? They needed a good talking-to. She turned, half planning to go to the door, but Grossmammi held her.

"You mustn't go out." Her grandmother's arm stole around her waist, and despite how calm she seemed, she felt very fragile as she leaned against Becca. They stood together, holding each other.

"Someone will hear. Someone will come." It

was an attempt to reassure her grandmother, who responded by squeezing her tightly.

"Yah, for sure." Grossmammi sounded calm, and it was Becca who felt reassured. "It's just boys' foolishness, when all's said and done."

A deep male voice shouted outside, and something clanked against metal, making their ears ring. Footsteps scurried across the porch, there was a confusion of voices, and an engine roared. In another instant a vehicle zoomed out the drive, screeched around the turn onto the road, and faded away.

Becca and her grandmother looked at each other, hardly able to believe it was over so quickly. A loud knock at the door made Becca jump.

"Becca? You all right?"

Surprised into laughter, Becca ran to the back door. She opened it to find her brother Matthew standing there with Nathan Mueller. They wore similar expressions, each of them looking half proud, half embarrassed.

CHAPTER NINE

"You two!" Becca feared for a moment that she might burst into hysterical laughter. "Komm in. What are you doing here? Not that we're not happy to see you," she added.

She glanced at her grandmother, who was already setting the kettle on the stove. Grossmammi's answer to everything was a nice cup of tea.

"I thought it'd be smart to take a walk around, just to look out for any Halloween tricksters." Matt gestured in the general direction of the cottage he and Miriam shared across the road. "I saw headlights, and then that pickup turned in to your drive. So I hurried over here and ran right into Nate. He had the same idea."

Becca turned toward Nathan, registering for the first time that he carried a pitchfork. She suppressed a nervous giggle as she stared. "What were you going to do with that?"

Before Nate could answer, Matt burst out, "He already did it. Clonked it right onto the hood of that pickup. That woke them up. They thought he'd use it on them next."

Nathan flushed. "I wouldn't, that's for sure. But I guess they didn't know that. I didn't even mean to dent the truck, but the fork got away from me. At least it scared them away."

"For sure. They really skedaddled." Matt was grinning from ear to ear.

Becca wasn't sure when she'd seen her brother look so pleased with himself.

"We're wonderful glad you showed up, both of you." Grossmammi patted them both on the cheek, to Nate's obvious embarrassment. "You'll sit down and have some tea and cake, yah?"

Matt shook his head. "Not for me, denke, Grossmammi. Miriam will be wondering where I got to. And worrying, if I know her." He grinned at Nate. "Glad we met up. Next time I'll bring a hoe."

Nate smiled back. "Better not. We don't want to get into trouble with the bishop." He turned to her grandmother, still smiling. "I must go, too. My bruder doesn't know I'm out, I think."

Becca realized Nate had smiled more in the last five minutes then he had since she'd known him. Somehow the incident had turned him and Matt into comrades. Why that should please them so, she had no idea. And if Nathan was still angry with her for her outspokenness, at least it wasn't showing.

Clearly they both wanted to be on their way, and she and Grossmammi shouldn't hold them back. But as they stepped outside, she followed them onto the back porch, her feet crunching on gravel.

"Thank you again, both of you. I don't think they meant to do anything worse, but it was a little frightening." Her glance toward the upstairs windows was involuntary.

"The babies didn't wake, ain't so?" Nate followed the direction of her glance.

She shook her head, relieved. "They slept right through it, thank the good Lord."

"Well, then, you can forget whole thing." Matt patted her arm. "I don't think they'd have the nerve to bother you again."

He strode off into the dark lane, but Nate lingered a moment.

"I'll leave my window open, so I'll hear if anything is going on."

"You don't need to do that . . ."

"I'm going to," he said firmly. "There'll be a mess to clean up in the morning. We'll stop by and give you a hand."

"You don't need to . . ." she began again, but realized it was useless to protest. He'd already stepped off the porch, brushing some dirt aside with his foot.

"What are neighbors for?" he said quickly as he moved away. "Don't worry. They won't come back." He disappeared into the darkness, as well.

Becca closed the door, making sure she locked it. Not that she was afraid, was she? Just jittery.

"Komm," Grossmammi said. "We'll have some of your cousin's chamomile tea. That will calm us down, yah?"

Becca slid onto a chair. "That's what Leah

says." She took the steaming cup her grandmother held out to her. Cradling it in her hands, she enjoyed the comforting warmth.

Funny. She hadn't seen Nathan in days . . . as far as she knew, he was angry with her, and yet he'd been right there when he was needed. And Matthew, too, of course.

"They're gut boys," Grossmammi said, settling down across from her.

Becca smiled. "Not boys. Matthew would be insulted if you called him a boy now that he's grown up and married. As for Nathan . . ." She thought through what she knew about him. "He's probably a year or two older than I am, I'd think."

"He's had some hard times, judging by the lines around his eyes and the tension in his face. That can make a person older." Grossmammi sounded as if she'd given some thought to their new neighbor.

"Yah. Losing his wife and baby the way he did was surely hard." She certainly knew what it felt like to lose a spouse. "His father died young, too. Now he's responsible for his little bruder. It's enough to put lines in anyone's face."

She wondered, just for a moment, if people saw lines in her face that hadn't been there before her loss.

Grossmammi nodded slowly, looking into her tea as if for an answer. "Seems as if he's lost his trust in life. That's a terrible thing to lose. Almost as bad as whatever caused it to begin with."

Becca had to think that through before deciding that her grandmother was right. When it came to people, she usually was. She'd instinctively seen what Becca had stumbled into.

How could you look forward at all if you didn't have trust? Trust in God, trust in life, trust that there were better things ahead. Even at the depth of her grief, Becca had always been able to dream that there was a peaceful tomorrow coming.

Of course, she'd had the children to comfort her and to plan for. Nathan didn't have that. All his hopes for the future had gone in a single incident.

That probably accounted for the back-and-forth attitude Nathan had shown toward all of them . . . as if he wanted to be friends but drew back, unable to.

She would be patient, she promised herself. If ever he wanted her friendship or her help, he would have it.

Nathan had promised himself he'd keep his distance from Becca, finding her too disturbing to his precarious peace of mind. The trouble was, it couldn't be done. At least, not unless he wanted to turn himself into the kind of hermit his uncle had been.

Finally he'd buried what she'd said to him about Peter. About trust. Gone, as if it never happened. Now he had to go on from that point.

He could hardly have ignored it on Thursday evening when he'd seen that pickup come careening down her lane. Or all the other times when life threw them together.

Now here it was Saturday, and he was setting out in the faint early morning light, driving a wagonload of pumpkins, squash, and Becca's apples into town for the festival.

When he turned onto the road, he drew behind a buggy carrying Becca, a couple of her brothers, and her parents. They'd loaded up all the other things they were taking to the festival. Behind Nate came Matt and Miriam, the lights from their buggy casting shadows on the road ahead.

The brisk morning air made him glad for the warmth of his jacket. It was a reminder that they were moving into November now, with winter not so very far off. Still, there was a lot to enjoy about autumn.

As the sun showed itself over the eastern ridge, and the light strengthened, the colors of the trees began to show in all their fall glory. A man had to be glad to be alive, watching the rising sun paint the valley with beauty.

Inevitably, he and Peter had become involved in the Stoltz family plans for the day, with him going early to set up. Only fair, of course, since he'd be marketing his produce with theirs. Peter had somehow managed to get invited to come later, driving Deborah, her sister, and Becca's twins. If he didn't watch out, he and Peter would be absorbed into the Stoltz family.

Still, even that didn't seem such a bad thing on a day like this. Why should he complain about being made welcome?

The festival site was at the township fire hall, a cement block building with bays for the fire trucks on one side and a large room for meetings and activities on the other. He'd come by earlier just to scout out what they'd have to deal with, and it didn't look bad. There was plenty of parking in the field, and rough stands were being set up quickly by folks, both Englisch and Amish, who seemed to have done it before.

Matt came up, waving for him to stop. "We can unload here and then move the wagon out of the way. Ours is the second stall in this row." He pointed.

"Sounds good." He set the brake and hopped down. "Looks like the weather will hold, but—" He sniffed, scenting something acrid in the air.

"Yah." Matt nodded, his pleasant, open face looking worried. "Grass fire last night, just beyond the bend in the road. Good thing they stopped it before it got this far, or we'd be looking at a cancelled festival."

"Again," he muttered, not liking the sense that something was out of control, threatening the peace of the valley.

"Again," Matt agreed. "So much for the theory that the trouble would end with Halloween. I don't like it." He echoed Nate's feelings, moving his shoulders as if to shake something off.

"Are you working or talking?" Becca called out, heading for the stand with an armload of boxes and baskets.

"All right, all right," Matt yelled back. "Don't be so bossy."

Becca grinned and went on her way. It was nice how close she and Matt were. Not twins, like their brothers and sisters, but still having a special link.

Nate considered his brother and sisters. He loved them, for sure, but he'd never had that kind of joking relationship with any of them. He tried to think it was because he was the eldest, but Becca was the eldest in her family, and it didn't hold her back.

He shoved the idea to the back of his mind to consider later and got busy with unloading and setting up.

A few minutes later, Nate was hauling a bushel of apples to the stand. He glanced at Becca's mother, who was spreading out some handmade pot holders on one corner of the counter, about to ask her where she wanted it. Someone grabbed it right out of his arms.

He swung around to find he was facing Becca's young brother-in-law, Abel.

Nate's first instinct was to snatch the basket back, but he restrained himself. Creating a scene was the last thing Becca would want.

"You're Abel King, ain't so?" He tried for a friendly smile.

Abel stared at him suspiciously for a moment before nodding. "Yah. Becca's brother-in-law. I'm going to help her."

By this time, Becca's mother had realized what was happening. "That's wonderful gut of you, Abel. Just put that on the ground in front of the stand for now. How is your mother? Over her cold yet?"

The question distracted Abel's attention from him. "She says it's gone into a chest cold, and Daad says if she doesn't go to the doctor, he'll bring the doctor to her."

She smiled knowingly. "I can hear them arguing. No Mammi wants to admit she's sick. You tell her we'll be making some chicken soup this week, and I'll send some over to her."

Seeing him safely occupied, Nate started back to the wagon, but before he got more than a couple of steps, Abel had caught up with him.

"I'll do the unloading," he said, scowling again. "You don't have to bother."

"Hey, we'll take all the help we can get," Matt said, seeming to jump to the right conclusion about the boy. Did everybody in the township know about his infatuation with Becca? Matt dumped one of Nate's oversized pumpkins into his arms, and Abel staggered at the unexpected weight.

Matt chuckled. "I think Nate should enter one of these for the heaviest pumpkin raffle, ain't so? After all, it's for the fire company."

"I guess. I mean, yah." Abel couldn't seem to make up his mind who annoyed him most. "Thomas was a firefighter. He volunteered because it was so important."

"Now that you're back, you can volunteer, too," Matt said. "We'd be glad to have you."

Abel frowned at Matt, who was obviously interfering in whatever plan Abel had for the day. Then he switched the frown to Nathan.

"I don't guess you're going to volunteer, are you?"

The way he said it was almost an insult, as if to imply that Nate was too busy butting in on Becca to do something worthwhile like volunteering. The right response would be to say that of course he would. Even to point out his years of service back home.

But that was something he'd never do again.

Becca, hurrying to the stand with another box of her mother's handwork, came to an abrupt halt. Matt, Nate, and Abel stood by the wagon, seeming frozen in the act of unloading.

Her frustration peaked. Abel, again. Couldn't

the boy for once act like a reasonable human being instead of a lovesick teenager? He was making both of them look foolish.

She moved toward them, caught a glimpse of Nathan's face, and her heart turned over. It wasn't so much his expression as his lack of expression that stabbed at her. Nathan seemed to wear an immovable mask, but even at this distance she could see the pain in his eyes. It was the way he'd looked the first time he encountered her small daughter. Not just pain, but grief and guilt.

"Are you boys going to unload that wagon or just stand there?"

Becca knew she'd spoken too loudly, but at least it had the result she wanted. All three of them turned toward her, the tension interrupted.

Her brother was the first to recover, and she felt a flood of gratitude for Matt.

"All right, all right. I already told you not to be so bossy." He looked both baffled and relieved, as if he'd been upset by something he didn't understand. "Here, Abel, get that pumpkin over to the stand. I'll bring the basket of squash, and we'll try to make it look like an autumn display."

With Matt pushing, Abel finally moved, and they both headed for the stand. Nathan turned away almost blindly, reaching for a basket of apples.

Should she speak, or would she just make things worse?

159

"Did Abel say something to upset you?" she ventured, hoping just to thaw that frozen look on his face.

For an instant it seemed to be working. His expression softened, and he put out his hand to clasp hers. The warmth of his touch flowed from her hand right into her heart. Affection and caring pulsed between them.

Now she couldn't possibly speak. She could only feel.

The moment shattered as quickly as it had come. Nathan thrust her hand away as if it were hot, grabbed the basket, and fled with it toward the stand.

Afraid of what her face might show, Becca bent over the box as if counting to be sure everything was there. Finally she had enough control of herself to start moving toward the stand, not letting herself even think of what had just happened.

With everyone working, the stand began to take shape quickly. Daad checked the cashbox and taped a list of prices to it, while Mammi counted and recounted the stacks of handwork she'd brought. Around them, friends and neighbors set up their stands or walked around, looking at everyone else's, stopping for coffee or a donut, picking out what they wanted before the festival officially opened.

Becca had always enjoyed this part of the

event . . . the sense of being part of the action behind the scenes instead of just a visitor. But today she felt as if she were enclosed within a glass bubble, viewing it all from a distance but unable to communicate.

Mammi nudged her. "Is everything all right? That's the second time I've asked if you want some coffee."

"Sorry, Mammi. Guess I'm not awake yet. Maybe coffee is just what I need." Surely her smile hid anything else she felt.

Her mother watched her with a trace of doubt, but then nodded and set off with Daad for the breakfast stand that was already open and probably doing a great business as everyone counted down the minutes until opening.

She double-checked the stock and set out some quart baskets, letting her thoughts stray. If her mother had persevered, Becca might have poured out her feelings and doubts, but it was a good thing she hadn't. Mammi's eagerness to have all her children happily settled close to her, getting married and having babies, was bound to affect any advice she gave.

Besides, it really had meant nothing at all, hadn't it? She'd been feeling sorry for Nathan's pain and doubly grieved at the idea that Abel might have had something to do with it.

As for the sensation of closeness and caring, the dawning affection that drew her closer to Nathan in those moments when he clasped her hand . . . well, that meant nothing at all, either. Sympathy, that was all it was.

By the time her mother reappeared with coffee and donuts, Becca had satisfied herself that she really did believe that. So everything was fine.

"Sorry we were so long, but your father found half a dozen people he had to talk to and he's still at it. And they blame women for being gossips." Laughing indulgently, she thrust a napkin toward Becca, using it to dust off some stray powdered sugar from the donuts.

Becca took it from her and finished the job. "Messy, but delicious. Denke, Mamm."

"Here, you go on back behind the stand and have your coffee in peace. We'll be busy enough in another ten or fifteen minutes, so take advantage while you can. I'll mind the stand."

Knowing what she said was true, Becca slipped out of the canvas side of the stand and went behind it. Their stand was in the last row on this side of the fire hall, making it easily accessible from the parking area. She could see Matt and Miriam walking hand in hand from where they'd parked the buggies, and somewhere beyond them was Nathan.

Abel was nowhere in sight, for which she was grateful. Goodness knew she loved the boy. After all, he was Thomas's little brother and precious for Thomas's sake. But until she could figure out how to convince him that his notion was foolish, she'd rather not see much of him.

She dusted off the remnants of donut and then downed a gulp of coffee. She'd best get back . . . but when she looked up, she found that Nathan was headed straight for her.

Seeking something to say, Becca could only smile as he approached. He seemed equally tongue-tied, and for a moment they stood, silently looking at each other. Becca's smile faded from her face as she took in his expression.

"Abel didn't cause trouble," he said abruptly. "Not much, anyway. He was prodding me about why I hadn't joined the volunteer firemen."

"Why would he do that?" Her exasperation grew. "It's not his business what you do."

"Don't." He caught both her hands in his. "It wasn't him. It was my own guilt that struck me." His hands tightened until she felt her fingers growing numb. "I won't tell him, but I have to tell you."

Caring rushed through her and out in a wave toward Nathan. "You don't have to . . ."

"Yah, I do. You've already guessed too much." His grip grew even harder, causing her to take a sharp intake of breath. "I was a volunteer. Before. That's where I was when . . ."

When his wife fell. When his wife died and their baby with her.

Becca seemed to read his mind. "It's not your

fault." She leaned toward him, needing to convince him even though she knew she couldn't.

"Yah, it is." His jaw hardened, if that was possible. "I made a choice. I chose between my responsibility to my family and my responsibility as a firefighter. I chose wrong." He seemed to struggle to say something else. "I won't ever put myself in that situation again . . . loving someone and letting them down. I won't trust myself. Not ever."

He didn't give her time to answer. He dropped her hands, spun, and surged away into the stream of people.

Becca could only stand there, facing the bitter truth. She'd thought she could never love someone again. She'd been wrong. She could.

But it wasn't any good, because the person she'd begun to love didn't have feelings for her. He couldn't. He was too caught up in guilt to have anything left for anyone.

CHAPTER TEN

Fortunately for Becca, she soon found herself too busy to think about what had happened. As the usual crowds began to flow into the festival grounds, she spotted Peter driving the buggy toward the parking area. And doing it as carefully as if he carried a cargo of fragile eggs.

She had to smile, even as she was grateful that the boy understood his responsibility with her two sisters, grandmother, and the twins on board. After some initial difficulties, Peter seemed to be fitting into the Promise Glen community, thanks mostly to her siblings, she realized.

They were good kids. She just hoped she raised her twins as well as Mamm and Daadi had raised theirs. Without Thomas . . . well, it would be more difficult, but she had plenty of help, and she could always trust that the Lord was with them. Comforted, Becca steered her way past any thoughts of what might have been.

Soon her sisters showed up at the stand with Grossmammi and the twins, and for a few minutes everything was chaos. The little ones were clearly excited about all the noise and movement, and she didn't think Deborah and Della were much better off. At the moment, they were arguing about who should watch the little ones first.

"Stop," she said, laughing. "Suppose you both go take a walk around to see what's here and which stands you want to visit. Then you can come back and take turns."

Della shrugged in answer. "That's easy. There will be exactly the same stands there are every year. And they'll be in just the same places. That never changes."

"You'll still find something to spend your money on," Grossmammi said, shooing them away. "Go, go. But come back in fifteen or twenty minutes. If we're busy then, we might need you."

"Come on," Deborah exclaimed, impatient and tugging at her sister's arm. "I don't care if it's exactly like last year. I want to get an apple dumpling."

"You always want to get an apple dumpling," Della retorted as they headed off.

Becca exchanged smiles with her grandmother, who shook her head. "Della always wants something different every day. She hasn't learned yet that it would be uncomfortable if she got it."

Picking up Joanna, who'd been tugging at her apron, Becca held her so that she could see the passing people. Fortunately, the twins hadn't realized that they could push their way through the canvas side of the stall and join the happy crowd.

She thought about Della again. "Well, it is nice to see a new sight or taste a new food sometimes.

Remember when we all went on that trip to Niagara Falls?"

She and Thomas had been newlyweds then, and a whole group of folks had taken a bus trip, visiting Niagara Falls, touring a museum, and riding on a canal boat nearby.

It was the majestic fall of water that she remembered most . . . that and huddling under a rain poncho together, laughing as the spray from the falls hit them. Thomas had held the jacket protectively over her head, shielding her.

Longing pierced her to have that back again, just for a moment. She had felt so safe, so cherished, in that moment.

"I remember." The intent look Grossmammi gave Becca seemed to say she noticed more than Becca intended. "A holiday is a gut thing, that's certain sure, but you wouldn't want one every day."

"Della thinks she would," Becca said, smiling.

But her grandmother swept on. "It's like the Sabbath. Six days you labor, and the seventh you rest and worship. We need that cycle to keep us balanced."

Grossmammi was still studying Becca, giving her a jittery feeling. Was she saying that Becca's life was out of balance?

Joanna gave a squeal and nearly jumped out of Becca's arms.

"Here, hold on, little girl." Thomas's father was

approaching, wearing a huge grin for his little granddaughter. "There now." He held out his arms, and Joanna dove into them.

"How gut to see you." Becca reached out to clasp her father-in-law's hand. "And Joanna obviously feels the same way."

Her daughter was laughing and patting his face, quite sure that she had his complete attention. Dear Jed, so helpful and cheerful. Thomas had been like him—stocky and strong. Jed's sandy hair had turned mostly gray, but his beard was still light. When folks teased him about it, he always laughed and pointed out that his beard wasn't as old as the hair on his head.

Jed kissed the baby's cheek and then tore himself away from admiring her. "Where's our little boy?" He leaned over the counter so he could see James. "What is he doing?"

"Trying to move a pumpkin that's bigger than he is," Grossmammi said. "Here he comes." She scooped up James, who gave one wail at being interrupted and then giggled, reaching toward his grandfather.

"Such a big boy," Jed crooned, taking him. "We'll see you both on Tuesday, yah?" He double-checked with a glance at Becca.

"That would be wonderful gut. They'll be excited to spend the time with you. But I thought their grandmother was still sick."

"I finally got her to the doctor. Don't ask me

how." He grinned. "One shot and a handful of pills, and she's better already. The doctor said it's not catching now that she's on the medicine. So Tuesday is on."

"I'm wonderful glad she's better. I thought from what Abel said that she was still sick."

Jed shook his head. "That boy's been mooning around so much that he doesn't know what's going on. We'll be there, I promise."

She nodded, not surprised that Abel had it wrong, but annoyed by the cause. Well, that would make things easier for her, because Miriam's doctor appointment was Tuesday afternoon.

She smiled at Jed, loving the sight of him bouncing both twins in his arms while Gross-mammi moved off to tend to a customer.

She'd been fortunate in her parents-in-law, Becca knew. Some people had challenges, especially in a situation where a spouse had passed. But Jed and Esther couldn't be kinder or more considerate.

Jed's expression caught her eye. Beyond his obvious joy in his grandchildren, something concerned him. As she opened her lips to ask what was wrong, he shook his head and moved a couple of steps away from the nearest people.

"Was ist letz?" she murmured.

"Abel." He gave another glance around, as if to be sure his younger son wasn't within hearing distance. "He's started his foolishness again, hasn't he? I saw him fussing with your brother earlier."

"Ach, it was nothing." She swept it away with a brush of her hand, not wanting to worry him. "Who has been talking about it? I wouldn't want Esther to be upset."

But he was shaking his head already. "You know how it is in the community. Everyone knows everything. That's why we urged him to go to his uncle for a time."

Becca felt a pang at the thought. They'd deprived themselves of their son's company, probably out of consideration for her. That was the kind of people they were.

"We prayed he'd be over it by the time he came back, but . . ."

"I know." She patted his hand. "I did, too. I thought some pretty young girls down there would distract him," she said, trying to make him smile. "But please don't worry about me, if that's what you're thinking." She hesitated. "I don't want Abel to be hurt, but all I can do is keep saying no."

"Now, Becca, of course we understand." He hesitated and then went on as if it was something he'd practiced saying. "It is our hope that God will send a good man to love and care for you and the kinder. That's what Thomas would want, too. But not a foolish boy like Abel."

Touched, she patted his arm. "Denke, but I'm not even thinking about that yet. As for Abel—"

"You must tell me any time Abel starts on that," he said, interrupting her. "It's fine for him to want to help you, but he has to stop pestering, talking about marriage. It's best I know, so I can deal with him. Though he's that stubborn I don't know if it does any good."

Joanna, sensing that she'd lost her grandfather's attention, took matters into her own hands and swatted him on the nose. Jed blinked and burst into laughter.

Laughing as well, Becca reached out for her erring daughter. "Don't worry. Abel will get over it one way or another."

She tried to sound confident, but she'd begun to wonder if it was ever helpful to try and change anyone's attitude. Some people seemed so set on their own ways, they weren't able to change. Or maybe they weren't willing to try.

Her thoughts flickered to Nathan, and she snatched them back. It was certain sure no use in trying to change him.

Nathan had walked clear around the festival area twice, but hadn't been able to settle to anything. He didn't like this feeling, but he'd committed himself to stay until the end and help the Stoltz family load up and head for home. And that was several hours away.

As he rounded the edge of the grounds nearest to the fire hall, he spotted Abel King ahead of him in the crowd, coming straight toward him. Almost without conscious thought, he turned and headed back the way he had come.

The last thing he wanted was another encounter with that young man, especially after what had happened that morning. And yet what was it to get him so uneasy? Nothing more than a minor disagreement.

Minor, yah. But not, it seemed, to Abel. Abel had glared at him as if Nathan were the worst enemy he had in the world. And that was ridiculous.

He remembered what Becca had told him . . . about Abel's foolish idea that he was meant to take Thomas's place as her husband. Foolish was right—the boy was not only too young for Becca, he was too immature to get married at all.

And why pick on Nathan as his rival? Nathan was nothing but a neighbor, trying to repay the family for their generosity and welcome. Abel might as well be jealous of elderly Henry Abbott, who lived a mile down the road and raised miniature horses.

Now he'd reached the far side of the grounds, and as he glanced behind him, he was relieved to see that Abel was nowhere in sight. Good. He didn't want to be caught up in a controversy with anyone in their new community.

Whatever had generated Abel's irritation with him, it should pass without any intervention on his part, especially if he could ignore the boy for a time. After all, it wasn't as if he were interested in Becca . . .

That thought trailed off as the memory of a couple of incidents surfaced in his thoughts. He tried again to brush them away, but they clung like cobwebs. There had been moments— moments he couldn't control and couldn't forget, either.

Trying to distract himself, he looked across the adjacent field to the tree line in the distance. Beyond it he could see the outskirts of town.

To his surprise, he could see some of the burned-over field from here, just beyond the spot where the tree line dwindled off. So the fire had come much closer than he'd imagined. Fortunately they'd gotten to it in time, or the Fall Festival would most likely have been cancelled.

He wasn't the only person taking an interest in the site of the fire. A few Amish boys emerged from the trees and stared at the charred field. As they moved into the open, he recognized the identical blue shirts of Becca's younger brothers. And the other boy—yes, that was Peter.

Nathan stood motionless for a moment, and then he started toward them. Any kid that age might be fascinated by what the fire had done, but still, he should be sure they weren't getting any wrong ideas.

One of the twins—David, he thought—was

running along the edge of the burned section when he came up.

"What's he up to?" He jerked his head toward the boy as he reached them.

"David?" the other twin said, and Nate recognized Daniel by his thoughtful expression. "He thinks he's going to find where the fire started."

"He might at that, but the firefighters have probably done that already, ain't so?" Nate's flicker of worry had vanished once he actually faced the boys. They were interested, that was all, as any boy that age would be.

"Nate, did you know that the firemen can figure out exactly what was used to start a fire?" Daniel's blue eyes lit with interest. "They might even have found something the fire-starter left behind, ain't so?"

"He wouldn't be dumb enough to drop something that would lead to him," Peter scoffed.

"Well? Who says he isn't? He can't be very smart if he thinks starting fires is a good thing to do," Daniel countered.

David came trotting back just then, looking disappointed. "I didn't see a single thing on this side. They must have started it somewhere else."

Peter was frowning in thought. "Which way does the wind come through here?"

Daniel pointed toward town. "From the west, mostly. Why?"

"If he wanted to burn this field—" Peter began.

"Yah, I see," Daniel interrupted, catching on quickly. "He'd use the wind to send the fire where he wanted it."

David was still looking blank, but then he nodded. "Okay, I got it. I didn't think of that. It would have started on the other side. Want to go look?"

Nathan interrupted before they could answer. "I'm thirsty. Komm on back. I'll buy you all a soda."

"Hey, great!" The twins looked identical in their enthusiasm. "Let's go." David jogged in place for a moment and then he raced off toward the festival, with Daniel right behind him.

But Peter hung back, walking with Nathan.

"Go ahead. I'll catch you up." Nathan gestured toward the other boys.

Peter didn't speak for a moment. Then he looked accusingly at his brother. "Why did you follow me over there?" He jerked his head toward the burned field.

"I didn't follow you, exactly." What was in Peter's mind? Maybe he shouldn't have shown so much interest, but after all, he was responsible for Peter now.

"Sure you did." Peter's voice had an edge of bitterness. "You thought maybe I was involved."

"No." Nathan said it sharply. "No such thing. You couldn't be."

Peter eyed him as if he wanted to believe that

175

but wasn't sure, and Nathan knew he couldn't leave it at that.

"Look, I . . ." He suddenly heard Becca's voice, accusing him of not trusting his brother, and changed what he might have said. "I know you weren't involved in that business back home. So why would I think you'd start up with it here?"

His brother studied the ground for a few minutes as they walked. "You don't trust me. Or anybody else, right?"

He started to say that wasn't true, but some innate honesty stopped him. He didn't trust himself. Was it possible he'd extended that feeling to other people?

But he didn't have time to do any soul-searching right now, because his brother was waiting for an answer. Hoping, maybe that some reassurance was coming his way. It didn't matter so much whether Nathan trusted himself, but he had to . . . had to . . . show his trust in his brother.

With an effort, he forced a smile to his face, reached over, and clasped Peter by the shoulder. "Ach, don't be so foolish. It's certain sure I trust you. You prove yourself to me every single day."

A smile dawned slowly on Peter's face and then expanded into a grin. Nathan gave him a little shake. "Come on. Let's catch up to David and Daniel. I want that drink."

Nodding, Peter headed off at a brisk trot,

and Nathan followed, images swirling in his mind. Why had his uncle popped into his head? Because Joseph Mueller had made a mess of his life? Was he in danger of turning into the same kind of person?

That was an ugly thought. He didn't want to look in the mirror one day and see an isolated, bitter old man staring back, looking a lot like Onkel Joseph.

Becca's hands tightened on the reins as Sweetie neared the lane to her house at the end of the day. Not that the buggy horse needed any guidance when it came to going back to her stall and her feed manger.

This day had been longer than she'd thought possible. And she was more tired than she'd ever felt after a festival. She slowed Sweetie down when the mare wanted to race into the barn.

"Komm, foolish one. You know I'm not taking the buggy inside."

Sweetie flicked her ears back as if annoyed and stopped at the usual spot for getting rid of her harness.

In a few minutes' time Becca had the mare in her stall, munching happily, and was lugging the harness to its place, then stepped on a trailing line and nearly dropped it.

What was wrong with her? Anyone would think she was getting old.

Foolish. It had been a good day, with more sales than she'd expected. She still had enough baskets of apples for the family's needs over the coming months, and Nathan had brought her a barrow load of pie pumpkins.

That would make Grossmammi happy. She could bake pumpkin pies and pumpkin bread to her heart's content.

She smiled at Nathan not knowing what to make of the small, dense pumpkins, thinking them just a baby version of the jack-o'-lantern ones. He hadn't known what to say when someone asked for a sugar pumpkin, so she'd handed it to him.

"What are you smiling at? All your profits at the festival?" Nathan had come in, carrying a basket of leftover apples, and she hadn't even heard him.

"Not really. Just wondering about people who don't know a pie pumpkin from a jack-o'-lantern."

"Give me a break. I never had much to do with pumpkins until Onkel Joe left me his." He set the basket on the rack where she kept them, safely out of reach of Sweetie's stall.

"Well, when my grandmother sees them, she'll probably offer you a pie."

He smiled, looking more relaxed than usual. "We won't turn it down. Nobody at our house knows how to make a pie."

A scrabbling from the cage drew Nate's attention. "Are you still tending that squirrel? You'll spoil him."

"Too late. I already did. Or rather the boys did. I caught Daniel in here the other day hand-feeding him peanuts." She shook her head. "If he had his way, this would be the fattest squirrel in the woods." She grasped the cage. "I meant to let him go this morning, but I was too rushed. I'd best do it now."

Nathan took the cage away from her, his hand brushing hers. "I'll help. But after your tender care, he'll probably cling to the cage. Why would he want to leave?"

Becca felt the heat rising in her cheeks. "It wouldn't be the first time an animal liked captivity best. Trust me, I have my ways to chase them off if I have to."

She started across the field behind the barn, heading for the woods near the orchard, and he kept pace with her.

"Did your ways of getting rid of a pest work with Abel King?" he asked, glancing sideways at her.

"I . . . not exactly." She was silent for a moment, thinking how complicated everything was. "I probably shouldn't have told you about it. It's your fault for being such a good listener," she added lightly.

"It's not a problem. Sorry if you didn't want it mentioned. But Matt said something about it this morning, too. He seemed to be losing patience with Abel."

"I'm not sure Matt ever had much . . . patience, that is. And I guess most of the community knows about it by this time." She blew out a sigh. "I hoped to keep it from his parents, but that didn't work."

"Word gets around fast. The Amish grapevine, yah?" Nathan raised his eyebrows in a question.

"Yah." She tried to laugh, but she didn't feel much like it. "The thing is that Abel's a worry— for his parents as well as for me. And he doesn't respond well to being tipped out of the cage and shooed."

"No, I guess not."

They'd reached the edge of the trees, and she motioned for him to set the cage down. The squirrel peered up at her as if he knew she was going to do something he didn't want.

"Stop looking at me that way." She scolded him, determined to take this lightly. And not to think about Abel King. "You have to get settled for the winter, you foolish critter."

"Matt says you've been doing this kind of thing since you were a kid . . . something about a baby owl under your bed."

"Matt should learn to keep his mouth shut," she said tartly.

Nathan shook his head. "No reason to be embarrassed about wanting to help a wounded creature. It shows you have a kind heart. Just make sure you don't end up getting bit."

Was he talking about wounded animals or about wounded human beings, like himself? She hurriedly grasped the cage door and opened it.

The squirrel looked at the door and then turned his back to it.

"Come on, now." She jiggled the cage, but the squirrel didn't respond.

Aware of Nathan's gaze on her, she picked up the cage, held the door open, and shook the cage firmly. Like it or not, he had to go.

The squirrel toppled out into the long grass. He hesitated, looked around, then looked back at the cage. Nathan picked it up and put it behind him.

With an almost human look of disappointment, the squirrel tried its leg . . . cautiously at first, and then more firmly. Finally he seemed to decide it worked. He abruptly darted for the nearest tree, sped up the trunk, and settled on a branch.

"Good job," she said, in much the same way she did to the kinder. "That's that." She turned, facing the orchard, and paused for a moment, dwelling on it.

"Your orchard's done well this year, ain't so?" Nathan asked.

"Yah. I hope so," she said softly.

"Just hope so?" he asked. "Don't you know?"

She shrugged. "The money has come in about like usual, but . . ." She hesitated, and started again. "This orchard belonged to my grandfather, you see. Some of my earliest memories are of being here with him." She smiled, letting her thoughts drift back. "He talked to me about it, even before I understood. His family were always orchardmen, and he planted these trees himself."

"It's more than just an orchard to you." He seemed to be trying to understand.

"Yah. It was always the place I came to when I wanted to be by myself. Even after my grandfather was gone, I felt close to him there." She looked from one tree to the next. "He talked about how the trees were like people, needing sun and rain, nourishment and care. And growing old like people, as well, so that sometimes they have to be removed to make way for younger growth."

"Sounds like you were close to him. I see why he left the orchard to you."

Suddenly aware of how much she'd been confiding in Nathan, she struggled to talk about something else.

"He would laugh at me for wanting to nurse any injured critters I found. But he was the one who made the cage for me, so I don't think he was too serious."

"Sounds that way." Nathan's voice had roughened, as if he were moved, and his hand encircled hers. "You do a kind thing with the injured. Just . . . like I said, don't get hurt."

She looked up into his face and knew what he was saying. He was warning her that trying to be kind to him could end up in hurt. That he wasn't a safe person to care for.

Too late, when his look stirred her as if it were a touch. And his touch went straight to her heart and took up residence there as if it were home.

Yes, she already knew it was too late for that. She wasn't just beginning to care for him. She was in love with him.

She'd never intended to do it. She couldn't believe it had happened. Losing Thomas still hurt just as much, but she was in love with Nathan.

CHAPTER ELEVEN

By Tuesday Becca felt that she could take a deep breath and relax about her job with the orchard. The festival marked the point at which her grandfather had always determined whether he'd made a decent profit for the year. She had met her modest goal and even bettered it.

She thought again about her parents' concern for her and felt a sense of gratitude to them and to everyone who had helped her get through the past year. Perhaps now her parents would agree that Grossdaadi had made the right decision in leaving the orchard to her.

Well, she ought to be reasonable as far as Mammi's opinion was concerned. She wouldn't be satisfied until Becca was either happily married again or had moved back home. And neither of those things was likely to happen.

Standing in front of the mirror in her bedroom, she slipped a dress over her head. Her everyday dress wasn't, she felt, suitable for the trip to the clinic with Miriam, so she changed to the newer one she usually saved for church Sundays.

Becca looked at her reflection for a moment. What changes had others seen in her in the past year?

As for her viewpoint, a year ago she had still

been so confused and shattered by losing Thomas that she hadn't been able to pay attention to the orchard or anything else except the babies. The need to take care of them had kept her going.

People had jumped in to help without being asked, that was for sure. Not just family, although they were always there, but neighbors, church members, people from other Amish communities, even her Englisch customers.

People were kind when there was trouble, and she had reason to know it. Now it was her chance to be there for someone else, and her heart filled with hope for her sister-in-law.

She was still a little surprised that Miriam wanted her to go to the doctor's appointment with her. Becca couldn't give herself any credit for it, not when so often it seemed she said exactly the wrong thing. Was it possible that just being open and accepting was even more important than words? Maybe she should try that more often. She'd hate to think she was becoming like Miriam's sister, always thinking she knew the answers to other people's problems.

Had she been that way with Nathan? Had she tried to fix his relationship with his brother? If so, she'd best worry about her own behavior instead of his.

Detaching her thoughts once again from Nathan, she focused on Miriam. She'd finally managed to get a few more details. Miriam thought she was expecting, but she'd been disappointed too many times to be confident. And she hadn't picked up a test kit. She'd blushed at the very suggestion. What if someone saw her?

Becca's lips twitched, remembering Miriam's attitude. Had she ever been as shy and insecure as that? Impossible. If she asked any of her younger siblings, they'd roar with laughter.

If . . . when . . . Miriam's sister found out, Becca could imagine the response. Abby was one of those women who took pride in always saying what she thought, and she was bound to be vocal about this. Abby declared that was being honest.

Maybe that kind of honesty wasn't always a virtue, to Becca's way of thinking. Where was the line between being interested and caring about others and being just plain nosy and bossy? She murmured a prayer that she could tell the difference in herself.

This afternoon was all about Miriam, she reminded herself. Even if Becca couldn't do anything more than hold her hand, she'd be there with her.

Hearing a car pull into the lane, Becca hurried downstairs. In the kitchen, Grossmammi and Thomas's mother Esther had gathered at the table with coffee cups and slices of the fruit bread that Esther had brought.

Jed, more interested in his grandchildren than food right now, sat on the floor with James standing on his legs while Joanna threw a ball at them.

"Mammi!" she exclaimed, and the ball missed its target and bounced off the cabinet. Joanna ran to her and pulled on her dress. "Up, Mammi, up!"

"Not now, lovey." She tousled her daughter's silky hair. "Mammi's going out with Aunt Miriam."

"I hope all goes well," Grossmammi said, and Esther nodded, scooping up Joanna. No one had told them anything about today's expedition, but by some secret known only to grandmothers, they seemed to understand.

"Yah, me, too." Becca pulled on a heavy black sweater against the chilly day and raised her hand in goodbye.

"Don't hurry," Esther reminded her. "We'll stay as long as you want us, ain't so, Joanna?" She bounced the baby in her arms, and Joanna nodded, giggling.

Becca took a deep breath, praying she was ready for whatever happened, and hurried out to the waiting car.

Dennis Warren, one of several retired men in the area who enjoyed driving the Amish when a horse and buggy wouldn't do, was holding the door for her.

"You ladies can sit in the back and chat all you want, okay? I'll get you to the clinic in plenty of time."

"Denke, Dennis." Becca slid in next to Miriam.

"How is Margo?" Dennis's wife was a constant customer at the fruit stand.

"Just fine. In fact, she said to tell you she could do with another basket of Winesap apples if you can spare them."

"For sure," she said, doing a mental count of what she had left. "You can pick them up when you drop me off, if you want. Or stop over anytime."

He nodded, satisfied, and slid behind the wheel. In a moment they were on their way.

Becca glanced at her sister-in-law. "Everything all right?" She spoke in Pennsylvania Dutch, knowing Dennis wouldn't understand them and wouldn't mind.

Miriam nodded, managing a smile, but her hands were clasped tightly in her lap. "I hope so," she said.

Remembering her thoughts about what she could do, Becca put her warm hand over Miriam's straining ones. "I know," she said softly. It wasn't easy to cope when the thing you wanted seemed so far out of reach. She knew that, as well.

Miriam blinked back a stray tear. "So many times I thought . . ." She shook her head, unable to finish. "It's not easy to keep hoping," she whispered.

"You'll be all right." She pressed their hands together. She'd like to say they both could keep hoping, but she didn't see her way clear to do that. "Dr. Ellison is wonderful kind, ain't so? The midwife asked her to check me when she realized it was twins. I really liked her."

It was easy to be reassuring about the woman obstetrician at the clinic. Becca had liked the confident, poised young doctor at first sight, and never found a reason to change her mind. Perhaps Dr. Ellison would be able to share some of her confidence with Miriam.

Somehow feeling the weight of Miriam's fears made Becca's seem light in comparison. Since admitting to herself that she loved Nathan, she had dwelt on it far too much, and it was time she stopped.

Miriam's problem could be solved, in one way or another. Even if she and Matt were unable to have a baby of their own, there were other babies desperate for a home and for the love of two parents. Miriam and Matt had so much love to give that she knew, one way or another, they would give it.

As for Becca's own private pain . . . she would bear it. She'd suspected all along that Nathan would not love again. Confident that she felt the same, she had missed the signs that her own heart was opening to him.

Now it was time to accept the truth. Whatever might have been between them was impossible. She still had a challenging job ahead of her, one that would need all the love she could give, in raising Joanna and James in the way she should. It was enough for her.

A glance at Miriam assured her that Miriam didn't seem inclined to talk anymore. They rode the rest of the way to the clinic in silence, hands clasped, and Becca prayed every mile of the way.

Carrying a CLOSED FOR SEASON sign to put on the fruit and vegetable stand and pushing a wheelbarrow, Nathan headed down the lane to help with the closing. Deborah had mentioned that Becca was out this afternoon, and it would be a nice surprise to find it finished instead of waiting for her.

He could hear voices from around the bend in the lane, so it sounded as if Deborah and Peter were already busy. Good. It wouldn't take long, in that case. He touched the sign to be sure the paint was dry.

When he'd told Becca he'd found a suitable sign in one of the sheds that he could repaint, she'd said not to go to much trouble—just the word *Closed* would do. But he enjoyed doing the lettering, and he'd added *Inquire at the house,* even though Becca seemed sure everybody knew that.

He hadn't expected, that first day when he'd upset her by assuming she wanted to sell the stand, that he'd ever become so involved with Becca and her family. Now it felt as if they'd been neighbors for years.

Just neighbors, he reminded himself. Nothing else.

Nathan rounded the bend and could see the stand. He also saw Peter and Abel King squared up against each other with flushed faces, while Deborah looked as if she was about to jump between them.

Easy, he told himself. He had to take it easy. The last thing Becca would want was some sort of confrontation between Peter and Abel. Or himself and Abel, for that matter. Whatever had brought those two to the boiling point, it was up to him to defuse the situation.

"Looks like lots of help today," he commented, walking between the two boys to set the sign on the counter. From the cloth bag he carried, he also set out the hammer and nails to put it up.

Taking his time gave him a moment to see how everyone reacted to his presence. Finished, he glanced at Deborah, smiling encouragingly. The strain left her face, and although she looked a bit pale, she returned his smile, clearly relieved to see him.

Unfortunately, neither of the two boys seemed to feel that way. *Boys* was just what they were, he thought as he surveyed them. He well knew that Peter was on the tipping place, where some days he showed a man's responsibility and the next he was as careless as a child.

Abel had a couple of years on him, of course,

but no one who'd seen the way he'd been acting could possibly mistake him for a man. What was more, he looked just as angry with Nathan as he obviously was with Peter.

Nathan turned to Deborah. It would do no harm to give Abel and Peter another few minutes to calm down. "I brought the wheelbarrow down also in case there are any apples to take back up."

"Yah, there's three baskets of them behind the counter." She hurried around the counter, looking happy to turn the situation over to him. "I think we can take those back to the shed."

"I'll do that." Abel had a belligerent tone to his voice that was going to be hard to ignore. "I'll take care of everything."

Nathan raised an eyebrow. "Did you talk to Becca about it? I don't think she expected you today."

"No reason you would know," Abel muttered, sounding sulky. "Becca's my sister-in-law. We're family. For sure she expects me to help with everything."

"Abel's mamm and daad are up to the house, watching the twins this afternoon," Deborah said, maybe hoping that would make the situation easier.

"That's right." Abel didn't look quite so red now, and his fists had unclenched. "We're family, like I said. Becca doesn't need to have neighbors helping her when she's got family."

Nathan's patience slipped a notch. The boy was determined to pick a fight. Well, Nathan wasn't going to satisfy that urge, if he had to present Abel back to his parents tied up with a bow.

"Oh, we're not just neighbors. We were partners over the produce Becca was selling for us." He picked up the sign and held it up to the center post.

"What do you think, Peter? A little higher?"

"Yah, I'd say so." Peter looked as reluctant as Abel to give up on their dispute, but at least he was sensible enough to cooperate with his brother. "You want me to hold it while you hammer it in place?"

Peter nodded, starting to move into position. Abel moved at the same time, jostling him so that he lost his balance. He stumbled on the wheelbarrow and was up again in an instant, heading for Abel.

Nathan was between them before anything else could happen. He grabbed the two of them by their shirtfronts.

"Enough!"

It was suddenly so silent that the call of a crow sounded like an alarm. Nathan glared from one to the other of them, feeling an urge to bounce their heads together.

"Isn't there enough trouble in the world without two Amish boys acting like hoodlums?"

Neither of them could look at him. Satisfied

194

that they were both as much embarrassed as angry, he let them go.

"We're going to finish this job with no more trouble. Anybody who can't do that can leave now."

Silence.

"All right. Peter, you and Deborah put up the sign. Abel, you can help me load everything else on the wheelbarrow. Now!"

They went to work without another word. He saw the look that Peter and Deborah exchanged, and he suspected they'd talk it over later. He didn't know who Abel talked things over with, but he'd best find someone, because he sure wasn't coping by himself.

As they loaded up the odds and ends of things left in the stand, he studied Abel's face. Without the scowl, it was young, not yet grown into the maturity he wanted so badly. He found himself wondering if Abel looked like his big brother.

At that moment it occurred to him that he did know who Abel had confided in . . . it would have been his brother, of course. Thomas. Now Abel was fumbling, trying to make up for it, telling himself he could take Thomas's place.

It wasn't possible. The boy probably knew that at some level, but he hadn't admitted it to himself.

He and Peter knew about losing someone, and Nathan felt sorrier for Abel than he'd have believed possible a few minutes earlier. After all, hadn't he struggled after Daad passed? Didn't he still, longing to have Daad's advice about dealing with Peter?

He and Deborah locked up the shutters, and he was reminded of doing that with Becca. Too many things reminded him of Becca.

As they started up the lane toward the barn, Deborah managed to come near enough to murmur something to him.

"Abel tripped him," she whispered, obviously eager to be sure he wasn't blaming his brother.

"Yah," he said, thinking what a nice girl she was. "Best to forget about it, ain't so?"

She smiled, then darted ahead to help Peter with the wheelbarrow load.

Abel was lagging behind, and Nathan slowed in order to walk beside him.

"Your folks are at the house, yah?"

Abel's scowl was back. "I suppose you're going to tell them about that." He jerked his head back toward the farmstand.

Nathan looked at him steadily for a long moment before he spoke. "It's not my place to tell your parents on you."

Dull red colored Abel's face, and he stared at the ground. "Denke," he muttered.

"But Becca will have to know," he went on. "It's her business, after all." He didn't suppose Abel would appreciate that, but he wasn't going to start lying to Becca for the boy.

That earned him another glare. "Why don't you leave Becca alone? She doesn't need you around."

Nathan met his glare steadily. "That's up to Becca, ain't so? Not me, and certain sure not you."

Abel's gaze went back to the ground. He muttered something, so softly that for a moment Nathan didn't understand it. Then he realized what Abel had said, and decided it was better to pretend he hadn't heard.

You want her for yourself.

Much better not to have heard that, because if he responded, he could only cause more trouble . . . both with Abel and for himself.

Responding to Miriam's wishes, Becca stayed in the waiting room while Miriam spoke to the doctor. It hadn't been her idea. She'd much rather have gone in with her, in case there were questions Miriam was too shy to ask.

But her sister-in-law seemed to have her courage screwed up to speak for herself, at least today, and that was surely a good thing. So Becca had contained herself as best she could until the door into the waiting room opened again.

Miriam came out of the office wearing a dazed look and clutching a handful of booklets and instructions from the doctor. Having been there herself, it didn't take much for Becca to understand what that meant.

Becca jumped to her feet, heedless of the other people looking on, and enveloped Miriam in a huge hug, trying to keep her tears from overflowing.

"I'm so happy for you," she whispered, her cheek against Miriam's.

Miriam drew back so that she could see Becca's face. She wore a smile so brilliant that it transformed her face from sweet to beautiful, and her eyes shone like jewels.

"It's true," Miriam murmured. "It's really true."

"It really is," Becca agreed. "Let's go home."

They left the office hand in hand and found Dennis waiting to pick them up. And if Dennis didn't know what was going on, then he wasn't as smart as Becca thought.

Knowledgeable about Amish customs as he was, he didn't say anything, but Becca caught his gaze in the rearview mirror a couple of times and found him smiling.

Miriam held Becca's hand again during the return trip from the clinic, but this time it was joy that flowed back and forth between them. Not only didn't Miriam have any problems that might hinder her in the future, but the longed-for baby was already on the way.

Miriam kept staring at the booklets throughout the drive, as if trying to believe that she had a right to them. Finally she showed them to Becca.

"I'm going to read every word," she declared.

"And I'll make sure Matthew does, too. We're going to do everything we can to be good parents. Matthew will be just as wise as your Daad, ain't so?"

Becca nodded, but she felt a giggle rising in her at the thought of her little brother trying to understand the information about pregnancy and childbirth. But the laughter was swamped by love . . . Matthew was going to be a father. How happy everyone would be.

The driver stopped at Matt and Miriam's house, and Miriam slid out, then turned to clasp Becca's hand. "Will you come in?"

"Ach, no, not now. You and Matt need this time alone together. I'll see you later, yah?"

Miriam was already turning away at the sound of Matt's voice calling her name as he came outside. Forgetting the two in the car, she rushed toward him, and they clung to each other, probably not seeing anything but each other.

Dennis turned to look at her, grinning. "I don't speak Deutsch, but I can sure understand that."

Nodding, Becca smiled back. She suddenly wanted to share the news with the world, but that wasn't the Amish way.

As they went back down the driveway and headed across to her place, Becca recognized a little touch of something that might be jealousy. She brushed it away. How could she be jealous? Then she realized it was longing.

Matt and Miriam were starting on a wonderful journey, and for an instant she'd wished to be back there again herself, at the beginning of her own journey.

When they reached the house, Becca got the basket of apples and settled with Dennis. She hurried into the kitchen, eager to share the news with Grossmammi. She'd missed Jed and Esther, she saw, since their buggy had gone.

Grossmammi was folding laundry at the table while Joanna made an effort to pull her finished work back down again. Fortunately she was just about an inch too short to do it.

"I'm back," she announced.

James, clinging to the table leg, let go and came toward her, for once staying on his feet instead of resorting to crawling. When he reached her skirt, she swept him up for a kiss.

"Gut job, James. Nice walking."

"Me, me." Joanna was there in a minute, so Becca held both warm, wiggling bodies close against her, love flooding her.

When she stood again, Grossmammi was smiling at her. "No need to tell me that it's good news. I can see it in your face."

"Yah, the best. She's telling Matt now. Imagine! My little brother is going to be a daadi."

Grossmammi wrapped her in a hug, laughing and thankful, and in a moment they were speculating on whether it would be a boy or a girl.

Eventually Becca sobered up. "How were things with Jed and Esther? Were the little ones good, I hope?"

"For sure. They had a good day with the twins, I think. I went over to help your mamm with some canning, so I had an excuse to leave them alone." She frowned slightly. "Abel showed up later, after I got back."

"He's not still here, is he?" Becca looked around apprehensively, half expecting him to appear from the closet with another proposal.

"No, no, he went when they did." She hesitated. "Actually, he came up with Deborah and Peter and Nathan from the stand. I guess you saw they closed up this afternoon and put up a new sign."

"Yah, I saw." She could only hope Abel had been on his best behavior. It was hard to count on it these days.

"Nathan did a wonderful good job on the sign," Grossmammi said, turning back to the laundry. "Seems like he's one to do his best with whatever he takes on."

Something about her voice made Becca look closer. "Was ist letz? Did Abel cause problems?"

Her grandmother considered. "Nobody said anything. But seemed like there was something going on between them. Abel was sulky, but that's nothing new, ain't so? And Nathan looked like he'd been holding on to his patience with all his might."

"Oh, no." She wondered what new problems Abel had found to stir up. If only she could convince him . . .

"The person to ask would be Nathan." Grossmammi interrupted Becca's thoughts. "He'd know, that's for sure, and you'd better find out." She glanced at the clock. "Run over now, while there's time before supper. Go on. You'll need to thank him, anyway."

Becca hesitated, but her grandmother was right. Whatever Abel was up to, it was best she knew about it. She remembered her conversation with her father-in-law. She'd promised to let him know of anything that happened, little though she wanted to.

Becca took the path along the field that would come out between Nathan's house and his barn. It was trodden down now in a way it hadn't been in years.

What would Joseph have thought about the frequent coming and going between the properties? Not much, most likely. No matter who tried to help him, he'd put up those barriers to keep people from interfering in his life, and he'd never let them fall.

Like Nathan? Becca felt a sudden chill. When Nathan wore that frozen, forbidding expression of his, he might as well put a *Closed* sign on his chest. He might be more like his uncle than he believed or wanted.

She spotted Nathan leading the horses toward the barn and followed him. Just a quick chat, she reminded herself. Best to keep it focused on Abel.

Poor Abel. The familiar combination of sympathy and annoyance reared up each time she thought of him. This wasn't what Thomas would have wanted for his precious little brother.

She paused in the barn doorway, letting her eyes adjust to the dimness within. Nathan, bending over the leg of the gray mare, straightened when her shadow fell across the floor.

"Becca. What brings you here?"

She couldn't tell whether that question was welcoming or not. "A little matter of saying thank you. Denke." She moved toward him. "It was a nice surprise to find the stand closed and ready for winter when I got home."

He shrugged, turning back to the mare, who tossed her head when he touched her foreleg. "What's happened to you?" he murmured, and it took a moment to realize he spoke to the mare, not her.

"I'll take her head." Becca grasped the mare's halter, stroking her neck. Should she come right out and ask about Abel, or try to talk about closing the stand and see what he said?

Nathan slid a firm hand down the leg, pinching a bit to encourage the mare to pick up her foot. She hesitated for a moment, then reluctantly did, and Becca felt the tension in her.

"Now, then, don't be foolish," she murmured, stroking the mare's neck. "It's all right."

"There it is. A nut, of all things, caught in the shoe." Using a hoof pick, he flipped it out. It lay on his palm, big enough to lame a buggy horse if she went on the hardtop road with it.

"That's better, isn't it?" She patted the mare again, and the horse responded by blowing damply on her neck.

"Gut," Nathan said, checking to be sure the mare was putting her weight evenly on the foot. "Denke, Becca." He glanced at her as he let the mare into her stall. "We're even now, yah?"

Becca smiled. "I think painting the sign and doing the closing is a bit more than holding the horse's head. The sign turned out wonderful gut, too."

"I liked painting the sign, so you don't owe me any thanks for that."

"What about for coping with Abel?" she asked. "Did you like that, too?"

His face clouded. "Ach, that boy's tiresome, I'll say that for him. He as near as nothing threw a punch at Peter."

Horrified, she sucked in a quick breath. "He wouldn't, surely." She shook her head, thinking how Thomas would have reacted to that. "You'd best tell me the worst."

His lips twisted in an attempt to smile. "Relax, Becca. It wasn't all that bad. I intervened before he could make things worse."

She eyed him apprehensively. "What did you do?"

"Took them both by the shirtfront and tried my best not to give them a good shaking. And gave Abel a choice between helping and leaving. He decided to help."

"You mean you pushed him into it." She rubbed at the ache in her temples. "Thomas wouldn't believe his little bruder could behave so badly. And I'll have to speak to Jed about it, though I hate to."

"It's best he knows." Nathan's voice was firm. "I know you don't want to cause him pain, but the next time, Abel might start that with someone who'll hit back, and then where will he be?"

"I know, I know. I'll talk to Jed." No matter what, this couldn't be allowed to go on.

"One other thing." Nathan stood looking down, his arm resting across the horse's shoulders. "Abel said . . . he hinted . . . that I am coming between the two of you."

Color flooded her face, and she didn't know where to look. "What . . . what did you say to him?" she asked faintly.

"I told him not to be ridiculous and put him to work. But whether that'll stop him, I don't know."

"I don't, either," she admitted, wondering if Nathan was worried about her reputation or his own. "But I will tell his father, I promise. Foolish boy. How could he think . . ." She couldn't seem to finish that sentence out loud.

"It's ridiculous," Nathan said again, as if to convince himself.

"Yah," she said, a flood of conflicting emotions tightening her throat. Nathan sounded determined to convince himself. And she couldn't say she felt very sure. Not about anything at all.

CHAPTER TWELVE

After another couple of days of arguing with herself, and trying to figure out the answers, Becca was on her way to town, where she hoped to have that difficult conversation with her father-in-law, Jed. She'd been unable to think of any way to contact him without either Abel or her mother-in-law finding out, and that would have led to an even more difficult conversation.

Finally she'd decided an errand to his place of business was the only possibility. Jed ran what he called his bargain store, saying he couldn't make it any clearer because he never knew what he'd have to sell from week to week. Hitting the wholesalers and the auctions, he picked up cases of canned food, sometimes a bit battered, plus odd assortments of paper products, cleaning supplies, bigger items like plastic chairs and folding tables with only an occasional dent, and anything else that he thought he could sell. She sometimes thought people showed up on his open days just for the thrill of the bargain hunt, never knowing what they might find.

Slowing down, Becca drove her buggy along Main Street, knowing that Friday tended to be a busy shopping day. But if she was nervous driving in traffic, at least Sweetie wasn't. The mare had seen it all before and plodded along until Becca turned in to the parking area at Jed's Bargain Store. Without prompting, Sweetie moved to the spot she wanted at the hitching rail, for all the world as if she looked forward to a chat with the buggy horse next to her.

Dismissing her thoughts as nervous fantasies, Becca climbed down quickly. If a person had to do something difficult, Grossmammi always said, it's best to do it first. Becca knew it was wise advice, but she had to admit it wasn't easy to follow. Still, if she did, the rest of the day should go smoothly.

Becca went inside cautiously, alert for any sign that Abel had come with his father today, but she didn't spot him. The teenager who worked the checkout line stopped lounging on the counter and put on a welcoming smile. Nodding to her, Becca moved into the rows of merchandise, on alert.

Stop being foolish, she lectured herself. Even if Abel was here, he'd behave himself in his father's presence. Jed was near a mountain of somewhat dented aluminum pans, talking to a man she didn't know, but he saw her and waved.

She kept going, knowing Jed would find her when he had a chance. Several people were sorting through the cartons of canned goods, and she walked past, greeting those she knew.

"Becca, just look at this." Emma Schmidt waved her hand at the pile of boxes. "You'd think Jed would at least sort things out so a customer could find what she wanted."

"He could," she agreed, smiling. "But then you wouldn't have the fun of the treasure hunt."

Emma grinned, beckoning Becca closer. "Shh. Look what I found." She showed Becca her shopping bag, in the bottom of which rested at least a dozen cans of beef chunks. "I found them first," she said, giggling. "There's a few left if you want."

"Gut work." They both knew perfectly well that Emma was enjoying the hunt for a bargain and wanted congratulations on her success. "We don't need any, cooking just for Grossmammi and me and the little bit the twins would eat."

"You might find some canned peaches in that pile," Emma pointed, obviously wanting to share her finds with Becca.

"I'll have a look in a minute." She turned away, seeing that Jed was free. "I want to have a word with Jed first. Maybe he'll give us a clue to find a special deal." She headed toward him, leaving Emma happily diving through another stack of cartons.

"Becca, it's wonderful gut to see you today." Jed clasped both her hands, beaming all over his broad face, eyes twinkling. Jed was always jovial, of course, but he did look especially happy to see her. Her heart warmed toward her father-in-law, making it even harder to bring up something that might hurt him.

"I had to see what great bargains you have this week," she said, delaying the difficult moment.

"Bargains you want, and bargains you'll get at Jed's Bargain Store. How about some beef chunks . . . a special price this week? I saw Emma showing them to you. Or maybe some pickled peaches? And there's a whole carton of bottles of coconut oil."

She was bemused for a moment. "What would I use coconut oil for?"

"Anything you use vegetable oil for. Very healthful," he said in his best salesman's voice, winking at her. He lowered his voice and whispered, "Don't bother. It's too expensive, but some of my Englisch customers like it. If they don't show up, I'll go broke."

"Don't kid me. You can sell anything, and you know it," she teased. Always ready for a laugh or a joke, that was Jed. She'd never seen him solemn until the day they lost Thomas. Her smile wavered at the thought.

"I know what you're thinking," he said softly. "But if I don't make a joke, how can I keep going? At first I felt guilty every time I smiled."

"Yah, I know." She squeezed his hand. "Me, too. But you can't raise happy children if you wear a grieving face."

His face grew serious. "You have something to tell me, ain't so? It's Abel, isn't it?"

She nodded.

"Ach, so I thought." He glanced around. "Komm. We'll go in the back before somebody decides to complain about something."

He ushered her to the door that led into the storeroom. Around several shelves stacked with boxes, there was a battered desk that had been an early bargain, itself stacked with ledgers and sales flyers.

Pulling out two chairs, he gestured for her to be seated.

"Now," he said once they were knee to knee. "You tell me what he's been up to with no glossing over it or leaving anything out."

Becca had to smile. How did he know she'd been thinking of how she could make it sound better? But Jed was right . . . only the truth would do.

"It happened on Tuesday, while you were with the twins," she said, choosing her words. "Deborah was at the farmstand with Nathan Mueller and his brother, Peter, who were helping to close it for the season." Maybe that needed a little more explanation. "You know they've been helping out with the stand sometimes in exchange for my selling their pumpkins and squash for them."

"Yah, yah, I know. Gut idea. The more variety

you have, the more you'll draw customers." For a moment Jed's salesman part took over from the concerned father.

"That's true. Anyway, Deborah wanted to surprise me by having it done when I got back. I had gone with Miriam to her doctor's appointment," she added.

"Yah, your grossmammi told us that," he said. "So how did Abel get involved? He was at home when we left. I didn't have any idea he'd follow after us."

"Well, Abel came to the stand, and Deborah says he wanted to do the closing. He was very insistent." She hesitated. "I wasn't there, but she said she and Peter were working and Abel actually tried to stop Peter from helping her."

She was having trouble looking at Jed's face, but he reached out to pat her hand. "It's all right. Just say it. Better to know."

Becca nodded. "Deborah was afraid they were actually going to fight about it, but Nathan showed up then. Apparently he had to physically separate them, and gave them both a scolding as if they were little kids. Then he pushed everyone into helping, and they got the job done." She took a deep breath. "Maybe it wasn't so bad, after all, but . . . well, Deborah was really upset."

"Ach, as she should be. We owe her an apology." Jed's lips were tight. "It is serious for someone Abel's age to be starting a fight. You might excuse it in a ten-year-old, but not at his age."

"I know. I'm just relieved that Nathan was there before it got any worse."

Jed rubbed the back of his neck. "It seems such a foolish thing to fight about. I guess he wanted to do it for you, but why . . ."

He let that trail off helplessly, and Becca's heart twisted in pain for him. Still, however she felt, she had to say the rest of it.

"I spoke to Nathan about it, wanting a grown-up's view. He said that Abel accused him of trying to come between Abel and me." She thought she'd be relieved at getting it out, but now the burden was transferred to Jed, and it still hurt. "Ach, it's foolishness," she added, "and so Nathan told him. There's been nothing between me and Nathan at all except business and . . . well, neighborliness."

The silence stretched between them, and she looked at the floor, studying the cracks between the wide boards.

"Foolishness is the word for it," he said at last, sounding very tired. He leaned toward her again, his face intent. "Becca, you must understand. That is what we . . . Esther and I . . . want for you."

She opened her lips to protest, but he swept on.

"You're a young woman with your whole life in front of you. It's only right and natural that you marry again, have more kinder, live the life God has planned for you. Thomas would want that, too." His face was very serious. "I'm as sure of that as of anything in God's world."

"Denke, Jed," she murmured. "But I don't have any plans for that now."

"You will, sometime." He smiled gently, his eyes warming. "But it will be a grown man who is able to love you and take care of you. Not a silly young fool like Abel who doesn't have an idea of what it takes to make a marriage."

"I'm sorry." It was all she could say.

"No need for that. It's we who must be sorry that Abel is behaving so badly. I should think Nathan Mueller did scold him, and he'll get a worse one from me. He may have to grow out of his feelings, but I'll make sure he doesn't bother you with his foolishness. That's certain sure."

"Don't hurt him." The words came out instinctively. "I mean . . ."

"Ach, I know what you mean, Becca. You're just like his mother in that." His expression grew more serious. "But hurt is part of growing up. And growing up is what Abel has to do, whether it hurts or not."

There was nothing more to say, Becca knew. Her heart was filled with sorrow . . . both for Abel, in his pain, and for his parents, suffering needless additional grief because of him.

"Ach, go on out and find some bargains," he

said, rising. "Make sure you get the family discount, mind. I'll be out in a few minutes."

Knowing he wanted to be alone, Becca nodded. There was nothing else to say, because nothing could make it easier.

Nathan finished working on the fence around the lower pasture, and as he started walking toward the house he saw Becca's grandmother beckoning to him from their back porch.

Frowning, he lengthened his stride, hoping nothing was wrong. He'd seen Becca leave about an hour ago, and apparently her grandmother was alone with the twins. But she didn't seem disturbed.

She opened the door for him with a smile, gesturing him in. James, sitting on the floor with a measuring cup in his hand, banged it on the wide wooden planks.

"Don't mind our Jamey. That's his idea of welcome. Komm, komm and sit a moment."

She moved toward the counter, which looked like a bakery shelf at the moment with several shoofly pies and loaves of bread cooling. Adding to the effect, her apron was decorated with streaks of flour, and another was brushed on her cheek.

"Everything's all right?" he asked, though it seemed clear there wasn't a problem. Maybe she wanted company.

"Yah, yah." The elderly woman lifted a coffee-pot from the stove. "Coffee?"

"Denke." He suspected he wouldn't find out what she wanted unless he let her feed him something. Smiling down at James, he sat at the table.

James dimpled and held out the metal measuring cup, but when Nathan reached for it he yanked it back, almost tipping himself over.

"Ach, Jamey, watch out," Grossmammi said. "He's just like a roly-poly, ready to tip over."

"He looks like he's gained a pound or two, ain't so?" He accepted the mug of coffee she held out to him and wasn't surprised when she followed it up with a wedge of shoofly pie.

"Yah, he's a chubby one now. That's all to the good. He'll slim down when he starts walking most of the time." She took one of the baskets that hung from pegs on the wall. "I'll put a shoofly pie and a loaf of fresh bread here for you to take home."

He shook his head, knowing it was futile. "You don't need to feed us, Mrs. Stoltz."

"Ach, who is Mrs. Stoltz? You'll call me Ada. Or Grossmammi, like all the young ones." Her round face was wreathed in smiles. "You must be without a baker at your house, unless Peter has a talent that way."

Nathan found himself laughing, partly at James, who was trying to hold both a cup and a ball in one hand, and partly at himself.

"Peter has a gift for eating, but not for baking. Or even simple cooking." He glanced around. "You're all alone with the twins today?"

"Just while Becca is in town. This one woke up early from his nap, so I'm trying to keep him from bothering his sister. She tires herself out scurrying around the house all morning while he sits and lets her bring him things." She tickled the boy's cheek, and he giggled, fat cheeks crinkling. "You're a lazybones, ain't so?"

"Maybe he just likes being waited on."

Nathan realized that it no longer gave him an uneasy feeling to be with Becca's children. He wasn't sure when that stopped, or why, but he knew it was a gut thing. After all, he couldn't live a normal life in the community while avoiding any small children. Not around here, that was certain sure.

The ball rolled away from James, so Nathan reached down and rolled it back. James grabbed at it, overbalanced, and toppled over, bumping his head on the chair.

Nathan froze. He'd hurt the baby—

Grossmammi scooped him up, crooning to James before he could burst into tears. She laughed a little at Nathan's expression.

"He's all right," she said. "Babies aren't that breakable. Especially chubby little ones like this." She squeezed James, planting a kiss on his cheek, and James turned his sorrow into a chortle.

217

"See? He bounces like a ball himself." She got up suddenly, looking toward the stairs. A moment later Nathan heard it, too. A little voice was calling out.

"Ach, I'd best get to Joanna before she tries to climb out of the crib herself."

Before he could think what she was about to do, she had dumped James in his arms and was headed toward the steps. "Just hold him a minute. Talk to him."

It was too late to protest. Nathan sat motionless, afraid to move. He and James stared at each other, and he suspected the boy was trying to decide whether or not to cry.

"Grossmammi says to talk to you," he said, not daring to change his grasp. "What should we talk about?"

James seemed to consider that for a moment. Then he reached up and fastened his fingers in Nathan's beard. He giggled, then tugged at it.

"Hey, take it easy." He unwound the little fingers carefully. "You've seen a beard before, ain't so? Grossdaadi has one, and Onkel Matt."

James came out with a few syllables which might have been an attempt to say Grossdaadi. Then he grabbed Nathan's beard again.

"I can see you're getting to be a handful." He pulled the hand free once more. "You're going to surprise everybody when you get to running around by yourself, ain't so?"

James giggled again, his warm, round body shaking, and turned so he could pound both hands on the table. Nathan had to let go with one hand in order to move the coffee mug out of reach. Fortunately, Nathan discovered he could hold James with just one arm around him. He tried bouncing him on his knee. James pounded his hands again, laughing, and Nathan relaxed, laughing with him.

"What is the joke in here?" Becca stood just inside the door, watching them as she took her bonnet off. "Looks like fun."

"Ma!" James declared. He wiggled like a fish, slid out of Nathan's grasp, landed on his feet, and trotted uncertainly to his mother.

"Look at you, walking clear over here," she exclaimed.

He grasped her skirt, and when she picked him up he turned and made grasping gestures toward Nathan, his fingers clutching.

"No, you can't have both of us hold you at the same time, silly boy." She squeezed him, planted a kiss on his neck, and put him down. He promptly repeated his trick by walking back to Nathan.

"It looks like he's mastered the walking game," Nathan said.

Becca's laughing eyes met his. "Yah, it does. And it also looks like you've made a friend."

Was that a little wonderment in her voice? Probably so. It certain sure surprised him. He rested his hand on James's silky hair, feeling it slide through his fingers, and his heart warmed. Something that had been tight inside his chest seemed to release.

Becca found herself staring at Nathan. His big hand was very gentle on her son's hair. He was actually touching James voluntarily, something she'd never expected to see.

She'd give a lot to know how this had come about, but was afraid to ask. Maybe she could find out from Grossmammi, who undoubtedly had something to do with it.

As if she'd spoken her name out loud, her grandmother came in, carrying Joanna, who was still wiping the sleep from her eyes.

Becca moved toward them. "Did you have a good sleep, Jo Jo?"

She kissed her daughter's silky cheek and sent a questioning gaze at her grandmother. Grossmammi smiled back with a satisfied expression.

Nathan shuffled his feet. Then, setting James on the floor near the handy table leg, he rose. "Thanks for the coffee. I'd better get going or Peter will think I got lost."

"Ach, let me finish getting the bread and shoofly pie ready for you." Picking up a snowy drying cloth, Grossmammi tucked it over the contents of a basket on the counter. Apparently she'd been feeding Nathan while Becca was gone.

Her grandmother handed the basket to Nathan. He thanked her with an expression caught between pleasure and embarrassment.

"Honestly, we're getting along okay, even if we don't have a woman to cook and clean for us."

"Get on with you." Her grandmother waved her hands at Nathan. "I know what men's idea of cleaning is. A lick and a promise, ain't so?"

He laughed, giving her the tender look he seemed to reserve for Grossmammi. "Just about. But we're okay." He bent to wave at the twins. "Bye-bye. You behave yourselves now."

James looked up at him solemnly, as if communicating something important, and then waved his hand in goodbye, showing the dimples in his cheeks.

"What a show-off he's turning into," Becca remarked, walking out to the porch with Nathan.

"James is just asserting his personality, ain't so?" Nathan raised the basket a little toward Becca. "Can't you persuade your grandmother not to press food on us? I'm starting to feel like a charity case."

She had to chuckle at Nathan's question. "Not even Grossdaadi could ever convince my grandmother to hold back on the giving—both of food and love."

Becca felt her cheeks grow hot at her mention of love. Still, that was how her grandmother felt about it. Food and love were synonymous in her mind. She carefully didn't look at Nathan.

"Yah, well, she's a generous woman. You're a generous family, for that matter." He had his foot on the first step, but still, he lingered.

"I hope you finished all your errands in town," he said.

Becca blinked. "Is that what Grossmammi said I was doing? Ach, well, it doesn't matter, since it's you." She flushed again. Why couldn't she stop tripping on her own tongue when she talked to him? "I mean, you know all about the problems with Abel."

"Was that what you were doing? Seeing him?" Nathan seemed suddenly alert.

"Ach, no. I was avoiding him so I could talk to his father. You know he wanted me to let him know about anything Abel did, and I couldn't ignore the way he carried on when you were closing the stand."

Nathan shrugged. "Abel's got some growing up to do. Sometimes nobody else can help you with that."

"You're probably right. Anyway, Jed's going to talk to him again. He wants . . ."

She let that trail off as she heard the sound of a car coming down the lane toward the house.

Nathan, looking in that direction, saw it first. "Have you been doing anything to attract police attention?"

"Not as far as I know," she said, turning to see

Jack Reynolds pulling up near the porch again. Feeling guilty at the sight of a police car was probably a common experience, but she didn't like it. "I hope it's not about those boys that made a mess at the stand again."

As Jack came toward them, Becca expected Nathan to finish his goodbyes and walk off. Instead, he stepped back up on the porch beside her.

"Becca. It's Mr. Mueller, right?" Jack's smile was as jovial as ever, but there was something a bit guarded in his eyes.

"Is something wrong, Jack?" Becca found she was pressing her hands against her skirt, and forced herself to relax.

"Well, that depends." He cleared his throat. "I guess maybe I should have a word with the both of you, if you don't mind."

Becca shook her head, stepping back and gesturing toward the door. "Will you come in for coffee?"

"This will just take a minute." Again, he looked uncomfortable. "Fact is, since Halloween there have been a couple more attempts at fires . . . barn fires, this time. They didn't succeed," he added hurriedly. "They weren't very good attempts, as it happened. The chief decided to ask the farmers to keep quiet about it."

"Isn't that what he said before?" she asked. "Somebody needs to take it seriously."

"I know, but his idea is if it's not in the papers there might be a better chance of catching the guy."

Nathan's frown had been deepening as Jack spoke. "Seems like it's an even better chance that the firebug might succeed the next time. People ought to be warned."

"That's what I said to him," Jack said approvingly. "Well, he's new, and it seems like he doesn't know the countryside so well. Anyway, finally he agreed to let me alert some of the farmers, especially ones who are a little isolated, like your place, Becca."

"Isolated?" She had trouble processing that. "But my parents and my brother and his wife are right across the road, and Nathan is just next door."

"Yeah, that's true, but your barn and sheds aren't visible from the road," he pointed out. "Seems like Mr. Mueller and his brother would be the only ones who might spot trouble here. That's what worries me. Your father would come when he knew, but how's he going to know in an emergency?"

Nathan nodded, turning to her. "He's right about that, Becca. We'll have to take extra precautions."

Becca stiffened. She didn't want anyone making decisions for her, but his use of *we* made her feel . . . well, not quite so alone.

"Just what I think." Jack was eager to agree.

"I'd feel better knowing you'd been warned. You might even take turns checking every so often at night. Okay?"

Becca nodded, realizing the depth of his concern. "Denke, Jack."

"We're doing all we can to find out who it is. Fact is, there are a couple people under suspicion, but we've got to have evidence."

"I understand. We'll all watch out for each other."

For the first time, her mother's desire to move them all back home had some appeal. But she'd never forgive herself if something happened when she wasn't here.

"You get on that phone the minute anything scares you," Jack said firmly. "We'd rather make a dozen useless trips than have something bad happen we could have prevented. And don't forget to ring the bell on your porch. Noise scares firebugs away fast. The louder the better."

Becca hoped she was doing a good job of hiding the shaking inside her. "We'll take care. You want me to pass the word along to my relatives?"

"Do that." Jack was already turning toward his car. "I'll get back to working on it. Those couple of farms up Dogtown Road are next on my list. They could have a whole marching band going up there, and nobody would notice it."

He'd reached the car and opened the door

before he spoke again. "You take care of each other."

"We will." Nathan's voice was firm, and somehow the sound of it calmed her nerves. Neighbors took care of neighbors here.

They'd be okay. Of course they would. With everyone on the lookout, nothing would happen here.

CHAPTER THIRTEEN

The next few days the weather changed, as it often did after Halloween. The bright, clear days changed to cloudy gray. Becca stood at the door, looking out as the rain came down persistently again today. She tried reminding herself that it was to be expected in November and that the creeks needed refilling, but it didn't help her disposition. She'd been nervous and jumpy since the day she and Nathan had spoken with the police officer together.

And it wasn't just about the threat of fire. There was another problem.

She'd become convinced that Nathan's attitude, especially about children, made it impossible for him to think about marrying again. She'd accepted that.

But then she found him with James on his lap, apparently enjoying the experience. If she'd had an opportunity to talk to him casually, she might be able to figure it out, but she hadn't seen him to talk to since then.

Joanna, as if reflecting her mother's mood, trotted to the door and smacked it with her hand. "Out," she declared firmly.

Miriam, who'd ducked through the rain with a large umbrella to help with the canning, laughed with delight at Joanna's expression. Actually, it didn't take much to bring on a smile or a laugh from Miriam these days.

She and Matt hadn't said a word to the rest of the family yet, and Becca tried to respect their privacy. But if she couldn't talk to her mother and grandmother about it soon, she thought she'd burst.

Still, each time she saw Mammi looking at Miriam, Becca knew it wasn't really a secret. Mammi knew how to interpret what she was seeing. And as for Grossmammi, well, she'd seemed to know even before she'd seen Miriam.

Mammi set a rack of jars on the table and turned to laugh at Joanna's expression. "It's raining. You don't want to get wet, do you?"

Joanna's bottom lip came out, and James toddled across the kitchen to join her. "Out," he confirmed.

Trying not to laugh, Becca scooped them up and stood where they could see out the window. "See? You can't go out. It's raining. In. Why don't you say *in?*"

James leaned forward until he pressed his face against the pane, squashing his nose. "Rain," he said, agreeing.

Mammi left the applesauce she was stirring to tickle him under the chin. "Rain, rain, go away, James and Joanna want to play."

James focused on her face and then clapped his hands.

"I don't know if that's applause for the poem or agreement that he wants to go out and play." Becca chuckled. "You used to say that to me and Matthew, remember? It never did make the rain go away."

"The good Lord didn't put us in charge of the weather," Mammi declared. "Maybe it's best. Anyway, at least with everything getting a soaking, it should discourage the firebug. If there is one."

Becca had passed on the warning to her family with mixed results. Daad, taking it seriously, joined Matt in patrolling around the properties once or twice a night, and Nathan did the same.

But Mammi seemed to look on the bright side, sure that the problem had passed with Halloween. Or maybe it was just that the idea worried her too much, and she felt better denying it.

Her grandmother concerned Becca the most, though. Grossmammi hadn't been sleeping well, and Becca sometimes heard her walking around during the night, maybe looking out the windows for an intruder.

"Matt says that folks are saying they found papers and trash splashed with kerosene against that old barn down on the hollow road." Miriam put down the jar she'd been washing and looked out the window.

Becca watched her grandmother, seeing the way she clasped her hands in silent prayer. Grossmammi had always been the rock in the family, holding everyone up, but in recent months she seemed somehow more fragile. Becca wanted to reassure her, but she didn't know how.

"We'll be fine," she said, knowing the words were inadequate.

"The water bath is ready for the jars." Mammi must have seen it as well, since she abruptly changed the subject. She adjusted the lid on the big canning kettle, letting out a puff of steam. "Let's get them in."

Whether Mammi had intended it or not, that worked. Grossmammi became engrossed in filling jars with the gently steaming applesauce. The thought of a firebug was drowned with noise and chatter. They filled all the jars, capped them, and finally lowered the rack into the boiling water.

Becca did a mental count of the number of jars on her pantry shelves. "Let's have a break." She paused to stretch her back. "This batch should make enough for the winter. And I have several baskets in storage if needed."

"You're sure?" Her mother set an apple walnut coffee cake on the table and began cutting it. "I could do a few more batches. The twins do love it. And you could share with Nathan and Peter, too."

The mention of Nathan's name let her doubts bubble up again. "I'm not sure he wants us giving him food all the time," she muttered, then wished she hadn't spoken. If she was going to react to every mention of the man's name, she might as well carry a sign saying she was interested in him.

"He's a good neighbor," Grossmammi said firmly. "Looking out for you the way he does."

Becca opened her mouth to protest and reminded herself to think before she spoke. Managing a smile, she kept her voice light. "You wouldn't be matchmaking, would you, Grossmammi?" That should divert her.

Her grandmother smiled and shrugged as if to say she'd never think of such a thing. But Mammi nodded . . . actually nodded.

"Mammi, not you," she protested.

"Why not?" her mother protested, her face red from the kettle's steam. "I'm not saying I'd push you into anything. Still, it's been over a year, and naturally folks will start thinking of you marrying again, especially with two little ones to raise. I'm sure Thomas wouldn't want you to go through life alone."

The mention of Thomas jolted her, reminding Becca of her mother's concern that she couldn't manage by herself.

"Thomas would be the last one to want me to rush into anything," she said firmly. "As for Nathan, I'm sure he's still struggling with how his wife and baby died."

Now all three of them stared at her, and she

heartily wished she'd kept her mouth shut. Drat the man, he had her so confused she didn't know what to say.

She hurried on before anyone could ask how she knew that. "Anyway, I could never love anyone else the way I loved Thomas." That was true enough, and maybe it would discourage them.

"I don't guess any of us ever get to feel the excitement of first love again." Grossmammi spoke from a lifetime of experience, her faded blue eyes wise. "But there are as many ways of loving as there are people in your life, ain't so?"

Becca felt her face grow warm. She knew that was true, because she'd felt it for herself. But . . .

Before she'd found an answer, her grandmother was smiling and shaking her head. "Ach, don't mind us. Mammis just always want to see their children happy and settled."

Grossmammi nodded toward Joanna, who was holding Becca's hand while she stared out at the rain. She spoke softly. "It's a wonderful thing to feel your little daughter's hand in yours. But you also look forward to the day when her hand just naturally goes to someone else . . . to a man who will love her forever."

For a moment tears were bright in her grandmother's eyes, and all of them knew she was thinking of Grossdaadi. And knew, too, that she never stopped missing him.

Mammi acted for all of them. She put her arms

around her mother-in-law and held her tight, and her own eyes glistened with tears.

Forever. All four of them had experienced that kind of love. Grossmammi and Becca had lost it. For Becca, it had been cut short, and she still didn't know whether it could come again.

Held in the arms of women who understood, she felt soothed and comforted.

The rain had finally stopped. Nathan stepped outside the house, glad to see that colorful leaves still clung to the trees, despite the numbers that had been stripped by the downpour.

Peter, emerging from the barn, came to meet him. "Did you hear anything about Thanksgiving from the Stoltzes? Deborah said they're going to invite us." A wave of color came up under his freckles. "I just wondered."

Smiling a little, Nathan nodded. "Yah, we're invited. Was that Deborah's idea?"

The flush deepened. "No . . . I don't know. I mean, she just mentioned it."

Taking pity on him, Nathan dropped the subject. He'd guessed the neighbors would invite them whether Deborah asked for it or not. Still, he should keep an eye on those two. They were both young to form a lasting attachment.

Weren't they? Hadn't he and Molly been about their age when he'd taken a fresh look at her and knew that she was the one for him?

But even if what Peter felt was the real thing, they were still too young to make decisions like that about their future.

This parenting business was more difficult than he'd thought. His own father had made it look so easy . . . never losing his temper, always ready to stop and listen to a problem, always fair. That was tough to live up to.

Gazing down across the field and tree line toward the road, his eye was caught by movement. It was Becca, he saw, carrying a shovel and walking toward the small white building near the creek.

He stayed, watching. It was their springhouse, he realized. Becca's grandmother had mentioned once that their water came from a spring off the mountain that surfaced at the side of the hill. The small building would keep the cistern clean and the water flowing, except in a severe drought.

But what was Becca attempting to do with that shovel? Not his business, he reminded himself. Besides, with his feelings in such tumult, it was far better that he stay clear of Becca and her twins as much as possible, wasn't it?

Even as he told himself this, he'd started moving toward her. He slowed for a moment and then strode on. After all, he couldn't be unneighborly when her family had been so generous with him.

When he reached her, Becca was trying to pull

open the wooden plank door of the cement block springhouse. The shovel was propped against the wall.

"Can I give you a hand?" He reached past her to grasp the handle of the door, his fingers touching hers. Becca yanked hers away as if they were scorched.

"You don't need . . ." she began, but he'd already pulled it open. A small amount of muddy water lapped over the threshold.

Becca shook her head. "Just what I thought. With as much rain as we got, I figured the cistern would be overflowing. And most likely silted up, as well. It always happens."

He stepped past her, noting that she wore a pair of bright yellow rubber boots that looked a bit big for her. His eyes took a moment to adjust to the dimness inside. She'd been right, the concrete cistern had overflowed.

Becca joined him, stepping onto the long two-by-fours someone had laid across the floor, supported by concrete blocks at each end. She dragged the shovel behind her.

"Please don't bother. I know just what needs doing, and it's better to have only one person in here working at a time. You'd just be in my way."

What was going on in her mind? She couldn't really relish the idea of slopping around in the icy water.

"How about if you step outside and tell me

what to do? Then nobody's in anyone's way."

"Nathan . . ." She sounded exasperated. And upset. "It's my job," she said firmly. "My spring-house, and my job. I won't have anyone saying I can't handle it myself."

He looked at her. Her face was turned away from him, and in the dim light he couldn't make out much, except that her jaw was set firmly. And that the back of her neck looked vulnerable, as white and fragile as a child's.

"Who's saying that?" he asked gently. "Not me."

"People," she said finally.

He touched her shoulder, encouraging her to turn back to him. "You're not a person who cares that much about what gossips say, so I imagine you're talking about family."

For a moment they just looked at each other, standing there on the rickety board in the damp. Then, quite suddenly, she laughed.

"All right. I'm being stubborn, I guess. But sometimes . . ." she hesitated. "Sometimes I feel I have to prove Grossdaadi did right by leaving the orchard to me."

He let her words drift through his mind. He could see where this came from, he guessed. Her mother was a good woman, he felt sure, but from what he'd seen she was inclined to want to control her children.

"Would your grandfather have been annoyed with you for accepting help to do a messy job?"

This time her smile came readily. "Of course not. I appreciate it very much," she said in a formal little tone that amused him. "Here's the shovel."

With Becca standing in the doorway giving directions while he worked, the job went quickly. She did know what was what, he reflected. Probably she and her husband had worked together the way he and Molly had. When you were young and in love, even doing a dirty job together could be fun.

It didn't take long to clear the silt from the cistern. He made sure the water was running clear where it came in, and then he eased the screened cover back over it. He thought he was beginning to recognize Thomas's handiwork when he saw it. Nothing he'd made was sloppy, everything served its purpose.

The screen, for instance, had been made to fit exactly over the cistern with a small hook at each end so that it couldn't be knocked aside by an animal. It was all as carefully done as the farmstand was. Thomas had left everything in order for his bride when he left.

He was tempted to say that to Becca, but he didn't want to hurt her inadvertently. He meant it as a compliment, but it might make for discomfort between them.

As soon as he thought that, he knew it wasn't true. Their relationship had moved so far so fast that he could already guess how she'd react to almost anything.

Relationship. Friendship, he added.

When he turned back to Becca, he found her with the shovel, making sure the drain under the side wall was clear.

"Here, you should have left that for me. You're getting all dirty." A long step from one plank to another brought him close to her.

"That's only fair." She took a look at her muddy hands and then wiped them on her skirt. "This will have to be washed, anyway. A little more dirt won't hurt anything."

"Would I be right if I guessed that you and Thomas used to do this together?"

Her smile trembled a little as she nodded. "When we were first married. But we usually did it early in the fall, so we didn't get too cold. I guess I fell behind this year. I should have kept up."

"Don't be ferhoodled." He clasped both her hands. They felt like pellets of ice, and he warmed them between his, longing for . . . something he couldn't even imagine. "You've got the jobs of two people on your hands. You can't blame yourself for not doing the impossible."

Becca stood quite still for a moment, and they looked at each other in the shaft of sunlight coming from the door. For a long moment he felt that caring shimmered in the air between them.

Then she moved away, holding the plank door while he came out.

He stepped out into the light, turned to fasten the door, and made sure any excess water was draining away. When he turned back to her, her gaze avoided his. In fact, she seemed to be looking at something far off that he couldn't see.

"It's hard," she said, her voice as distant as her gaze. "One morning life is fine, and you're filled with plans for the future. And by evening the entire world has been turned upside down, and you know it will never be the same again."

She might have been speaking for him. He knew exactly what that felt like.

The reminder emphasized the chasm between them. But at the same time, it created a bond . . . as if a light chain across that chasm connected them.

He didn't know what it meant or whether it could last. Still, at the moment it seemed to give him some remnant of hope.

Becca awoke to a dusting of frost over the yard and the pasture. She opened the bedroom window for a moment, enjoying the scene as the sun rising over the ridge picked out sparks of light from the grass. The gray, dull days had passed for the moment, and the air was crisp with the scent of fall.

Closing the window, she hurried through

dressing, hearing the twins babbling to each other in their cribs. What were they saying? They seemed to think they were making sense, and the rhythm of their babbling was that of Pennsylvania Dutch speech. She had to laugh. One thing about twins she knew from experience . . . they might quarrel and tease one another, but they were also good company. And even when they fought, they would instantly turn against any third party when needed.

By the time breakfast was over and the babies settled in a corner of the kitchen with their toys, Grossmammi was tying on the large work apron she wore for cooking.

"Remember your mammi is coming over to make dried apples with us," she said. "She'll be here early, I think."

Becca hadn't forgotten, and she scrambled to her feet, pushing a toy train toward James. "I'll go take care of the animals and then bring the apples in. We wouldn't want Mammi to think we're not ready for her."

Her grandmother chuckled. It was a family joke that the closer a holiday came, the faster Mammi moved until no one could possibly keep up with her.

"You're getting faster all the time yourself," Grossmammi teased. "Ach, there's the phone. Better check to see if it's your mamm."

Becca grabbed her heavy black sweater and

headed out the door, enjoying the scent of crisp fall air. She reached the phone shanty in a few steps and grabbed the receiver.

"Mammi?"

"Sorry," a laughing voice said, and Becca recognized her father-in-law. "I won't keep you if you're expecting her, but you'll want to know. Abel is coming over sometime this morning." He gave a gusty sigh. "I hope he's coming to apologize for his behavior lately. That's what he's supposed to be doing, anyway."

Becca tried not to show the dismay she felt at the prospect of another encounter with Abel. Did the boy realize how unpopular he was making himself with his actions? Probably not, or he wouldn't persist.

"Denke. I appreciate your letting me know." She tried to think of something encouraging to say, but unfortunately she couldn't think of a thing.

Jed didn't seem to expect it. The poor soul was as discouraged about Abel as she was.

"Now, you'll call me if . . . well, if you need me, ain't so?"

"Yah, for sure."

But when she'd completed the call and walked toward the barn, she wondered if she should. Maybe it would be better if they all just ignored Abel. She hated feeling as if she was telling on him to his father.

In the meantime, anticipating a difficult conversation took a little brightness out of the day.

When she came back lugging a basket of Jonathan apples, her mother had already arrived.

"Ach, gut!" Mammi took an apple and squeezed it, then sniffed it. "Perfect. We'll have a fine time making enough dried apples for Thanksgiving, ain't so?"

The anticipation on her face restored Becca's good humor, at least for the moment. Mammi really loved each and every step of getting ready for a holiday. Even Thanksgiving had its traditions, like the dried apple chips.

"Don't let the boys near them, or there won't be any left by Thanksgiving," Becca pointed out. "Maybe we should keep them here until next week."

Grossmammi nodded. "We'll make as many pans as the oven will hold," she said, getting out the large flat baking pans. The warmth that filled the kitchen said she'd turned the oven on as well.

"I love the smell of apples," Mammi declared. "Apples and cinnamon . . . what could be better?"

Joanna obviously heard the magic word. She scurried to her grandmother and tugged on her skirt. "Apples?" She held out her palm, her head cocked to the side.

Mammi laughed, patting her cheek, and then looked questioningly at Becca.

"Yah, fine. If they have a couple of slices, maybe they'll leave us alone long enough to get the cutting done."

Her mother was already washing an apple and slicing it, and while she did that, Becca warned them about Abel's impending visit.

"I hope he's on his best behavior," Grossmammi said, sounding as if she didn't believe it.

"If not, he'll get a good talking-to." Mammi always said that as if a good talking-to was the cure to every problem. "Now let's get at these apples."

With one person washing, one slicing, and one arranging the slices on the waiting pans, the operation went smoothly. Becca's mother loved using the slicer that produced one thin, even slice after another. Becca flicked out the seeds, pleased by the star shape in the center of every slice.

Chattering about anything and everything, the work went quickly for them. Once every pan was filled and every slice sprinkled with cinnamon and sugar, the pans were ready to go in the oven.

"I love this nice big oven of yours," Mammi said, as she did every time she used it. As she straightened, she glanced over Becca's shoulder, and her face tightened. "Looks like Abel is here. Do you want us to go in the other room?"

Becca gave a nervous laugh. "I'd rather you stayed, I think. Unless, well . . ."

The truth was, she didn't know what was best.

She just knew that between Abel and Nathan, her heart was being wrenched nearly in two. They were both stubborn and both wrongheaded, and she couldn't seem to deal with either of them.

Her mother patted her arm. "Don't worry. You can handle him, and if not, we will."

Becca couldn't help but laugh. If Abel knew he had her mother to deal with and her grandmother besides, he'd run the other way.

Sobering, she said a silent prayer she could discourage Abel without hurting him and went to the door.

Abel stepped inside, reaching out as if to grasp Becca's hand. Then he saw her mother and grandmother. He blinked, swallowed, and his hand dropped to his side.

"We just got dried apples in the oven," Mammi said. "Sit down and tell us all about what you're doing now. Have a cup of coffee."

Abel had really been thrown out of step by Mammi's welcome, but Becca saw him steady himself. He straightened, smiling at the two older women. "Denke, but I don't have time. I need to say something to Becca." He stepped toward the door. "Maybe out on the porch?"

Since they'd be in full view, Becca nodded, pulling her sweater around her. Perhaps this was best. At least he wouldn't be humiliated by apologizing in front of her kin.

She hadn't seen Abel acting so grown up since

he'd come back. Becca felt a flare of hope. It looked as if his father's lecture had finally convinced him he was behaving foolishly. She stepped out onto the porch and waited while he followed her.

Once the door was closed, Abel stood for a moment, maybe looking for words. "I'm sorry." He blurted the words out, and then he blinked rapidly.

Becca studied him. "Do you mean that, Abel?"

He grimaced. "I guess you have a right to ask. But Daad made me see that I've been behaving wrongly. He said Thomas would be angry with me for badgering you. Honestly, I never thought of it that way. I just thought I could take care of you and the babies."

His voice cracked suddenly, and just as quickly as that, he again became the little brother that Thomas had loved.

"Abel," she began. "It was just a year in the spring. I can't . . ."

He nodded, cutting her off. "I know. I'm sorry. I just wanted to help you."

"That's good of you." Was it really going to be this easy after all of his persistence? "I'm glad to know I can call on you when I need help."

She bit her lip, wondering if she should tell him again that he was too young for her. Maybe not. It only seemed to upset him. She took a step back, hoping that was all he had to say.

Abel stood very still, looking mournful. He finally nodded. "I should go."

Relieved, she kept herself from agreeing openly and reached for the door, eager to have this embarrassing conversation over. "Goodbye, Abel."

He turned away and abruptly froze, staring. Glancing past him, she saw what had startled him. It was Nathan, pushing a barrow loaded with a couple of pumpkins and several gourds. She even knew why—because Mammi had asked for them to decorate for Thanksgiving.

Becca opened her mouth to explain. Then she caught a glimpse of Abel's expression and the words caught in her throat. She had never before seen such a look on Abel's face. He looked at Nathan as if he hated him.

Then he ran toward his buggy without a word. Becca felt like bursting into tears. For a moment it had felt as if the problem were solved. But if just the sight of her neighbor affected Abel this way, it was nowhere near resolution.

CHAPTER FOURTEEN

Becca realized Nathan had stopped where he was, watching Abel's retreating figure. He turned to her, and she struggled to compose her face, hoping he wouldn't see how upset she was.

"Did I scare Abel away? What's happening?" He set down the wheelbarrow he was pushing, and the pumpkins in it jostled one another.

"No, no, it was nothing. Are those for my mother? She'll be—"

Becca realized she was babbling and pressed her lips together. Nathan must already know all there was to know about her difficulties with Abel. Trying to hide it at this point was ridiculous.

But that didn't mean she wanted to discuss Abel's foolish ideas about Nathan.

"Sorry. I guess when I saw Abel I should have turned right around and gone home." His lips twisted a bit, and she knew he thought her foolish to be so concerned about what he saw as a boy's crush on her.

"Don't be ferhoodled," she said crossly. "We can't tiptoe around him. Just forget it." She took a breath and reminded herself it wasn't Nathan's fault. "My mother is here. Do you want to bring those in?" She gestured toward the pumpkins and gourds.

He shook his head, and his expression relaxed. "No need to clutter up your house with them. I saw she was here and thought I'd ask if this is enough, that's all."

"Come ahead in, then." She found herself relaxing, too. Regardless of what might have been, she still found Nathan a comfortable person to have around.

She opened the door, and they both stepped into a kitchen that was filled with the aroma of apples and cinnamon. "Mammi, Nathan brought some pumpkins and gourds and such for you."

"Ach, wonderful." She came to peer out the window and smiled. "Just perfect. You can leave them on the porch, yah?"

Nathan nodded, inhaling deeply. "What good things are you folks cooking now?" He smiled, and Grossmammi hurried to usher him toward a chair.

"Sit, sit. We can't offer you any dried apples until Thanksgiving, but you'll have coffee and shoofly pie."

"Thanks, but I didn't really come to eat." He smiled down at her grandmother, and Becca noticed again the special tenderness he extended to her each time they were together.

Not surprising. Everyone loved Grossmammi. But she was still impressed. Nathan had come a long way from the stone-faced man she'd first met.

Heedless of Nathan's refusal, Grossmammi was pouring coffee and cutting pie. There was never any point in trying to talk her grandmother out of feeding everyone who came in the door.

Succumbing to her grandmother's pressure, Nathan sat down and let her put coffee and a slice of pie in front of him. "Denke." He took a gulp of the coffee. "This reminds me of home."

The instant the words were out, his expression changed. He'd moved from smiling at a happy memory to remembering pain so quickly. They all saw it, but it was Mammi who spoke.

"It's gut to think on the happy memories," she said, almost at random, it seemed. "And funny sometimes what reminds us. Whenever I smell dish soap, I remember washing the dishes with my sisters, the four of us chattering all the while as if we hadn't seen each other in a month instead of being together every day." Mammi smiled. "Good memories."

Becca was surprised, and touched, as well. It wasn't usual for Mammi to pause in the midst of her busy day to indulge in memories, but it looked as if Nathan had touched something in her heart. That thought of herself with her three sisters—was it her next younger sister, Alice, who died early, that drew her?

Meanwhile the twins, apparently thinking they'd been ignored too long, came toddling over to Nathan, with Joanna beating her brother by inches.

She immediately tried to climb into his lap.

"Hey, wait a minute." If he was startled, Nathan covered it well. "You don't want to fall." He pulled her onto his knee, leading to an immediate outburst from James.

"Up," he demanded. "Me."

Nathan smiled at him. "You, that's right." He lifted James onto his other knee. "Satisfied?"

Becca felt something that had been tight within her relax. Whether he realized it or not, Nathan's attitude toward children was not what it had been. That didn't mean anything, she told herself quickly, but she couldn't help feeling a tiny flare of hope.

Nathan bounced the twins on his knees between sips of coffee and bites of shoofly pie. James grabbed a fistful of crust and crumbs and stuffed it in his mouth, making them all laugh. Joanna, of course, had to have some as well, and when Nathan put them down, they had sticky hands and smiles.

"I'd best go before I make any more of a mess." Nathan stepped quickly out of range of sticky hands, and Mammi caught the nearest twin with a wet washcloth in her hand.

"Becca, you go out with Nathan and empty out the wheelbarrow for him," Mammi said.

Aware of her mother's matchmaking, Becca went quickly outside with Nathan, wishing Mammi weren't so obvious. She hurried to scoop the gourds from the wheelbarrow.

Nathan was suddenly next to her, so close she imagined she could hear his breath. His hands brushed hers as they finished the job, and her heart seemed to be thundering in her ears.

She should move away, she thought, not moving. Nathan seemed unaware that he held her hands. In fact, his big hands enveloped hers warmly.

"You're cold," he murmured, so soft she barely heard it.

She glanced up, intending to say something, but she couldn't seem to think. His eyes were intent on her face, as if he memorized it. She could feel his fingers moving on the back of her hand, then her wrist. Warmth spun through her from every touch, overcoming her power of speech. She could only look at him and sense some wordless communication going back and forth.

And then, in an instant, the moment was over. He took a step back, looking bemused, and she wondered if she also wore that glazed expression.

"I . . . I should go," he murmured, but his hands clung to hers for another long moment. Finally he released her, shaking his head slightly. "We'll talk soon, ain't so?"

She nodded, then watched as he pushed the wheelbarrow away. She didn't know what to think. Or what to feel. But the tiny flare of hope she'd felt earlier was blazing now, consuming her common sense.

A little later Nathan stood in what he still saw as Onkel Joseph's kitchen, still feeling dazed. Shaking his head, he forced himself to concentrate on his surroundings instead of drifting off into dreams.

To this point he'd just seen the farmhouse as providing a roof over their heads. Suddenly he saw it as he thought Becca would see it. It wasn't dirty, that was for sure. He had enough self-respect that he wouldn't tolerate that. But it certain sure wasn't anything like the bright, comfortable kitchen at Becca's house.

He'd thought this room depressing the first time he entered the house, but after a time he'd gotten used to it, not really seeing any longer that the wooden cabinets needed to be cleaned and waxed or that the dishes were mismatched and chipped. The sink could use a good scouring, as well. Seemed like a man ought to take a little more care of the place he lived in. He couldn't imagine any of the women in Becca's family entering it without wanting to pick up a scrub brush.

Becca . . . not just her family, but Becca herself. Since he'd come back from seeing her, he'd been trying to hold at bay thoughts of the moments when he'd held Becca's hands in his and their eyes met. But he couldn't.

He had hovered on the brink, so near to

tumbling into love that he'd struggled for balance. Even now, he felt that incredible yearning to lean forward and claim her lips, to hold her warmly against him and spend his life protecting her.

That was where the dream came to an abrupt end. He couldn't. He couldn't risk again the chance of loving her and letting her down. And even if he dared, one thought of the babies sent him reeling away from the possibility. He didn't dare risk the twins.

Peter clattered in the back door and found him scrubbing the sink furiously. "Hey, Nate. What are you doing?"

Pulling off his jacket, he tossed it on the nearest chair, where it hung for a moment and then slid off onto the floor.

Nate glared down at it. "Since when do we hang jackets on the floor? Put that on the peg where it belongs."

His brother stared at him in surprise, and then the sullen look settled on his face. "Okay, okay. Didn't know we were that fussy."

While he scooped up the jacket and hung it on the appropriate place, Nathan pulled himself together. His problems weren't anything to do with Peter, and he shouldn't let himself take them out on the boy.

He pictured his father in his mind . . . always patient and steady, always fair. Peter deserved more than Nathan's feeble best.

"Sorry," he muttered as Peter came back and stood watching him. "Guess I just realized what a mess we've been living in."

"It just seems comfortable to me," Peter said, shrugging. "But I guess it would drive a woman berserk." He gave Nathan a measuring look. "Are you expecting visitors?"

Nathan shook his head, feeling regret for a moment. "No. What have you been up to?"

"Just over at the dairy farm. You know, helping David and Daniel with a couple of things," he said casually. Still with that casual air, he wandered around the kitchen, touching one thing and then another.

Nathan dropped the sponge and turned to face him, leaning against the sink. He might be oblivious of a lot of things, but Peter clearly had something on his mind.

"Okay, so what is it? It's plain as the nose on your face you're wanting something."

"Not wanting," Peter snapped, and Nathan realized he could have said it better.

"Right, sorry. What's up, then?"

Mollified, his brother nodded. "Well, it's this way. Seems like Daniel has a chance at being an apprentice at that hydroponic outfit that Eli Fisher runs. You know, where they raise those fresh vegetables that new way. Daniel's all excited about it, so his father's going to let him try."

"Gut for him." Nathan wasn't sure why the boy would want to, but the Amish-owned business looked like an interesting operation from the little he'd seen of it.

"So anyway," Peter went on, carefully casual, "Daniel's daad asked if I might want to work for him a few days a week. He could use an extra hand, he says, and I could learn about the dairy business."

That idea was totally unexpected, and Nathan reacted with a frown, trying to think it through. Maybe he should have been looking out for an apprenticeship for Peter, but he hadn't. Was that another gap in his ability to take care of his brother?

"I guess that's true," he said slowly, "but I thought you were set on running the farm with me."

"Yah, but you said yourself that there wasn't going to be much we could do until spring planting, so why shouldn't I?" Peter's voice was growing impatient, like it always did when he didn't think he was going to get his way.

"Why do you want to?" Nathan countered. Did this mean Peter wasn't satisfied with the life they'd taken up after Mammi's remarriage?

"Just because I want to!" Peter made an angry gesture. "I like being around the guys, and I could earn a little money of my own. Isn't that a gut enough reason?"

Nathan rubbed the back of his neck, telling himself to relax. It wouldn't do anyone much good for him to lose his temper, as well. And shouldn't he be showing Peter that he could talk something over instead of quarreling? *Daad would have done this better,* he reminded himself.

"Seems like it might be a good idea," he said slowly, seeing the brief flare of anger fading. "Suppose I talk to Abram about it."

Peter's irritation flared up again. "I don't see why I can't make my own decisions about it. You don't trust me, that's what it is. I'm not a little kid."

"It's my job to look out for you," he began, but Peter wasn't listening.

"It's just like what happened back in the spring. I didn't do anything wrong, but you didn't trust me anyway. You don't trust anybody."

Peter barreled out of the room. A good thing, Nathan realized. He was in no mood to be tactful, and he certain sure didn't want to talk about trusting, either Peter or himself. But life kept challenging him.

He braced his hands against the counter, blowing out a long breath. *Patience. Think about how Daad would have handled this.* But he and Daad had been closer than he and Peter were, and Daad hadn't been haunted at the idea of making a mistake that would hurt those he loved.

• • •

Becca had lingered outside, cherishing that bit of hope, until the cold air forced her back inside. The warmth and the scent of apples and cinnamon wrapped around her like a comforting quilt holding her.

Afraid someone would say something about Nathan, she longed to plunge into speech about something or someone else. Unfortunately her mind was stuck on the feel of Nathan's strong hands on hers and his gaze that seemed to look into her heart.

Her grandmother and her mother still sat at the table with cups in front of them, but they were both looking up at her. Amusement twinkled for a moment in Grossmammi's eyes, and she and Mammi exchanged looks that put Becca instantly on guard. If they were going to tease her . . .

But Joanna started tugging at Mammi's sleeve, pointing toward the shoofly pie and smiling, so Becca's mother held out a bite of sticky molasses and crumbs for her. Instead of eating it from the spoon, Joanna picked the sticky piece up in her fingers and nearly shoved her whole hand in her mouth.

"Greedy one," Mammi crooned, stroking her silky hair.

"Mine," James said, wiggling his fingers in a clutching motion and then resting his head on his grandmother's lap.

Grossmammi chuckled. "I think the smell is making James sleepy." She leaned back, sounding as if she were getting tired, as well.

"Seems like everyone should have a nap early today." Mammi was looking at Grossmammi as she spoke. Becca followed the direction of her gaze and had to agree. Her grandmother was tiring. She hadn't shown it while they were busy with the apples, but now that she was sitting, she sagged a bit in her chair.

"Grossmammi, why don't you go in and rest for a bit?" Becca moved toward her, shaken again by how suddenly her grandmother showed fatigue these days.

Grossmammi stiffened at once, her shoulders straightening and eyes snapping. "Ach, I'm not one of the kinder, ain't so?"

Becca held out her hand. "No, of course not," she said, in her most soothing tone. "But you were up early getting apples ready, so why not rest a bit?"

Still grumbling softly, Grossmammi grasped Becca's hand and levered herself up. Then she gave Becca a swift hug, her eyes regaining their twinkle.

"Guess I should stop complaining. That just shows I am tired, yah?"

"Yah." Becca put her arm around her and walked with her to the door leading to the grossdaadi haus.

"Just for a little bit," Grossmammi said, releasing her, and went willingly.

Becca closed the door and went back to the table, smiling.

"Denke, Becca." Mammi went to wipe the stickiness from Joanna's face and hands. "She listens to you better than me." There wasn't any resentment in her voice, just acceptance. "She always did. The first granddaughter . . ." She let the words trail off, and Becca caught her smiling at Joanna.

"Yah, and you'll be just as bad," Becca teased.

"Most likely," she agreed. "Now, tell me. Was Nathan all right when he left? I was afraid I'd said the wrong thing."

Becca shook her head, seeing the warmth in Nathan's eyes in those few minutes outside. "It was gut for him, I think." She hesitated. "You were talking about your sister Alice, ain't so?"

Mammi looked startled for a moment. "I guess I was. She went so early—only eight when she passed. I can still see her giggling when she had a soap bubble on her nose." Mammi's expression was soft as she looked at the picture in her mind. "It's gut when you can remember those happy times."

Impulsively, Becca touched her mother's shoulder. It seemed that her mother, who was always the comforter, needed comforting herself. "You never talked much about her when we were younger."

Mammi rose, slipping her arm around Becca's waist. Tears glistened lightly, but she smiled. "You were little. I didn't want to make you sad."

She should have seen that for herself. Mammi had always wanted to protect them, sometimes when they didn't need it.

"I'm all grown up now, Mammi. You can talk to me about anything."

Her mother patted her. "You'll have to remind me of that when I forget." She hesitated. "You've done such a fine job . . . raising the twins, taking care of your grandmother, running the orchard . . . Daadi and I are proud of you."

The words startled Becca, and it took a moment to respond. Did Mammi really feel that way about the orchard? That wasn't what Becca had heard her say.

"I thought . . . I was afraid you thought the orchard was too much for me. That maybe Grossdaadi should have left it to someone else."

Understanding swept over her mother's face. "Ach, Becca, sometimes I wish things were different, that's certain sure. I hate to see you carry such a heavy load. Just wait . . . you'll feel that about your kinder, too. No matter how old, they're still your babies."

Becca looked at the twins, knowing she'd probably be just the same. She'd have to guard against it.

"I know," she began, "but—"

"But your grandfather knew what he was about," Mammi said quickly. "He knew you were the one with the love for it, just like he had."

Now it was Becca whose eyes were filled with tears. "Denke, Mammi," she whispered, wiping her cheeks and finding that her mother was doing the same.

"Look at us." Mammi laughed a little. "So foolish. Besides, sometime maybe you'll have a partner to help carry the load, ain't so? It's not a burden when it's shared."

Mammi was hinting . . . that was clear. She had seen something of what was happening between Becca and Nathan, and she was hoping.

Like me, Becca thought. She was hoping, too. Just a little, but it was enough for now.

CHAPTER FIFTEEN

It had been nearly two days since she had seen Nathan, and Becca was beginning to wonder if those moments between them had been nothing more than a dream. A gust of air pulled the corner of a sheet from her hand, whirling it in the wind before she could peg it to the clothesline. Scrambling after it, Becca snatched the sheet before it could hit the ground.

Scolding herself for her inattention, she put the clothespin on it firmly. It was a good day for drying laundry, and a fun day for the twins. James had paused in his play to watch her chasing the sheet, giggling to himself.

"It wouldn't be funny if I had to wash it again," she informed him, smiling.

Wearing their warm jackets, James and Joanna had been chasing the colorful leaves that swirled in the breeze. The sun was bright and the air brisk . . . she shouldn't ask more of life at this moment than watching her children's happiness.

We'll talk soon, Nathan had said. She hadn't expected him to take this long. If he felt the way she did, surely he'd want to talk about it.

Maybe that was the answer. Maybe he didn't feel what she did.

Perhaps he thought everything was happening

between them too quickly. She sometimes feared that might be true. Was this really a love to build a marriage and family on?

Loving had been different with Thomas. She hadn't felt this heady mixture of longing and doubt with him. She had loved him as a playmate, and that love had matured as they had grown. It had been deep and satisfying and it hadn't produced this surge of doubt . . . not just doubt about Nathan, but doubt of herself, too.

Maybe she'd been wrong to think what she felt for Nathan was love. Maybe her own longing had gotten in the way of her common sense.

Joanna stopped throwing leaves at her brother to point toward the barn. "Horsey," she declared.

"That's right. Aunt Deborah's bringing Sweetie out."

She glanced toward the barn to see Deborah leading the mare toward the paddock. Deborah stopped, and Sweetie tossed her head and danced a little, responding to the crisp breeze with a desire to run. But Deborah was waiting for something . . . no, someone. Peter came along after her, closing the barn door as he came out.

They put Sweetie in the paddock and leaned on the gate, watching as she threw her head up, galloped a few yards, and then kicked back before apparently remembering that she was a grown buggy horse and not a silly foal. Almost as if she wanted to be sure no one was watching, she looked around and dropped her head to crop at the grass.

Deborah laughed. Grabbing Peter by the hand, she tugged him along to where the twins ran to meet them. Deborah picked up Joanna and swung her around. When Peter didn't respond to a tug at his leg, James smacked it, shouting, "Up!"

"James, don't be bossy," Becca said, but Peter's serious expression relaxed in a laugh as he picked him up and swung him around, too. In an instant, all four of them were spinning and laughing in enjoyment.

Becca watched them, smiling indulgently. The problem would come when Peter and Deborah decided to stop. They'd tire out before the twins, she felt sure.

She was wondering how Peter would respond if she asked about his brother when Deborah intervened.

"Go ahead, Peter. Tell my sister about it." Deborah sounded sure of herself. "She won't blab to Nathan."

Becca gave her what they'd always called the Mammi look in the family, and Deborah grinned.

"Well, you won't, will you? If Peter tells you something private, I mean."

"I guess not, as long it's not something like planning to jump off the barn roof," she replied. Peter was looking sullen, so she added, "You don't have to do what Deborah says, you know."

The boy laughed, the sullen expression vanishing

as if it had never been. He reminded her of Nathan suddenly. Nathan hid behind the stony face he did so readily, like Peter slipping behind the sullen expression, determined not to talk. They were more alike than she'd thought . . . more than they thought, probably.

"It's nothing," he muttered. He glanced at Deborah. "I just thought that, maybe if you wanted to, maybe you'd talk to Nathan about me. Make him see that he's wrong."

She brushed the sheet she'd just hung with the flat of her hand, buying time. "What is it you think he's wrong about?"

Peter stared at the ground, frowning, and James, apparently thinking the frown was for him, clouded up to cry. Deborah snatched him up, tickling him so that the sob turned into a giggle.

"Go on, Peter. Don't frown at the baby. Just say it."

Becca wasn't sure she'd heard her baby sister being so bossy before. Bossiness was usually Della's routine. Deborah must feel sure about her friendship with Peter. And it seemed to work, because Peter nodded and met Becca's gaze.

"You maybe know that your daad said I could work for him sometimes once Daniel starts his apprenticeship?"

She nodded. She'd thought it a good idea of Daad's, but maybe someone didn't.

"Well, I really want to. I never thought Nathan

wouldn't agree. I mean, he already said we wouldn't have much to do this winter because of not having any stock yet, so why shouldn't I?"

Becca had to admit she was surprised. It seemed a logical thing that would benefit everyone. She'd never have thought Nathan would object. But maybe she hadn't heard the whole story.

"Did your brother actually say that he didn't want you to work for my daad?"

"Well, not exactly. But he didn't say yes, either. Why should he care?"

Peter sounded like her sister Della, reacting before there was anything to react to. She did want to talk to Nathan, but not about something like that. It would sound like interfering.

Peter was going on, nursing his grudge. "It's not his business, anyway. He's not my father."

She winced. "I hope you didn't say that to him."

That stopped him mid-complaint. He stood there, his mouth open in surprise.

"I didn't. But it's true."

If she said what she was thinking, Peter would be mad at her . . . and maybe Deborah would, too. But she certain sure wasn't going to jump into the middle of Nathan's private business without trying to get Peter thinking straight.

"From what I've heard, your father was someone to look up to," she said casually.

"Yah, he was." Peter blinked, as if thinking of his loss.

267

"Seems to me your brother has a big job in front of him, trying to fill your father's shoes when it comes to raising you. Do you think he might be worried about doing it right?"

She held her breath, hoping that was the right thing to say.

Peter stared so hard at the ground in front of him that it was a wonder he didn't bore a hole in it. Finally he shrugged. "I don't know. I guess maybe." He met her eyes finally, and he seemed to be taking it pretty well.

She put her hand on his shoulder. "Tell you what. I'll promise to speak to your brother, if you'll try to get rid of that chip on your shoulder. Is it a deal?"

After a moment of silence, Peter's lips twitched. "Okay. I'll try. Honest."

Becca hoped he would. They were both so sensitive about their relationship with each other. She thought she understood it, but it was a chancy thing to interfere in someone else's relationship.

She began to wish she'd said no to begin with. Where could you find balance in a situation like this? She just hoped she wasn't making a mistake that would destroy her fragile relationship with Nathan.

Standing at the top of a ladder to reach the henhouse roof, Nathan realized he had a complete view of Becca's property. He could see from the orchard on the slight hill behind the house all the way across the pasture to her house. Behind the house stood the barn and several sheds. Everything was in good order. It didn't take much to see that the owner of the property cared about it.

He'd hate to think what this property said about him.

Repairing the roof had been on his list since the first inventory of what had to be done. Too bad Onkel Joseph hadn't kept his buildings in order. He wondered, not for the first time, what had turned his uncle into a person who didn't care. It still seemed strange to have come into his property without having known him at all.

Nathan grasped a shingle that crumbled in his hand. He'd hoped at first it might not have to be done until spring, but judging by the amount of water inside after the last rain, he'd best do it now. Otherwise he'd be replacing the whole thing in the spring.

Maybe Peter didn't understand that, with his talk about there not being much to do at this time of year. Sure, they wouldn't have any residents for the chicken coop until spring, but . . .

He shook his head, cutting short the argument he was having with himself. He knew full well that Peter could manage a few days a week at the Stoltz farm and still have time to help him. He'd let his own uncertainty get in the way of saying yes to the boy.

On the other hand, there'd been no reason for Peter to flare up the way he did. No reason except that he was a teenager, he guessed.

Pounding a nail into the last of the shingles he was replacing, he glanced down toward Becca's place again. She was hanging laundry on the line, while Peter and Deborah chased the twins between the lines of sheets and clothes. Obviously that was more fun than standing on a ladder in the wind.

Okay, now he was feeling sorry for himself. Pitiful. Just like Peter. Only Peter had hurried down to Becca's for sympathy. He could imagine Becca's response. She'd already all but told him he wasn't handling the boy the right way.

He climbed down and set the ladder carefully on its side to put away later. That could be Peter's share of the work.

The twins' high voices carried clearly on the air. "Mine! Mine!"

He stepped out from between the henhouse and the barn to see what had James and Joanna shouting their new favorite word. It seemed one of the sheets had come loose and was flapping in the breeze with both of them chasing it.

Mine. He guessed that was the age they were. Come to think of it, if Peter paid more attention to what the family needed than what he wanted, they'd get along better.

Daad had always stressed the importance of

the family. He expected each of his children to understand that . . . faith first, family second, and yourself last. Daad probably hadn't thought there'd be a time when he and Peter would be on their own.

Now he had to fill in for Daad with Peter, and he hadn't been doing much of a job of it. He'd have to make peace with Peter sometime, and it might as well be now.

He looked again at the happy group and listened to their laughter. Yes, it might as well be now.

The closer he got, the more guilty he felt. He'd said something to Becca, something that seemed right after those dizzying moments they'd shared. There was no denying what had happened. They'd both felt it. When the world shakes around you, you can't pretend it hasn't.

He'd said they'd talk later. But they hadn't. Naturally she'd have expected him to make the first move. Instead of doing so, he'd been caught in a quagmire, unable to move forward or back.

Becca looked up, saw him, and smiled. For an instant, her sweet, honest smile chased away his doubts, and he didn't see anything else.

With a squeal, James saw him and barreled toward him, his legs pumping. He nearly crashed into Nathan's legs, but Nathan caught him in time, swinging him up into his arms.

"Hey, watch where you're going, little man." He bounced him, making James chortle with laughter. "He's getting awful sure on his feet, ain't so?"

Becca nodded. If she struggled to face him after what happened between them, she didn't let it show. "He's faster every day. Grossmammi and I are constantly on the run."

Peter had been swinging Joanna around. Laughing, he set her down. She took a couple of wobbly steps before reaching up to him again. "More."

Peter laughed, flopping down on the grass beside her. "I can't. I'm too dizzy."

Joanna wasn't one to take no for an answer. She grabbed his arm and tugged at him. "Up."

Deborah rolled a ball toward Joanna, distracting her, and in a moment James was wiggling to join them. Nathan set the boy down and watched all of them running after the ball.

Say something, he ordered himself, glancing at Becca and then looking away. *She's expecting you to say something.*

His tongue seemed stuck. How could he believe in a future with Becca, with all that entailed—the twins, the family—and yet let this moment slip away? He watched that sweet smile fade away and her face set. He'd disappointed her.

Becca bent and picked up the empty basket, holding it against her hip. "If you have a minute, there's something I'd like to talk to you about." Her gaze went right past his face, and her voice was cool. "It's about the job my daad offered to Peter."

He gathered his wits as best he could. "Yah. The job."

"We probably should have asked you about it before Daad spoke to Peter." Again, that cool tone. It was clear that she didn't really think so. "Peter seems to think you don't want him to do it."

So he'd been right. Peter had come looking for sympathy. No doubt, based on the fact that Becca looked at him as if he'd just come out from under a rock, that she agreed with his brother.

He stiffened. "I'm sorry Peter brought our quarrel to you. He shouldn't have. That's a family matter."

Nathan realized his error immediately. He could have put that better. Should have, in fact. Truth was that he wasn't very good at any of this. Not at being a father, not at communicating with a woman.

He'd made it sound as if he was closing her away from anything to do with his family. What else could she think?

She'd clearly been waiting for him to follow up on those precious moments they'd experienced, but he couldn't. The old, painful memories wouldn't let him. He couldn't trust himself to take care of anyone, especially not Becca and those two precious children.

He had to get away from her before he made promises he couldn't keep. He turned away. "Please send my brother home by four."

For an instant he almost hoped she'd make a move to stop him, or to say something else, but she didn't. She carried the basket toward the house, and he walked away.

Becca did her best to put a pleasant face on things after she'd gone inside, but she feared it hadn't worked very well. Her grandmother was only too careful not to mention Nathan, while Deborah and Peter were embarrassed and uncomfortable. She didn't blame them.

In fact, once the twins were in bed for their naps, Deborah and Peter went off for a walk and Grossmammi decided to take a nap herself. She did look tired, and Becca suspected that it was as much worry over Becca as actually needing sleep.

She put her arm around her grandmother and walked with her to the door into the grossdaadi haus. "I'm all right, Grossmammi. Please don't worry."

Her grandmother patted her cheek. "Yah," she murmured. "Even if you love someone, you can't solve their problems. They have to do that for themselves."

Becca nodded, not sure whether she was talking about Becca herself, or Nathan, or someone else in the family. Her grandmother didn't say more, just went off toward her bedroom.

Trying to think what she should be doing, Becca

discovered that her mind was a blank. So she sank onto a kitchen chair and put her face in her hands. She wasn't sure how much of this situation was her fault and how much was Nathan's or even Peter's. But however it happened, it seemed to have brought their relationship to a dead end.

Rubbing her temples, she blinked back tears. Why did Nathan have to be so hard on Peter? And why did Peter have to flare up so quickly over anything and nothing? They should be together against the world instead of against each other.

A footstep sounded out on the porch. She straightened, looking out the window and expecting to see Deborah, but it was Miriam, wearing a winter bonnet and clutching a heavy black sweater around her.

Becca hurried to the door. "Miriam, how nice of you to come over. No need to ask how you are . . . you're blooming."

Miriam certainly fit that description. Her cheeks were rosy, her dimples showed, and her blue eyes sparkled. "Ach, this is the best thing ever. I had to come tell you. I've started being sick in the morning. Isn't it wonderful?"

Becca burst into laughter, her worries sliding away. "I'm sorry," she said when she could speak. "I don't remember being so happy about it myself, but if that's how you feel . . ."

"You know what I mean." Miriam giggled, shedding her bonnet and sweater. "I guess it isn't exactly fun, but oh, Becca, you can't believe how sweet Matthew is. He keeps telling me to sit down and rest, or eat some crackers, or go back to bed and let him bring me some weak tea."

Secretly thinking she'd like to see it of her brother, Becca nodded. "That is sweet. And you are expecting for real."

She drew Miriam down to a chair and put the kettle on. "Now you can tell me all about it, when there's nobody around to hear. And I'll give you some tea that isn't weak."

"I'm just about bursting to talk about it. Do you think anyone else has guessed?"

Becca's lips twitched. "I think it's safe to say the women in the family know. If you look, you'll see scraps of fabric for baby quilts in Mammi's workbag, and Grossmammi has gotten out all of her finest yarn to make sweaters and caps . . . pink, blue, yellow, pale green . . . maybe you should mention what colors you like before she gets carried away."

Miriam pressed her palms against her rosy cheeks. "Ach, I didn't realize. How did they know? Did you tell them?"

She shook her head. "I didn't need to. They have great instincts." She put her hand over Miriam's. "There's so much to be thankful for this Thanksgiving, ain't so?"

Miriam's eyes shimmered. "Yah, for us. You . . ." She let the words trail off, but Becca knew what she was thinking. Sweet Miriam wanted everyone to be as happy as she was, and her instinct told her something was wrong where Becca was concerned.

"I'm all right. Or if I'm not, I will be." The longing to confide in someone overwhelmed her. "I just . . . I was starting to care about Nathan. Maybe too much."

Miriam clasped Becca's hand in both of hers. "I could see that. We . . . Matthew and I both . . . we felt he was caring for you. It would be so good."

The tension eased out of Becca in the warmth and caring she felt from her sister-in-law. "Maybe. But I don't think Nathan is ready to love again. He's still tied up inside himself. He can't seem to open up . . . not to me, not even to his own little brother."

"You see him hurting and you can't help him," Miriam said softly.

"What makes you so wise?" She managed a smile as the kettle whistled, and she got up to make the tea.

Funny, she thought, as she made tea and set out cookies. Miriam had said the same thing Grossmammi had, only in other words. It wasn't possible to fix things for another person, even someone you loved. Oh, you could keep your children from falling and kiss their hurts when they were little, but they had to learn to do the fixing themselves as they grew.

Was that a fault in her . . . jumping in to try and fix things for others? If so, she was the one with a lesson to learn.

The thought didn't soothe the hurt, but somehow it made it a little easier to accept. Nathan had shut her out of his heart. She could go on loving him and praying for him, but he had to be the one to open his heart again.

CHAPTER SIXTEEN

Peter wasn't talking to him the next morning, Nathan realized. Or, at least, not talking unless he had to answer a question. Nathan shoved down the annoyance he felt. How could he expect Peter to discuss anything calmly if he couldn't himself? He'd failed. That insight came to him sometime in the night, when he'd been waking and sleeping and then waking up again. Finally he'd gotten out of bed and walked around the house.

The place had started feeling familiar, even if it didn't feel like a home. Nathan had moved to the windows, looked out at the dark. Then he'd glanced down toward the road, seeing a faint gleam in the distance from the cottage where Matt and Miriam lived. Closer, the glow from a lamp had sent a yellow glow from Becca's kitchen window.

He chased away the memory of that light shining in the dark. It was better not to think about Becca at all right now. Peter was enough to deal with at the moment.

Even as Nathan thought it, Peter gathered up breakfast dishes and carried them to the sink, careful not to look at his brother. Determined to do a better job this morning than he had the

279

previous day, Nathan got up and joined the boy as hot soapy water filled the sink.

Talk to him, he told himself, picking up a dish towel and trying to figure out how to start.

Just do it, he guessed. He cleared his throat.

"Look, about that job with Abram Stoltz."

"Yah?" Peter eyed him cautiously, but at least he didn't flare up.

"Sorry if I . . ." He took a breath and tried to sound sorry. "Well, anyway, I guess I over-reacted."

"Yah. You did." Peter's tone didn't sound very friendly, but maybe Nathan deserved that.

"I guess I was surprised when you came out with it." He slid a sideways glance at his brother, looking for signs of softening.

This was Peter, he reminded himself. The little brother who'd followed him around constantly, trying to be like him. Now he was trying to turn into a man.

"Do you want to learn something about dairy farming?"

Peter shrugged. "Maybe," he muttered, not looking at him.

"Sounds like a good chance, then." Nathan tried to infuse some enthusiasm into his voice. "If you want to work with Abram this winter, it's okay by me."

The stubborn look in Peter's face didn't change, but then slowly it eased away. "Okay, then. Gut."

Nathan had hoped for a friendlier response, but he'd take it.

Then, surprisingly, Peter produced a smile, the little lopsided grin he'd had as a small child . . . just like he'd had the first time Nathan let him take the reins in the pony cart. Warmth seemed to flow between them.

He could have stopped there, satisfied, but there was something more Nathan wanted to say if he could get it out. His throat was suddenly tight.

"You know, when I was younger it seemed like Daad always figured things out pretty fast . . . like he always made the right decision. He knew how to be a daad." His throat eased. "Me, I'm not even sure I know what that is."

That caught Peter's attention, his eyes widening. "You know what? Becca said something like that."

The last thing Nathan wanted to do was talk about Becca just now. The mention of her name had a disintegrating effect on him. "Anyway . . ."

Before he could go on, Peter repeated the words. "I said, Becca said something like that."

Nathan's jaw clenched. It took an effort to speak. "Yah? She's a smart woman, I guess."

Peter eyed him the way he used to, when he was trying to talk his brother into something. "Really nice, too."

Nathan had to respond. He couldn't walk away just because the subject made him uncomfortable. "Are you trying to be a matchmaker?" He tried for a light tone. "I'm the big brother, ain't so? I'm supposed to be the one to give advice."

Peter's blue eyes suddenly sparkled the way they used to before he turned into a teenager. "Deborah says she thinks you two might be good together. I think so, too."

Peter was being honest, he thought, and after all, he had a stake in what Nathan did.

"It's not as easy as that," he muttered.

"You mean because you were married before. And Becca was married before, too." Peter didn't want to let it go.

"Something like that." If he could get out of this conversation . . .

"From what I remember about her, Molly would want you to be happy, ain't so?" Peter looked like he believed that, and Nathan didn't have an answer.

He struggled with it, knowing what Peter had said was true. Then he dropped the dish towel and clasped his brother's shoulder, giving him a gentle shake. "If I agree, will you stop bugging me about it?"

Peter laughed, a sound Nathan didn't hear very often. "Okay, okay. But I won't stop thinking about it."

Neither will I, Nathan realized. He couldn't.

Glancing out the kitchen window, Becca saw the kind of bright, crisp, sunny fall day that invariably made her happy. If it didn't quite work today, that was her fault.

She couldn't lose what she didn't have, she reminded herself, and turned to join her grandmother at the kitchen table. The early morning chores were finished, and the twins were playing happily in their corner . . . for the moment, at least.

Her grandmother was pouring two midmorning cups of tea, a sure sign that she wanted to talk. Becca slid into her chair, knowing that even if she managed to smile and pretend everything was all right, Grossmammi wouldn't believe it.

"Drink it," she urged. "Hot tea with sugar is good for everything." She hesitated. "Even broken hearts."

Becca obediently took a sip, cradling the hot mug between her hands. It did feel comforting, and she welcomed comfort just now.

"I don't have a broken heart. Maybe just bruised."

She tried to smile, but it didn't come out very well. "I thought . . . I guess I hoped things were going somewhere with Nathan."

"Maybe they are. Things take time, ain't so?"

She'd like to believe that it was just a matter of time, but she couldn't. "Nathan never really said anything. It was just looks, and touches, and feelings."

Grossmammi put her hand gently over Becca's. "And you responded. I could see that."

"Yah." Had she been that obvious? But then, she never could hide anything from Grossmammi, and there was no point in trying now.

"All those things showed me that I could love again, but he can't. He can't . . ." She broke off for a moment, struggling to find the right word. "He can't trust, that's it. Without trust, how can you have love?"

Grossmammi shook her head. "Poor man. You could have been good together, each of you bringing what would heal the other. But if he won't let you in, then he's the loser by it."

"Yah. It feels kind of like losing on my side, too," she said, almost smiling.

Her grandmother's hand squeezed hers, and Becca clasped it warmly. She could feel the fragile bones, but there was strength in her grandmother's hand, as well. Grossmammi had been through it all, and come out stronger than ever.

If only she could say the same for herself.

"I have enough to make me happy," she murmured, feeling her way around the hurt that lodged like a solid rock in her heart. "I have the twins, and my family, the orchard, the church . . . if that's all I have, it's enough."

"Yah." Grossmammi jerked suddenly as the back door rattled. In another moment it burst open, and David hurtled in, as usual never slowing down.

"Anything left from breakfast? I'm starved."

He shed his jacket, throwing it toward the hook. It missed and dropped to the floor.

Grossmammi's look stopped him midway to the table. She didn't speak . . . she just looked at the jacket.

David flushed. "Sorry, Grossmammi." He went back, picked it up, and hung it where it belonged.

Becca had to chuckle. "I hope my look is that effective one day," she said, and Grossmammi laughed, too.

"What do you mean?" David asked, straddling the chair he jerked out.

"Never mind." Becca got up. "You want some eggs and scrapple? Or coffee cake?"

"Yah, please," he said cheerfully. "It's been a long time since breakfast."

Shaking her head, Becca put the skillet back on the stove. While she did, the twins had discovered their uncle and were pulling him off the chair to play with them. Funny for the twins to have an uncle not so much older than they were, but good, too. They could learn a lot from Daniel and David.

"Didn't you have breakfast at your house?" Grossmammi said, getting out the coffee cake. "I can't believe your mammi didn't feed you."

"Yah, sure." He looked up from balancing a block on Joanna's head. "But that was ages ago. Since then I mucked out stalls, fed the chickens, gathered the eggs . . . lots of things."

"Where's Daniel? I thought he usually did the chickens." The twins had a complicated system of deciding whose turn it was to do what, and Becca had never really tried to figure it out.

"Not here." David didn't look at her but concentrated on the babies. "Daad said he should go over to the hydroponics plant to get an idea of what they want him to do. If I know Daniel, he'll be gone the whole entire day, and when he does come home, he won't be able to stop talking about it."

All of that came out in one breath, and Becca exchanged looks with her grandmother. It was easy to see what was wrong, but not so easy to fix it.

"He'll be excited, ain't so?" Grossmammi's soft voice held affection and understanding.

"Yah." David scowled. "I don't see why he wanted to do something like that, anyway."

"You like a lot of the same things," Becca said, dishing up eggs and scrapple hot from the skillet. "But you like some different things. He'd rather have bacon than scrapple any day."

He got up and came to the table, his eyes lighting up at the sight of his scrapple. "Denke, Becca." He sat, shoveling a forkful into his mouth before his bottom hit the chair.

"But this is like being a real apprentice," he said around a mouthful.

Joanna and James grabbed his pants, pointing

to the scrapple on his fork and stopping his complaint, if that's what it was. Distracted, he grinned and popped a piece into each of the two mouths that opened like birds.

"When you decide what you want to do, Daadi will—"

She stopped, because David was halfway out of his chair, staring out the window.

"Look! The barn!" He scrambled for the door and Becca rushed after him, her heart racing at the alarm in his voice.

They burst onto the back porch, and she saw then what her brother had seen. Smoke was curling out the open door of the barn.

David raced toward the barn, and she bolted after him. Barn fire—and Sweetie was still penned into her stall. She grabbed David as he plunged for the door.

"Get the hose. Quick!" When he still strained against her holding arm, she shook him. "The hose first. Schnell!"

Relief swept over her as he obeyed, running for the spigot on the side of the house. Grabbing the shovel that leaned against the barn wall, she beat at the sparks nearest her, moving toward the stall.

She could hear the mare now, squealing, feet kicking against the stall. Panic lent strength to her arms. David was yelling something, and a stream of water burst into the barn, soaking her skirt. Beyond the sound of his shouts, the horse's cries, and the crackle of fire, she heard the bell on the back porch clanging wildly. Grossmammi had gotten to it. It would alert anyone in earshot, and relief swept over her.

But she had to get Sweetie out. Another few feet and she could—

A hand caught at her shoulder, spinning her around while an arm encircled her waist. She was swept off her feet and held so tightly she could scarcely breathe, knowing instinctively it was Nathan's strong arms around her. She could feel his labored breath and hear his strong heartbeat. She hadn't been so close to another person since Thomas.

She struggled against his strength. "Sweetie."

"We'll get the horse. You get outside now."

A few long strides, and he set her, coughing, on her feet. He turned, and she saw his tall figure disappear into the smoke.

Figures brushed past her, and then David thrust the hose into her hands. "Keep it on us, yah?"

She nodded, but he was already gone . . . her little brother, becoming a man in front of her.

Her eyes burned. She could hardly see through the smoke, but she focused on aiming the water where they were fighting their way toward the stall. She managed to spray David, then Nathan and another person she could see beyond him . . . Peter, of course. She heard him yelling, and then they were converging at a point beyond the stall.

"Get Sweetie," she shouted, and then burst into a spell of coughing that doubled her up.

As she recovered, she sensed others around her, crowding into the barn. Hands grabbed the hose from her, and someone else pushed her out the door, where Miriam clutched her and pulled her farther away.

Miriam. How did Miriam get here so fast? "It's all right, it's all right," she kept saying, hugging Becca and batting at her skirt at the same time.

Becca looked down. An errant spark had it smoldering.

"The mare . . ." she began again, but then she saw Peter and David coming out, the lunging horse between them. Behind the boys and the horse there were others coming through the smoke, stepping out into the clear air. It was Nathan and Matt, and they were carrying something between them.

Not something, someone. She hurried toward them as they lowered their burden to the ground. Kneeling, she brushed the soot and smoke away from the face, praying he was breathing. It was Abel.

CHAPTER SEVENTEEN

A half hour later Becca realized that her teeth were still chattering against the rim of the mug of hot tea Grossmammi had brought her. Someone had wrapped her in a coat that was too big for her, and she snuggled it around her, trying hard to get a grasp on everything that had happened.

Abel sat on the edge of the porch, coughing frequently. He was wrapped in a blanket while paramedics checked him out for the third or fourth time after giving him oxygen. Someone had reached his father, and Jed stood close by his son, his expression a mixture of worry and anxiety.

Daad sat down next to Becca on the porch step, wrapping his arm across her shoulders. "It's going to be all right, I promise. Everything can be replaced and rebuilt."

She nodded, but doubted that things could ever be the same. So many people crowded the yard and worked at clearing out the barn, even as the volunteer firemen packed up. The acrid smell of charred timbers tainted the air as women bustled in and out with coffee and cold drinks, eager to find someone to tend to.

Becca let out a long breath. "Abel . . . ?" she began, making it a question.

"It seems certain sure that he started the fire."

Daad squeezed her. "I can't understand it, or how he could start those other fires . . ."

"But he didn't!" David, who had been trying to get someone to listen to him for the past half hour, finally seized his chance. "That's what I kept trying to tell you. I heard the police arrested the guy—and after all the things folks thought, he wasn't a teenager. It was actually a member of the Jonestown Volunteer Fire Company." David seemed to pale. "They think he liked watching things burn and then putting out the fires."

"I'll never understand that," Daad said, shaking his head. "But whatever else he did, that man didn't start this fire. You found Abel. You saw the stuff he used to start it."

"Yah." David sent a glance toward Abel, as if seeing him change in front of him. "I saw it. Abel did it."

"Why?" The word burst out of Becca. "Why would Abel do that to me?"

"I didn't mean it to be so bad." Abel had heard, and he spoke directly to her, despite the other people gathered around him. "Honest. I thought . . . I thought . . ." His face screwed up as he tried not to cry. He seemed to force himself to go on. "I thought I would put the fire out and rescue Sweetie and then you'd see that I could take care of you."

His words hung on the air. All around him was silence. Everyone seemed afraid to speak.

"I'm so ashamed." Tears rolled down his cheeks, making tracks in the soot. "The fire started so fast, and then I tripped and knocked myself silly and somebody else had to haul me out." He choked on a sob before he could continue. "Who got me out?"

She saw Nathan and Matt exchange glances, and then Matt spoke. "David spotted you, and then Nathan grabbed you and pulled you away from the flames."

Abel looked at Nathan, and Becca thought he'd almost wished he hadn't been saved rather than know that Nathan had done it.

Abel's father turned to her, his face ravaged with grief. "How can I say how ashamed I am? Thomas's wife, the mother of his children, and my son does such a thing—"

"Don't." Becca reached out to grasp his hand and hold it tightly. "He didn't mean it to hurt me, you know that. He . . . he's all mixed up."

The men began to shuffle their feet, as if embarrassed by all the emotion pouring out.

"Becca's right," Nathan said abruptly. "It was a mistake. We all make mistakes. All we can do is try to make amends and do better."

"Yah," Daad added, averting his eyes from Jed's face. "We'll have to rebuild part of the barn."

"We will work on that," Jed said. "If you'll let us."

"For sure," Becca said, longing for anything

that would bring about peace with Thomas's family. "Abel, too, yah?"

Jed nodded, his face drawn. "He'll have to go before the bishop and the people." His voice broke a little on that. "If you can forgive . . ."

He let that trail off, as if he couldn't say anything more.

She put her hand on his arm, her heart aching for him. "It will be hard for him, but even if he must be under the Bann for a time, he will find his way back. Believe that."

There was a murmur that might have been agreement from the others who stood there. They all knew what happened after a wrong like this. Abel would have to beg forgiveness of the whole church and accept whatever punishment was given. And he would be forgiven, his sin wiped away.

Looking at Abel's tearstained face and swollen eyes, she didn't doubt that he would repent . . . was already repenting. God would see him through this, and they would help.

Becca let out a deep breath, relieved that she could do it without coughing. It would be a long time before she could forget this day, and she still didn't feel she was thinking straight. But one thing she must do.

She moved so that she could touch Abel's face. He winced away instinctively, but she wiped away the traces of tears.

"It's already forgiven," she said softly. "Now we'll move on, ain't so? It's what Thomas would want."

He couldn't meet her eyes, but he sniffled a bit and nodded.

She ought to check on the twins, but at that moment Deborah and Della came out with trays of sandwiches, followed by Miriam with the coffeepot.

"The babies are fine," Miriam said, pausing beside Becca. "I got them both down for a nap." She smiled as if surprised at herself.

"It's gut practice," Becca said, her voice croaking a little.

Miriam giggled. "Grossmammi recruited everyone else to make sandwiches. She says you should come in and change and eat something."

Becca shook her head. Given how raw her throat felt from the smoke, she couldn't imagine choking any food down. She shook her head at the coffee Miriam tried to give her.

"I'll go inside soon. I have to thank everyone first."

"Yah, I understand." Miriam pressed her cool cheek against Becca's. "I'll try to keep her from coming after you."

They exchanged a smiling, sisterly look, and then Becca began moving from one group to another, determined to thank everyone there.

When she reached the firemen, the chief drew

her aside. "I saw . . . well, where the fire started. You know it looked like it was deliberate."

She met his eyes and a message passed between them.

The chief nodded. "Guess it could have been either way, right? I guess we can leave anything else to the bishop and the church."

"I can't thank you enough." Her gaze included the others, who were helping themselves to sandwiches. "All of you."

They shuffled and muttered something indistinct, as if it was embarrassing, making her want to laugh. She looked around the farmyard, making mental notes of all those who'd rallied around . . . mostly neighbors, taking care of neighbors.

A little distance from them, Nathan stood talking to Matt. From their gestures, they seemed to be planning the repairs to the barn. Peter stood next to Nathan, and as she watched, Nathan put his arm across his brother's shoulder and gripped it tightly. Peter grinned, leaning against him. It seemed the brothers were okay.

As for her . . . well, she couldn't look at Nathan without feeling his arms around her in the midst of the flames, holding her tightly, keeping her safe. She tried to tell herself that he would do that for anyone he rescued. Tried, but didn't succeed. She couldn't help feeling that it meant more than that, and the hope that had died in her began to flicker, just a little.

• • •

Nathan and Peter walked down to Becca's barn again the next morning as soon as their own chores were done, including taking care of Becca's mare. Sweetie had spent the night in their barn.

Today was another sunny, brisk day with a light breeze blowing. That breeze should wipe away the acrid smell of burning that ruffled nerves and sent images of flames darting through his mind. Probably everyone else's, as well.

Matt and his daaad were there already, and the two boys, as well. From what he could tell by the gestures, David was explaining the events to his twin.

Matt greeted them with a grin. "Poor Daniel. He had his visit to the plant about his apprenticeship yesterday, and that had to be the day that something exciting happened around here."

"David has plenty to talk about, that's certain sure," Abram said, joining them. "Well, they're growing up and taking on responsibility fast, ain't so?" He nodded toward Peter, who had gone to join David and Daniel. "Your boy, too, I hear."

Nathan nodded, still feeling that little flare of fear in his heart when he thought about Peter charging in. But he'd done the right thing, and if he hadn't spotted Abel when he did . . .

"Yah, David and Peter did men's work here yesterday. David was the first one to spot what was happening, I hear. He was already taking charge when we showed up." He knew Abram would understand the praise for his boy without another word said.

Abram's eyes softened as they rested on his son. "Have to say that we always thought Daniel the more mature, but the truth is, they all mature in different ways and rates."

Matt, who'd moved closer to the starting point of the fire, made a face and uttered a disgusted sound. "That smell's too much. Let's get the rest of the burned stuff out of here. Then we'll see what has to be done."

Nathan pulled on a pair of work gloves. "Let's get at it, then. We have to give Sweetie her home back."

Matt laughed. "Yah, she's a spoiled girl, all right. Good thing Becca didn't have any wounded squirrels or birds in here yesterday, or we'd have been hunting for them."

Nodding, Nathan began to marshal the boys to cart things out, sending them to round up a couple of wheelbarrows.

"Sweetie can stay at our place as long as needed, but that's not very convenient for Becca." He grabbed hold of a stall plank and pulled it free. "Looks like the stalls will have to be rebuilt."

Matt joined him, and together they pulled and pried the boards free while the boys loaded the wheelbarrows and carted them off to a spot well behind the barn.

Nathan found himself glancing toward the barn doorway more than once. He hadn't forgotten the feeling he'd had when they'd hauled the King boy out into the air. He'd stood there, coughing and choking, and his mind had gone back to finding his Molly. This time he'd been able to save, not lose.

Not that one life paid for another; he didn't think that. But still, he felt somehow lighter than he had in a long time. After Molly, he'd been convinced he couldn't take responsibility for another person ever again. And yet the good Lord kept pushing him into places where he had to do just that. First with Peter, then with Becca and her family, and even with that foolish boy yesterday.

If God could trust him with others, who was he to say that he wouldn't try to live up to it?

He looked at Peter, laughing and talking with the twins while they did a job of work. Peter had shed a burden, as well, he thought. He hadn't looked that happy in months or even longer.

I didn't understand what was happening to him. Nathan could only shake his head at that. He should have seen how many blows his brother had taken, with Daad's death and Mammi's leaving and the betrayal by boys he'd thought were his friends.

Becca had seen far more than he had. She'd tried to talk to him about it, and he'd been fool enough not to let her in. She would have helped, but he'd done what he always did—shut people out. Especially people who cared about him.

Nathan approached that thought carefully. Did she forgive him after everything that had happened between them? Could she forgive and give him another chance?

Matt nudged him. "You going to sleep on the job?" he asked, grinning.

"Just thinking," he replied, looking again toward the doorway, half hoping and half dreading seeing Becca again.

An outburst of laughter came from Peter and the twins, and then they came jogging over, carrying something in a pail.

"Look what we found," David called out. "Already cooked apples. Maybe Becca would like to make a cobbler with them."

Despite the charring, the fruit they'd come up with did have a nice scent. "All you need is some cinnamon," Nathan said. "But I don't think Becca would find it funny."

Before the boys could reply, Becca's voice floated in from the door. "What is it? Are these three planning a trick on me?"

Laughing and elbowing each other, the boys descended on her, all of them talking at once. Nathan just stood back and watched. He felt better for seeing her, but he could hope not to feel so tongue-tied when he tried to apologize to her.

Maybe she wouldn't think it necessary, but it was to him. He had to make up for his refusal to listen to her when she tried to help.

After a moment she sent the boys off, laughing, probably to dump the apples on the compost heap. Then, catching his gaze, she came toward him.

"This is good of you," she said, gesturing toward the barn. "I know you have work of your own to do . . ."

"Nothing more important than helping a neighbor," he said, and then rushed on before he could lose his nerve. "Especially a neighbor I wouldn't listen to when I should have. At least I've learned that."

"About Peter, you mean?" For an instant her lips seemed to tremble, but the impression vanished as quickly as it had come. "I butted in where it wasn't any of my business."

Somehow he couldn't come out with the fact that it was her business—that caring for each other made it so. But that was assuming too much—assuming that what they knew was between them was big, and serious, and life-changing. No, he couldn't do that, especially not here, with family apt to interrupt any minute.

So instead he took her hand and held it for a moment. "Maybe so, but you know a lot more about little brothers than it seems I do. If I had listened to you . . ."

"It's nothing." Looking somehow disappointed, she pulled her hand free. "I'll have lunch ready for everyone in a little while. Make sure you and Peter come in and eat."

Becca turned away, and she left him wondering why he couldn't ever manage to say what he really felt where Becca was concerned.

Alone in the kitchen a little later, Becca watched the beef vegetable soup swirl in the pot while she stirred it. The soup was ready, the fresh loaf of bread cut, but still she delayed in calling everyone in. She wanted to hang on to the relative silence for just a little longer.

Not complete silence, of course. It would be foolish to expect that in her busy household. Still, with Grossmammi watching the twins in the living room and everyone else outside, she did have a moment to think.

She ought to be concentrating on how she could help poor Abel in the fix he'd gotten into, but instead her mind was caught up in her own problems—with Nathan.

Putting the wooden spoon on the stove rest, she got out large, heavy bowls for the beef vegetable soup. Thick and hearty, it was practically a meal all by itself, and she loved the aroma. It seemed to promise comfort, warmth, love . . . all in a bowl.

Nathan had been trying to tell her something,

she'd thought. Something other than the fact that she'd understood Peter better than he had.

And that wasn't even true. He'd definitely know and understand his brother best, if not for the stubborn blockade he put up to keep out anything like sharing or loving.

Unless he could let down the barriers he'd erected to protect himself from pain, she couldn't get in and help to heal it. No one could.

Her heart twisted. She'd seen . . . felt . . . what a future with him would be like. She wanted that for herself, for the twins, and definitely for Nathan. Could she really be that patient?

The back door opened. Nathan walked in and stood there, alone, looking at her. A flush rushed up from her chest to her temples, and she hoped he'd think it from her bending over a hot kettle.

"I . . . I'm about ready to call everyone for lunch . . ." she began, hardly knowing what she was saying.

"I know you didn't call us yet." He moved slowly toward her, his face filled with determination. "When you do, everyone will rush in, ain't so?"

She nodded, not sure what to make of his mood.

"I'm very fond of your family. And my family. But some things I'm not going to say to you in front of them."

Becca's breath caught, and her thoughts fluttered, bouncing here and there like a ball thrown by a toddler. Before they could settle, Nathan had taken both her hands in his, wrapping his fingers around them to hold them tight. His were warm and sure, strong against her skin, and she had to struggle to draw breath.

"Becca, I've been trying to tell you something since yesterday. I've gone over it and over it in my mind, trying to find the words."

A clatter of little feet yanked their attention to the opposite kitchen door . . . the one that led to the living room. Joanna and James burst through. They caught sight of Nathan and paused for a moment. Then, gleeful at seeing him, they flung themselves across the floor to grab hold of his legs, one on each side.

"I'm sorry," she began, stumbling over the words, as Nathan looked down at the twins. His look of determination eased, and he laughed.

"I guess I'll have to say it in front of these two." He rested a large hand on each silky head. "It concerns them, all right, but they won't understand."

He looked at her, his face wearing the rare, gentle smile he'd seemed to reserve for her grandmother and the twins. Now it was for her.

"Ach, Becca, I've learned a lot in recent weeks, and some of it I didn't even recognize. I should have. But yesterday, when I came out of the barn and saw that we were all okay, I knew. The burden lifted from my shoulders, as I knew the truth." He let out a long breath, maybe of relief.

"I don't have to worry about Molly and the baby, or keep reliving their dying. Because they're safe now in the Lord's hands . . . safe and happy."

His words seemed to pierce her heart. If he had reached that point of peace about his wife and baby, she couldn't ask for anything more. And if she'd had any part in it . . . well, it would be the Lord's doing, not hers.

"I'm wonderful glad you see that," she whispered, tears glazing her eyes.

"I thought I couldn't trust any longer—not God, not other people, not myself. And if I couldn't trust, I couldn't love." He seemed to be looking into his own soul, and he shook his head. "So ferhoodled, when all along you've been teaching me to trust again. To love again."

Becca struggled to speak as the tears spilled over onto her cheeks. "I would never want you to forget them, any more than I could forget Thomas . . ."

"Up!" Joanna, losing patience with her elders, swatted Nathan's knee. "Up!" she demanded. "Up, up!"

"Up!" James agreed.

"What were you saying about family interrupting us?" Laughter spurted out through her tears, and wasn't that what life and family was all about . . . good things and bad things all mixed up together?

Chuckling, Nathan bent to scoop up one twin

in each arm. He stood, holding them so that the three of them, together, faced Becca.

"I love you, Becca King. And I love these two noisy little ones. Will the three of you have me?"

Becca hesitated for just one second, questions flooding her thoughts. But the love in his eyes swept them all away . . . all the doubts and fears for the future. The future would be what it was, and they'd be able to cope with it together.

Slowly she stepped forward. She put her arms as far as they could reach around Nathan and her children. No, their children now.

Nathan pressed his cheek against hers in a hug that promised love, and companionship, and family, and all the things that made a blessed life. Their arms in a tangle, the children giggling and squealing, and now with Grossmammi watching from one door and the boys from the other, Becca felt his lips on hers and knew they were all home, together.

EPILOGUE

Thanksgiving Day filled Mammi and Daad's house to overflowing with family and friends, as always. Becca and the twins had arrived early, and Deborah swept the little ones off to play where they wouldn't be underfoot.

The rest of the women descended on the kitchen, laughing and talking and cooking and getting in each other's way. From the kitchen window Becca saw Nathan and Peter pull up by the barn. Nathan looked toward the house as if to catch a glimpse of her. She waved, but before he could respond, Matt grabbed his arm and turned him away.

Miriam paused next to her, seeing what she did. "No doubt Matt's telling them to stay outside with the rest of the menfolk. They don't want to come near the kitchen until they're called to eat. Afraid we'll put them to work."

Grossmammi chuckled. "Ach, they're all alike when it comes to that. They don't want to get in the way of a bunch of determined women."

"Determined is right," Mammi said, gesturing with a wooden spoon. "This year we're going to feed everyone at the same time and at the same table. We had to set the tables up end to end into the living room, and that's what we did."

Della paused in the act of counting silverware. "What difference does it make as long as everyone gets to eat? Maybe if we set up separate tables it would be faster."

"Faster isn't what's important," Grossmammi said. "It's sitting together around the table as a family and giving thanks for our blessings."

Mammi's expression softened at her mother-in-law's words. "Yah, that's it. I want to see the whole family around me at once. We can see how it's growing." She smiled at Becca and then touched Miriam's cheek lightly, and Miriam blushed.

"We'll do it, Mammi. Don't fret." Deborah paused, carrying a huge stack of plates. "If we have to sit two to a chair."

"That's right." Della elbowed her sister, following with a tray of silverware. "Deborah and Peter can share."

"Stop it or I'll tell everyone about that boy you met at the hardware store," Deborah said, and before anyone could ask, they'd hurried out of the room.

"Careful with that tablecloth," Becca heard Della saying. "We don't want the babies pulling it down on themselves."

Startled, Becca took a step in their direction, but Mammi shook her head. "I clipped it to the table first thing. She's just being bossy." She smiled, glancing out the kitchen window to where Nathan stood with Daad and Matt. "I'm so wonderful happy for you and Nathan. And Peter, and the twins. You'll be a wonderful gut family."

She whisked off to inspect the tray of rolls that were ready to go in the oven before Becca could answer, but Becca warmed at her mother's words. And if part of Mamm's happiness was due to her feeling that Becca needed someone to support her . . . well, that didn't matter. She and Nathan knew that they would be supporting each other, and that was what was important.

Becca detoured casually past the window, her gaze searching for the figure she could pick out in any group of Amish men anywhere. To her surprise, Nathan was on the porch, gesturing to her.

Startled, she grabbed her jacket from the peg and slipped outside. "Was ist letz? Is anything wrong?"

Nathan's hand closed reassuringly around her wrist. "No, what could be wrong?"

She had to laugh. "Everyone inside is agreed that none of the males will come near until called to eat, and yet here you are."

His blue eyes laughed back at her. "I'm not just any male, ain't so?"

"Not at all. You're mine." Becca's heart seemed to swell as she said the words.

For just a moment they were silent, with wordless speech vibrating in the air between them.

Then Nathan seemed to force himself back to the present.

"Abel is over here." He nodded to the driveway where it curved around several large pines.

Startled, she leaned forward until she spotted the buggy that waited there. "What is he doing? Why doesn't he come to the house?"

Nathan shook his head. "He won't come in. I already tried. I'd guess he's embarrassed to face everyone, but he wants to give you something from his mother."

"Poor boy. He doesn't need to feel embarrassed. I thought we were all over that since he's been helping with the rebuilding all week. Has something else happened that I should know about?"

"Not guilty," he said promptly, making her laugh.

"Sorry," she said. "I didn't mean . . . well, that anyone had made him feel bad."

"Not that I know of." He held out his hand. "Are you coming?"

She nodded, taking it, and stepped down off the porch. Nathan moved with her, still speaking. "Maybe he feels like working with two or three people is different from encountering your whole family gathered in one place. Komm, we'll see what he wants."

"You think I'm being foolish, feeling so responsible for Abel, ain't so?" In a lot of ways, it had begun to seem that Nathan understood the boy better than she did.

"No, I think you're being loving, like always." His gaze touched her face, reassuring her.

Together they walked over to the buggy where Abel waited. Flushing a little, he handed her a basket with a snowy white towel covering its contents.

"This is from Mammi. She wanted you to have some of her apple dumplings and her pumpkin squares."

"That's wonderful gut of her." She took the basket from him. "You know it would be fine for you to come in and see everyone. You're always welcome."

The flush came again. "Not today."

Nathan squeezed her hand, and she knew what he was saying. *Not now. Don't push it.*

"Tell everyone a very happy Thanksgiving for us, then. And thanks so much."

Abel ducked his head in acknowledgment and clicked to the horse. As he moved off, she looked up into Nathan's eyes.

"Do you think he'll ever feel normal around us again?"

"One day," he said, taking the basket from her. He lifted her hand and pressed a kiss against her wrist, sending a flood of warmth straight to her heart. She seemed to feel every separate movement of his lips, as if her skin was sensitized to his touch.

"Three weeks," he murmured. "Three weeks

until we are married." He smiled gently. "That's a gut thing about autumn love, ain't so? We don't have to go through all the preliminaries of getting married the first time. We go right to the important thing."

"Yah," she said softly. "Our promises . . . to each other and to God."

He nodded, again understanding, and bent to find her lips in a kiss . . . a gentle, longing kiss that left her wishing for more.

"Three weeks," she murmured. "Seems like a long time."

Laughter bubbled out of him, making Nathan look like a young boy. "It will come soon. And then we'll be a family."

She linked her arm with his as they headed back toward the house. "A family with one teenager, two toddlers, one grandmother, and the two of us. Are you sure you're ready for all of that?"

Nathan chuckled again. He seemed to have lost forever the stern, stone-faced expression she had seen the first day she met him.

"More than ready," he said. "Ever since the day I met you. I just didn't know it then."

Neither of them had, Becca thought, smiling at her first impressions of Nathan. Who would have guessed that so soon they'd be finding love together? Not first love, no, but love just the same. Love to last a lifetime and beyond.

GLOSSARY OF PENNSYLVANIA DUTCH WORDS AND PHRASES

ach. oh; used as an exclamation

agasinish. stubborn; self-willed

ain't so? A phrase commonly used at the end of a sentence to invite agreement.

alter. old man

anymore. Used as a substitute for "nowadays."

Ausbund. Amish hymnal. Used in the worship services, it contains traditional hymns, words only, to be sung without accompaniment. Many of the hymns date from the sixteenth century.

befuddled. mixed up

blabbermaul. talkative one

blaid. bashful

boppli. baby

bruder. brother

bu. boy

buwe. boys

daadi. daddy

Da Herr sei mit du. The Lord be with you.

denke (*or* danki). thanks

Englischer. one who is not Plain

ferhoodled. upset; distracted

ferleicht. perhaps

frau. wife

fress. eat

gross. big

grossdaadi. grandfather

grossdaadi haus. An addition to the farmhouse, built for the grandparents to live in once they've "retired" from actively running the farm.

grossmammi. grandmother

gut. good

hatt. hard; difficult

haus. house

hinnersich. backward

ich. I

kapp. Prayer covering, worn in obedience to the biblical injunction that women should pray with their heads covered. Kapps are made of Swiss organdy and are white. (In some Amish communities, unmarried girls thirteen and older wear black kapps during worship service.)

kinder (*or* kinner). kids

komm. come

komm schnell. come quick

Leit. the people; the Amish

lippy. sassy

maidal. old maid; spinster

mamm. mother

middaagesse. lunch

mind. remember

onkel. uncle

Ordnung. The agreed-upon rules by which the Amish community lives. When new practices become an issue, they are discussed at length among the leadership. The decision for or against innovation is generally made on the basis of maintaining the home and family as separate from the world. For instance, a telephone might be necessary in a shop in order to conduct business but would be banned from the home because it would intrude on family time.

Pennsylvania Dutch. The language is actually German in origin and is primarily a spoken language. Most Amish write in English, which results in many variations in spelling when the dialect is put into writing! The language probably originated in the south of Germany but is common also among the Swiss Mennonite and French Huguenot immigrants to Pennsylvania. The language was brought to America prior to the Revolution and is still in use today. High German is used for Scripture and church documents, while English is the language of commerce.

rumspringa. running-around time; the late teen years when Amish youth taste some aspects of the outside world before deciding to be baptized into the church.

schnickelfritz. mischievous child

ser gut. very good
tastes like more. delicious
Was ist letz? What's the matter?
Wie bist du heit? How are you?; said in greeting
wilkom. welcome
Wo bist du? Where are you?
yah. yes

RECIPES

Pesto Raioli Chicken

1 pound chicken breast strips
2 Tablespoons olive oil
¾ cup chicken broth
9 oz. package refrigerator cheese ravioli
3 small zucchinis, sliced
1 red bell pepper, sliced
¼ cup basil pesto
Parmesan cheese

Cook chicken strips in oil at medium heat until browned.

Add broth and ravioli, cover and cook for 10 minutes.

Stir in remaining ingredients, bring to a simmer, and pour into a greased casserole dish.

Sprinkle with Parmesan cheese.

Bake at 350°F for 30 minutes. This makes 6 servings.

Butternut Squash Bake

This is a little trouble to make since you have to cook the squash first, but the combination of winter squash and raisins is perfect for your Thanksgiving meal.

2 cups cooked mashed butternut or acorn squash
1 cup sugar
2 eggs, beaten
⅓ cup orange juice
⅓ cup dry milk
½ cup raisins
Dash of salt
¼ cup melted butter

Combine all ingredients and mix well.
Pour into a greased 1½ quart casserole dish.
Bake at 350°F until set, about 1 hour. This makes 6 servings.

Dear Reader,

I hope you'll let me know if you enjoyed my book. You can reach me at marta@martaperry.com, and I'd be happy to send you a bookmark and my brochure of Pennsylvania Dutch recipes. You'll also find me at martaperry.com and on Facebook at Marta Perry Books.

Happy reading,
Marta

Center Point Large Print
600 Brooks Road / PO Box 1
Thorndike, ME 04986-0001 USA

(207) 568-3717

US & Canada:
1 800 929-9108
www.centerpointlargeprint.com